I0541614

A PROPER YOUNG LADY

a novel by
Lianne Simon

FAIE MISS PRESS

A Proper Young Lady
Lianne Simon
ISBN 978-0-9851482-1-8

Copyright © 2015 by Lianne Simon

Published by Faie Miss Press
Springfield, Tennessee
www.faiemiss.com

PUBLISHER'S NOTES

This is a work of fiction. Names, characters, places and incidents either are the product of the author's imagination or are used fictitiously, and any resemblance to actual persons, living or dead, business establishments, events, or locales is entirely coincidental.

The publisher does not have any control over and does not assume any responsibility for author or third-party websites or their content.

Individuals depicted in the images are models and used for illustrative purposes only.

Set in Bridone and Hero

Printed in the United States of America

To my loving husband,
who first encouraged me to write.

A
Proper
YOUNG
LADY

CHAPTER 1

Melanie

The boy will never come back again, yet I dream of his kiss as I blow out the candles. Another birthday—another year with him gone.

Mom hands me a present. I mumble my thank-you and tear off the wrapping paper. No way some little presentation box holds the carburetor parts for my dad's motorcycle. Or a new helmet. An audible sigh escapes my lips. Rude, yeah, but jewelry's the last thing I need for my birthday. Okay, so maybe perfume would be worse.

Mom grins at my sister Beatrice. I'm sure they conspired on what to get me—girly stuff no doubt—a polite way of saying nineteen's too old for me to still be a tomboy.

Yeah. Whatever.

The lid to the velvet case springs open with the faintest pressure from my thumbs.

Whoa! My heart stutters before my trembling hand grabs the silver chain and the case tumbles to the floor. I haven't seen my locket since Dani's family moved away. I was so pissed at her for leaving that I broke the thing trying to get her picture out.

Treating the heart like a family heirloom, I click the latch to open it. Dani's grinning face peeks out at me. Like a fool, I sit here mute till Mom speaks. "Danièle's coming to spend the summer with us—at least if that's all right with you."

"For real?" I scowl at my mother. Fury wars against a desperate longing. Dani and I were best buds, but she skipped town and never contacted me again. Five eternal years without even a stupid text. "No, Mom. Not her. Not whatever horse she rode in on."

My mother pulls me close, like I'm gonna start crying or something. "Don't be too rough on Danièle. Her doctors thought it best you two not see each other again, and we were all foolish enough to go along with them. We owe you both an apology."

"Mom, I don't—" The old wound splits open then, and a yearning I've almost forgotten overwhelms me with the need to see Dani again. "Oh, all right."

Mom's face remains serious. "Danièle's engaged now, honey. She needs someone she can talk to about surgery."

Doctors have stalked Dani since the day she was born, intent on making her body and mind conform to their idea of normal. Any other girl could have a life without everybody harassing her. Not *Danièle*. Not with psychologists and crazed parents analyzing her every move.

She fled once to avoid having parts cut off. Why cave now? Her body might look normal when the surgeons are done, but will anything be left of the free spirit I knew? "Mom, even the doctors admit that surgery sucks."

My mother's expression lays the burden on me. "All the more reason for her to be certain what she wants."

"But why marry some jerk who won't accept her the way she is?"

Beatrice eyes me from behind Mom. "Mrs. Welles says it's Danièle who thinks she has to be the perfect woman."

"Can't you tell her how messed up that is?"

"I'd love to, but I need to get back to Fred and the kids." My big sister hugs me the way she always does before leaving. "Look, Melanie, nobody even knew I was intersex until I got that inguinal hernia. Finding out I had testes in my abdomen was pretty traumatic. But at least my body looked female on the outside. Danièle's had to deal with sexual ambiguity from birth. I understand why she might want to have surgery."

"So why's the girl my responsibility? You're the one who's intersex."

"Didn't you promise to always be her friend?"

"Well, yeah." *I am so gonna regret this.*

Danièle

Daddy points to his wrist while looking at me—fair warning that we'll be boarding soon. I stroll into the ladies' room, check my hair, and touch up my lipstick. The company jet is well equipped and spotless, but who wants to use a restroom on an airplane?

On the flight I sleep the best I can. And read. But each time I gaze out the window, the clouds grow darker and thicker. In the Miami afternoon sky, they stretch to the horizon. Summer lightning flickers out over the ocean.

As we begin our approach, the plane lurches, sending a cup of Jasmine down the front of my dress. *Brilliant. Just brilliant.* Not hot enough to burn, but the tea will leave a stain.

My father smiles encouragement and caresses my hand with his.

Yes, Daddy. I'll be brave. For you. And Mum.

Surgery has lurked in the dark corners of my world since the hour of my birth. At times, the threat seemed distant—almost fanciful—but the monster crouches on my doorstep now. His restless blade stands between me and consummation. What choice have I but surrender if I wish to marry?

We land without incident and taxi to a stop in front of the general aviation hangar. After one of the crew opens the door, I unbuckle and follow Daddy outside into unexpected sunshine.

A dark-haired technician with a clipboard meets my father with some urgent matter, and they head inside.

I pace next to the aircraft while the crew searches for my luggage. With so few passengers, how difficult can locating my bags be? Yet they find nothing. So I wander inside to the break room.

My father glances up from his reading. "Something wrong, love?"

"They've lost my bags."

"Didn't Ethan carry your luggage out to the limousine for you?"

"Apparently not."

"Well, chin up, love. Think of this as an opportunity to add to your wardrobe. I'm sure Miss Fairbairn can recommend some suitable boutiques."

Yes. Melanie. Rambunctious little redhead with green eyes and a non-stop grin. *If she still cares, she'll help me though this.*

My father sets down his book and hugs me tight. "Are you certain you don't want your mother or me here for your surgeries?"

"I'll be fine, Daddy. It's best I face this alone."

His eyes search my face, but they hold more doubt than mine. "All right. If you change your mind—if you need anything at all—ring me. All right?"

"Sure." *Not a word about security. Which means you have that covered somehow.*

An hour later, Uncle Randolph drives up in his BMW. I still don't have my license. Daddy wants me to wait. For how long, though? Mum never drives, but at least she knows how.

Randy speaks with my father before approaching me. "Got your bags?"

"No. They've gone missing. Would you mind stopping at Dadeland on the way to the Fairbairn home?"

He rolls his eyes as though I've asked him to take me to Paris instead of a local mall. "Do you know what my time's worth?"

I grin at my big-shot uncle. "Counsellor Welles, the young ruffian Ethan Davis is responsible for my misfortune. Sue him for damages if you like."

My uncle shakes his head in mock agony, opens the passenger-side door, and waves me in. "After you, princess."

Melanie

The rusty pair of Vise-Grips drops from my throbbing hand. I sit on the ground, squeeze my eyes shut against the pain, and suck on my bleeding knuckles. I stripped the stupid threads. The machine shop on Flagler might have a replacement bolt, but a glance at my watch tells me they're already closed for the day. And besides, I've got no wheels.

Grey clouds slide across the sun, and the mosquitoes start a feeding frenzy, so I roll my dad's motorcycle back into the garage.

The tools—most of them somebody else's rejects—go into a plastic bucket.

A new set of metric wrenches waits on the dresser inside. My father bought them for me just before he went back to Afghanistan. *Dad, if you were ever home, you'd know I was working on your stupid bike. Hello? Ancient British motorcycle. As in not metric?* Of course, if he was here, he could fix the piece of junk himself.

Whoa, buddy! A black BMW M5 pulls into the driveway, a sweet custom job with tinted windows and wicked fender flares.

The driver gets out—a stocky guy with black hair and a well-trimmed goatee. Dark glasses keep me from seeing the dude's eyes. One hand holds back the side of his jacket, like he might have to draw and shoot somebody. The guy scowls at the entire neighborhood before flashing me a lopsided grin. Kinda creepy.

The passenger door swings open. Out steps a model—well that's what she looks like—with her fair skin, an almost white blonde mane floating around her shoulders, and a body way too thin for her height.

"Dani?" One hand creeps up to my throat. Careful of the grease on my fingers, I click open the locket and compare the photo inside with the young woman strolling toward me.

"Yeah. Guess so." My former best friend's become a beauty queen.

Shame floods me. *I was the prissy one back then. What am I now?* I wipe both hands on my T-shirt, but only manage to start my knuckles bleeding again.

In spite of my sweat and grease, she hugs me tight. "I missed you." After the girl lets go, she waves a carefree arm toward her driver. "This is my uncle, Randolph Welles."

The guy nods at me and wags a finger at Dani. "The motorbike's off limits, princess."

She lets out a plaintive sigh. "If you say so."

He scans the area again before heading back to the car. When he returns with an armload of shopping bags, I show him to my bedroom. "She's staying in here...with me."

He gives me another crooked smile, drops the stuff on my bed, kisses Dani on the cheek, and walks out the door. I wait for him to bring back a suitcase or something, but he just drives off.

"Don't mind him. Uncle Randolph's not one for chatting with people unless they're his clients."

My polite smile fades when I notice the dark streak on the front of her dress. The fabric appears to be silk. *Wonderful. The thing probably cost more than my entire wardrobe.* I brush a grubby finger across the stain. "I'm sorry I ruined your dress."

Head down, she picks at the fabric. "This? I spilled tea earlier. On the plane."

Yeah. Right.

Dani grins like we're best buds.

Not even a message in all that time, and you think we're still friends? "Mom says you're engaged."

I forgot how well Dani reads my body language. Her violet eyes beg for understanding. "I'm sorry, Melanie. Mum still blames me for what happened."

"Are you serious? That was ages ago." I study her face, in search of any hint of the old Dani. "Why should people expect you to be perfect, anyhow?"

For the proper young lady standing in front of me, even a shrug displays her grace, like maybe she's already a Stepford wife or something. She brushes a delicate fingertip across the locket at my throat. "My guess is that Mum's betting against me going through with the surgery. Help me prove her wrong, will you?"

"At fourteen you wouldn't even let them touch you. Now you wanna cut off body parts? What are you—crazy?"

Her face turns grave, almost desolate. "I'm calling Dr. Pierson in the morning."

What did the psychologists do to your brain, girl? Only hunger keeps me from yelling at her. "Mom's working late. Are sandwiches okay?"

"Sure."

After we eat, I show Dani where to put her things. My dresser and closet are small, but it isn't like I have a bunch of stuff. While she unpacks, I throw my grubby clothes into the hamper and go into the bathroom to wash up.

I work on my dad's old bike. Okay? That doesn't mean I like crud all over me. By the time I scrub off the grease and blood, and finish my shower, Dani's sitting on my bed in a fuzzy pink robe.

I'm not gonna spend my entire summer worried about her seeing me naked, so I drop my towel, grab PJs out of the dresser, and get ready for bed.

With the lights off, I sit on the mattress, lean against the wall, and draw my knees up close. Five years since Dani left. Five. "So tell me about your beau."

The girl's violet eyes glow in the moonlit darkness, triggering faded memories of the time I spent with her family while my mother was doing chemo. Dani kept me from going crazy. Or worse.

The bed shakes as she changes position. "Ethan and I met while I was studying at Oxford."

"In England?"

"Yes. My junior year of college."

"Oh." And I didn't even finish high school.

"I'll be a senior at the University of Richmond this fall. Ethan has one more year at Oxford before he finishes his PhD."

"Is he from the UK?"

"Actually, he's from Massachusetts. His mother lives in Cambridge."

"Did you tell him yet?"

"About being intersex? Yes."

"And?"

"He says he doesn't care, but I want to make sure. I don't want any surprises on our wedding night."

"Yeah. Guess not."

CHAPTER 2

Danièle

Sleep eludes me. A restless Melanie turns over every few minutes. Once in a while, an arm or a leg bumps me. It's been a long while since I've had to share a bed with anyone.

Melanie rises early and dresses. I roll over, spread my arms and legs, and press my face into a pillow. After soft-spoken words, the floor creaks and a door shuts. Moments later, a car starts and drives away.

Feet pace in the kitchen. Dishes rattle. A cabinet drawer slams.

The bedroom door squeaks open again, and Melanie sticks her head into the room. "I got some errands to run. I should be back before one."

I nod acceptance and roll out of bed. While the air's still cool, I jog around the University of Miami campus. After showering, I'm as ready as I'll ever be. If I delay even once, I'll never follow through with surgery, so I pull up Dr. Pierson's contact information on my phone and dial the number.

Dr. Sharon Pierson—I remember her as a friendly old woman who always got me to say more than I intended. Unlike some of my other physicians, she never lied to me, and always asked my permission before examining me.

"Santa Clara Medical Center. How may I direct your call?"

"I'd like to make an appointment with Dr. Pierson."

"I'm sorry, but she no longer maintains regular hours. Dr. Villanova handles her patients now."

"Oh...all right." I hang up and drop my cell phone on the bed.

Before Mum found Dr. Pierson, I went to pediatric specialists at the hospital. Unpleasant memories of lying naked on a table in front of a dozen medical students send a chill through me. I swore I'd never go back.

The sensation of being trapped pushes me outdoors. A chorus of songbirds greets me there. The Florida sun burns hot across my skin, even as a tropical breeze brings the scent of rain. Another pleasant summer day in Miami—almost enough to make me forget what lies ahead. I sit down on a bench, lean my head back, and relish the warmth on my face.

An approaching shower drives me back inside. I settle into an overstuffed chair in the Fairbairn living room, gather my legs under me, and close my eyes.

All this surgery to make everyone else happy. Perhaps Melanie's right about my being daft. Are marriage and children really worth the cost?

Better than being forever alone.

Melanie enters the house with a slam of the screen door and a cheery hello. After a glance my way, she drops her tote on the counter. "Why the sad face?"

"Dr. Pierson no longer takes patients."

"She turned you down? You were her favorite."

"I don't think she was there."

"Oh...yeah." Inspiration lights Melanie's brow. "Let's go bug her at home then."

"What? Now?" A wisp of memory tickles the back of my mind. Long ago, Mum took me with her to the Pierson residence.

"She lives on the other side of campus. On Granada Boulevard."

Yes. Of course. The support group met there. But I can't let her see me like this. "Wait right here." I rush to the bathroom and pop open my cosmetics case.

Melanie follows, a smirk on her face. "Why can't you go as yourself?"

"This is serious, Melanie." I set my lipstick on the counter and frown at her. "If she thinks I have any doubts, she won't approve the surgery, and I won't be able to marry Ethan."

"Oh, and like makeup's gonna convince her?"

"The psychologists in Virginia analyze every last detail. You can get away with being a slob and a tomboy. I can't."

"Slob?" Melanie punches my shoulder with her middle knuckle. Hard.

"Hey! That hurts."

"Then don't call me names."

"Ow. Okay." I rub at my arm. No doubt it will bruise. I check my face one last time, grab my purse, and head outside.

For several blocks our path leads us beneath flowering trees and sunny skies. We cross San Amaro Drive and stroll across campus. After we turn on Granada Boulevard, Melanie stops in front of a pale yellow house. "I think this is where she lives. Mom used to bring my sister here for the meetings, and I tagged along sometimes."

Old memories take on a more familiar shape. Melanie's sister has a condition similar to my own—a more complete form of androgen insensitivity that doesn't require surgery.

We walk up the drive and ring the bell.

Nothing. Twice. No answer.

"She's not home." I tug on Melanie's sleeve, but she folds stubborn arms across her chest and plants herself on a bench next to the door. "We can afford a couple more minutes."

An hour later, a car pulls into the driveway. I fidget while the doctor parks her old Toyota and walks up the brick path toward us. "Why, Danièle! You look fabulous. And Melanie. How are you both?" She opens the front door and waves us inside. "Make yourselves comfortable."

After she brings us sodas and shortbread cookies, Dr. Pierson sits in a high-back chair across from me. "Last I heard, your family moved north. To Virginia. Am I right?"

"Yes, ma'am."

"Oh, don't ma'am me. You're all grown up now. What brings my favorite patient back here anyway?"

"I'm getting married."

"Well, congratulations! I don't suppose you dropped by just to tell me that, though."

"I was hoping you'd supervise my surgery."

"Would you prefer to discuss this in private?"

I shoot a glance at Melanie. "She's my support group now."

"Very well. What exactly were you planning to have done?"

"I want to be normal between my legs."

Melanie makes a soft snorting noise. The doctor closes her eyes a moment and breathes out a muffled sigh. "I never suspected you of being unhappy with your body."

"I'm not."

"Then why cut up healthy tissue?"

"Most guys want to have intercourse."

"Granted. You may be able to do that without vaginal surgery, though. Why the rest?"

Because I'm a coward. Half woman and half little boy. Pseudo-hermaphrodite—like I'm not even real. "I don't want my husband reminded of what I am every time he sees me naked."

"You realize surgery may damage your ability to enjoy sex?"

But everyone else will be happy. "I thought the procedures had improved."

"They have. But the surgeon will cut off most of your clitoris. Do you think the remainder will be as sensitive as what's there now?"

"No." *But the world requires it of me to be considered normal.*

Beyond the picture window lies blue sky and bright sunshine. Across the street, two children frolic under a sprinkler while a young woman watches. *Is a family of my own too much to ask?*

A deep groan works its way up out of my soul. If I don't have surgery, Ethan might not marry me. My parents would try to hide their feelings, but they'd be heartbroken. My psychologists all but said that a real woman gets married and raises a family. Our culture provides no place for hermaphrodites—other than as medical oddities or circus freaks.

Dr. Pierson takes a long sip from her glass before continuing. "Have you and your boyfriend tried to have sexual relations?"

"I'm not—" *Am I so afraid of Ethan seeing my body the way it is?* "No. We haven't."

"Have you experimented with anyone else?"

The blood drains from my face. What might my parents have told her?

Dr. Pierson gets up and walks to the kitchen. She returns with a can of ginger ale and a glass of ice. "I don't care about your sexual preferences or your gender. What concerns me is whether or not you're making a well-informed and rational decision. Understood?"

"Yes, ma'am."

"Now, then. Have you had sexual contact with anyone?"

Heat blossoms across my face. Why didn't I come alone? "Yes. When I was young."

"Did your clitoris play a part in that?"

At the edge of my vision, Melanie gapes at me, her green eyes wide. Mine blink—a slow-motion rejection of reality. "Yes." My shoulders slump, all my energy gone.

"Enough for now." Dr. Pierson's eyes gleam calm satisfaction.

"Does that mean you'll help?"

"You're certain you wish to proceed?"

"I have to do this."

"Very well. I'll line up a team. We'll perform your surgery at the clinic." She pulls a smart phone from her purse and hits a few buttons. "There's an opening July 1st. We can always cancel if need be, but I'd like to get you on my calendar."

Nearly a month away. Time to prepare.

Shouldn't I be excited? They always promised that surgery would make me like other girls. Yet none of the intersex adults I've met are glad to have had their genitals modified—mutilated, some say. Not one.

Dr. Pierson gathers the empty glasses and carries them to the kitchen. When she returns, she hugs us both goodbye. "Come to the clinic Wednesday at one. We'll discuss this further. I want to make sure you're ready."

Hysterical laughter bounces around inside my skull. I may cut off a bit of flesh that once gave me pleasure. For Ethan. For my parents. But I'll never be ready.

Melanie

Dark clouds roll across the faded blue sky, threatening an afternoon shower. Palms trees dance a slow ballet in the wind. I grab Dani's hand and rush down the driveway. The girl doesn't even notice when we take a different route home.

At Stanford Drive I pause long enough to get her attention. "You're not the one who's crazy, you know. It's all these freaking people who think every girl has to look the same between her legs."

When Dani's eyes rest on mine, I flinch at the despair flowing from them. "No one's forcing me to do this, Melanie."

I grab the girl's arms, shake her hard, and try not to scream. "What do you think all the psychologists are for? To help you decide between male and female—so you'll remove your breasts or cut down your clitoris." Heart thumping, face hot, I bite my lip to keep from swearing. "Didn't any of those creeps ever tell you it's okay to be intersex?"

Dani runs her fingertips down the side of my face, like she's calming some hysterical little kid. Her eyes grow tender. "I want to be normal. All right? If that takes surgery, well then..." Pain grows in her eyes till she turns her head away.

There's gotta be a way to reach you. "Has Dr. Pierson ever gone back on her word?"

"No. Why?"

"She promised to arrange your surgery. Isn't there anything you'd like to do now that the gender police aren't watching?"

Her lips slow-morph into a smile. "Will you teach me to ride a motorbike?"

I flash her a teasing grin. "Isn't mine off-limits?"

Some of the old Dani—the high-spirited tomboy I so loved—shines past the barrettes and makeup. "How much does a dirt bike cost?"

Motocross or not, she'd still have to drive it on the road. "Honda makes a street-legal 250. With a helmet and all—about four grand new."

She purses her lips and appears to reconsider. "That's a lot for something I'd only use for six weeks—ten at the most."

"Wouldn't you keep it?"

Her face turns sullen. "Mum says a proper young lady doesn't ride motorbikes."

Guess I'm not one then, huh? How many other things is Dani giving up in the name of being a woman?

We walk on in silence. When she turns to me again, the tender concern in her eyes surprises me. "Are you who you want to be?"

Me? My gut sends a quiet snicker up my throat. Hardly. The stupid bike keeps my hands rough and my nails chipped. All the money I get I spend on parts. Would I rather be a princess like *Danièle*? Well, yeah. Who wouldn't?

After the Welles family moved away, rumors about the two of us spread. Without Dani's friendship and encouragement, I went from wearing flowers in my hair to swearing and having fistfights with the bullies. All the taunts of the past five years sweep over me in an emotional tsunami. I try to hide my tears, but Dani pulls me close and holds me. "It's all right. Be whoever you want. You're still my friend."

I push away and start walking again—as much to flee the memories as to get home. When Dani catches up, she grabs my hand and pulls me to a stop. "Let's find a used motorbike. All right?"

"Okay. Yeah. Tommy will know where to get the best deal." A smile creeps back across my lips. Even if the girl isn't serious, she distracted me long enough for the emotions to fade. Okay, so she might still be my friend.

"Tommy?"

"Yeah. Some guy I met at a motocross event Dad took me to last year."

"Boyfriend?"

"Nah. Just somebody I hang out with."

As we cross San Amaro Drive, a car pulls out of my driveway. The house is still too far away to do more than guess what they wanted. I pick up the pace a little.

"What's up?" With her longer stride, Dani has no trouble keeping up.

"Dunno. A delivery maybe."

We're still a block from my home when I recognize something in our front yard—one of those fancy real estate signs on a wooden post. Selling the house can only mean one thing—Dad's not coming home. "No!" A wave of adrenaline pushes me into a sprint that leaves my lungs burning and my heart pounding. "I told you not to go."

"Melanie!" Dani catches up a breath later and grabs my arm. "What's wrong?"

"Yeah. For Sale. Stupid leaflets and all." I throw myself against the post, but it won't budge, so I beat at the sign with my hands till Dani grabs my shoulders and yanks me backwards.

"Stop it!" She seizes me in a tight embrace before I can take a swing at her.

"He has to come home." My anger shatters. I press my eyelids closed to hold back the torrent of grief. Adrenaline fades and leaves my body trembling. After my diaphragm spasms end and my heart settles down, Dani releases me.

The girl studies my face, the way she used to when we were little, like she can read my thoughts there. Dani appears about to lecture me, but only shakes her head. "You're bleeding."

Inside, I scrub my hands while Dani rifles through the drawers in the master bathroom. She returns with antibiotic ointment and some bandages.

The girl lays a towel across my hands and places a small bag of ice on top of each one. A mother's concern shines from her eyes. "I don't recall you having a hissy fit before."

It's called puberty. Mood swings have tormented me for so long I've almost gotten used to the roller coaster ride. "It's my stupid hormone medication. Tommy calls them my bitch pills. If I'm not yelling at him, I'm crying."

I try to brush my runny nose against my sleeve. Dani gives me a look like I'm some disgusting little kid, grabs a paper towel from the kitchen counter, and wipes my nose and upper lip clean. I scowl at her, but tamp down my anger. "Thanks."

"Perhaps you should stop taking them."

If you were female, you'd understand.

Pain flashes hot across Dani's face, like she might have read my thoughts for real this time. At least I didn't share them out loud.

"My periods were wicked bad—cramps, bleeding, nausea. The PMS alone drove me nuts. Tommy says I was worse before I went on the pill."

Eyes full of concern scan my face again. She takes a quick peek at my knuckles. "I assume you'll want help fixing dinner."

Both of my hands throb. "Well, yeah." *Mom is gonna kill me.*

CHAPTER 3

Danièle

After rinsing the blood stains from my blouse, I put on a new top, brush my hair, and check my makeup. Exhausted from the day's ordeal, I collapse on Melanie's bed. What became of the cheery—and often cheeky—ginger-haired pixie I knew?

My phone chirps. *Why do I get a message every time I have something important to think through?*

<< *Ethan—call me*

He answers right away. "Hey, babe. You all settled in?"

"I am. How's the internship going?"

"Boring. I practically have my PhD, but they treat me like a high school freshman."

Ethan's voice holds restrained anger. He's never been the most humble man. My fiancé expects to lead. He rarely asks for anyone's advice. Even mine. I roll my eyes at the phone. "I'm sure you'll win them over, love."

"That may take some doing. How are things on your end?"

Let's not talk about my surgeries. "Melanie and I have been renewing our friendship. She went with me to my first doctor's visit."

Silence follows a soft grunt of acknowledgment. "You can't have children."

My stomach tightens. "That's true. I don't have a uterus. We'll need to adopt."

"Can't we use my sperm and your eggs and have someone else carry our child?"

I explained all of this months ago. I don't have any ovaries either. "My—" The pediatric endocrinologist called them twisted ovaries. Testes would have been more accurate, even though they gave me a feminine puberty and don't produce sperm. "We'd need to get donor eggs as well. Is it that important? Surrogacy would be twice as expensive as adoption."

"Worth the cost to be certain what we'd get. And when."

Why are we talking about a family now? I have a year of college left to finish before becoming a mother. "Why the sudden interest in children?"

"I've been thinking a lot about Dad lately. He died when I was eight. I swore I'd marry young, have kids, and spend as many years with them—and my wife—as I could."

"And you want our children to be from your own sperm."

"Yeah, babe. You understand that, don't you?"

At times, my infertility cuts deep. "Yes, love. I do."

"The company also considers kids a huge plus—an indication of stability and maturity. They look for that when considering executive placement."

You've got a year left in graduate school, and you're already planning on a vice presidency? "Where will we get the money?"

"Don't worry about the finances. Okay, babe? I'll handle that. You work out the details."

"I guess I'll look into surrogacy then."

"Thanks. You're the best. This means a lot to me."

We say our goodbyes, but I stare at the phone long after he hangs up.

Melanie pokes her head into the room. "You gonna help with supper, or what?"

Her hands are bruised and lacerated, but most of the swelling has gone away. "Do they hurt much?"

"Nah. Let's use yours, though. Okay?"

The teachers at Knox Preparatory School instructed me on home economics theory. Mum taught me how to orchestrate a banquet. I've never cooked an actual meal, though.

Some of the old Melanie finds her way out as she directs my spaghetti sauce preparation. A fine line separates good-natured teasing from making fun of me, but her contagious laughter never hurts my feelings.

I've just put on water for the pasta when Mrs. Fairbairn walks in the door. She rushes to embrace me. "Danièle! Welcome back to Florida. Sorry I missed you yesterday."

Only five years have elapsed, but the woman in front of me has aged at least a decade. Dark circles under her eyes speak of a lack of sleep. Or ill health. Perhaps both.

My chest constricts as I remember a time—years ago—when Melanie lived with us for several months. Doctors treated Mrs. Fairbairn for an aggressive form of breast cancer. As her mother's health deteriorated, Melanie became increasingly distraught. At one point she wouldn't talk to anyone but me.

When I glance at Melanie, her mother rests a gentle hand on my arm and whispers, "Please don't upset her."

I meet the concern in her eyes and dip my head. Her daughter has enough issues.

Melanie hands me a box of angel hair pasta. I dump it into the boiling water and start a timer. She snickers when I get out china plates instead of plastic, and again when I explain why setting spoons on the table is proper, even if no one uses them.

Mrs. Fairbairn takes three bites of spaghetti before dropping her fork and rushing around the table. "What happened?" She removes her daughter's bandages and examines her hands.

"I'm okay, Mom. I ran into that stupid sign. Why are we selling the house, anyhow?"

"I'm sorry, honey. They were supposed to wait until I'd spoken with you." Mrs. Fairbairn returns to her seat and pokes at her spaghetti. "I'm sending you to a private school in September, and we have to pay the expenses somehow. I'll stay with Beatrice and Fred."

"But Dad..."

"Honey, you know your father's not coming home."

Melanie drops her glass and bounces up out of her chair. "Liar! He is so." Her eyes blaze, and her whole body trembles for a moment before she bolts for the door.

I set down my fork and stare at Mrs. Fairbairn.

What should I do?

Melanie

Dad promised to retire from the military after one final tour in Afghanistan. Six months later, some guy comes to the door and tells us my father died a hero.

Who cares about them or their crummy war, anyhow? Weren't two tours enough? I begged him not to go.

Dad said he loved us, but he had a duty to perform.

Now we're all alone.

I climb on his motorcycle and slump against the garage wall. What will I do without his hugs and his stories and his motorcycle rides?

The icy numbness wears off, and my hands wake up again. My throbbing right thumb remains swollen, like I mighta sprained the thing. I flash a scowl at the real-estate sign and show it that my middle finger still functions perfectly.

Movement in my peripheral vision turns out to be Dani. *Right. Like I need you to bug me right now.*

She hugs me and pats my back. "I'm sorry about your father."

Dani used to hold me whenever I hurt and Dad wasn't around. Wouldn't Mom? Well, yeah, but I kept getting mad at her. "Life sucks. Okay?" I'd push her away, but my hands hurt too much. So I rest my head on her shoulder and cry instead.

When my hiccups stop, I back away from the girl. "Gotta get hold of Tommy." I run back into the house and find Mom. "I'm sorry for calling you a liar."

She pulls me close and kisses me on the forehead. "I know you didn't mean it, honey."

Yeah I did. But I meant the apology too. "One of Tommy's friends wants to buy the stuff in the shed—Dad's motorcycle parts and all."

Mom studies my face for a long while before nodding. "All right, but I have no idea where your father keeps—where he left the key."

You too, huh? Wish I could fix things for you, Mom. I squeeze her hand. "Doesn't matter. Tommy can cut off the lock."

One eyebrow drifts up her forehead, but she nods agreement.

I walk into my room, grab my phone, and send Tommy a message.

>> *Melanie—Alan wants bike parts?*

The boy never lets go of his phone, so I plop down on my bed and wait.

<< *Tommy—your dad's stuff?*

>> *Melanie—yeah*

<< *Tommy—u sure?*

>> *Melanie—yeah*

<< *Tommy—bike 2?*

Keeping my father's old motorcycle isn't gonna bring him back.

>> *Melanie—yeah. tues am?*

A minute passes. He might be in traffic on South Dixie Highway.

<< *Tommy—k c ya*

So that's it, Dad. I toss the phone aside, then kick off my sneakers, curl up on my bed, and dream of a boy who promised to love me always.

Sunbeams fade to moonlight and shadows to dark emptiness. Somewhere in the house Dani's lilting voice raises a question.

Mom's soft reply follows a moment later.

Footsteps pad across the living room and up the hallway. The door creaks open a slit. "Are you all right?" The girl walks right in, flips on the light, and plops down on the bed beside me.

"Does it matter?"

"Yes." Violet eyes overflow with tender concern.

Hold me. After five long years, I refuse to ask anything of the girl.

Yet she reads my desire. As she always did. Dani pulls her dress over her head and drapes it across a chair. After slipping on a night-gown, she runs to the bathroom for a minute. When Dani gets back, she turns out the light, lies on the bed beside me, and works her arms around my waist. For a moment, the girl presses her face into my hair. Hot breath tickles my ear. "I'm sorry I haven't been a better friend."

A broken promise stands between us, but her warm hands against my arms sooth my anguish. Back when Mom had cancer, Dad came home from Afghanistan, but he still had to work long hours. Beatrice went to stay with my Aunt Margaret. And me with the Welles family. Dani was all I had back then. She held me and listened to my pain. She told me things would be okay.

In the darkness I seek the girl's eyes again. "Dad's gone, and now Mom's sending me away to finish school."

Violet eyes shine like pale moonlight. "You didn't graduate from high school?"

"No. They expelled me for fighting. I got a year to make up."

"Prep school isn't so bad. You'll be all right." Her assurance fades as my eyes challenge her. "You're welcome to stay with my parents," she says. "I'll be in college, but home most weekends. Mum would love to home-school you."

Yeah, make a proper lady outta me. Like that'll happen.

I pull myself closer and nuzzle into her shoulder. Dad's never coming back, but that doesn't keep me from entertaining an impossible dream.

CHAPTER 4

Danièle

Work day. Melanie scrounges through a pile of clothes she dumped on her bed and hands me a paint-stained T-shirt. "Mine. Should fit you okay." Next, she picks out a ratty pair of jeans. "Mom's. You'll have to try them on. Mine might fit you better." Last of all, she hands me some old gardening gloves.

Most of the next several days we spend scrubbing the house, sorting through the family's possessions, and generally preparing for an agent to show the property. With my hair in a loose ponytail, and grime my only makeup, a grin takes up permanent residence on my face. The daily phone calls from Ethan assure me of his love.

Tuesday morning, as I'm carrying out a box of trash, a couple of young men rattle up the driveway in a decrepit Ford pickup. Melanie introduces the driver as Tommy. Tall and beanpole thin, he's a cross between a backwoods farm boy and a college-educated nerd. The hug he gives Melanie lingers. A hand wanders up her back. "You sure you wanna sell the stuff?" he says.

Melanie's jaw muscles tighten. She steps back, easing out of his embrace. After a sharp nod, she glances at me. My cheeks warm as I turn my attention to the other man.

Tommy's friend Alan might be in his late thirties. "Well, kid, let's take a look at what you got," he says. Despite being a bit sloppy, and having beard stubble, he proves as businesslike as my uncle Randy.

Tommy hefts a pair of bolt cutters longer than his arm. He snips the lock off, as though it's soft plastic, sets the tool aside, and waves her forward. "After you, kid."

It takes us an hour to sort through and load everything, but less than a minute for Melanie and Alan to agree on a price. All she keeps are a few cafe racing trophies, a box of photos, and an old set of motorcycle racing leathers—pants and a long-sleeved jacket.

As the truck drives off, my phone chirps again.

<< *Ethan—call me*

I say a short prayer for his sanity and press connect. "Are you there?"

"Hey, babe. Finances are a done deal. You got a surrogate lined up yet?"

I roll my eyes and glance at Melanie. "Is someone with red hair and green eyes satisfactory?"

"Is she pretty?"

My gaze wanders back to Melanie and lingers. She carries an extra fifteen pounds. Her wavy hair—always unruly—snakes about her shoulders. A touch of facial asymmetry curls her grin up a bit further on one side. Her true beauty—and what makes her pleasant company—is her empathy. Compassion learned through pain shines from her emerald eyes and whispers in her laughter. Who better to be the biological mother of our children? "Yes. She is. Should I ask her?" Almost—almost I regret that her mother will never allow it.

"Yeah. I want to get moving on this right away."

What? "Weren't we planning to have our wedding next summer?"

"I've got this job nailed down—just as soon as I have my degree. I figure we get married the first of March. That gives us three months to find a house and get settled in with the kid before I grad-uate and start working."

Nine months before April means embryo implantation in July. Does an IVF cycle take a month? We need to start now. Today. A smile—sure proof of my insanity—creeps across my lips. "I'll let you know what she says."

"One more thing, babe. Your father says you want to face your medical stuff on your own. I won't push my way in where you don't want me, but I can take time off and would love to be with you when you wake up from surgery. Whatever you need, babe, I'll do for you."

"Thanks, love. I'll be fine. It's enough to hear your voice every day. And know you love me."

"So long as you're sure. My heart will be there. You know I love you."

After Ethan bids me goodbye, I dial my mother's number. "Mum?"

"Yes, sweetheart. Enjoying your holiday?"

"Ethan wants us to have a child right away."

"Wonderful! I'm certain you'll make a brilliant mother."

"No, Mum. He asked me to arrange a surrogacy now so the baby arrives right after our honeymoon."

"That sounds a bit unusual, but—"

"He's looney." *So am I for wanting a baby before we get married.*

"Why of course. Men aren't the most rational of God's creatures."

"Daddy's sane."

"Theodore's a brilliant husband and father, but he's as mad as the rest."

"How do I talk Ethan out of it?"

"Sweetheart, if the young man's to be your husband, you must accept his idiosyncrasies. Give wise counsel, but support him when he doesn't heed your advice."

"With an infant, I won't have time for college."

"Perhaps Melanie will agree to stay on as nanny after the child's born."

The phone slips from my fingers and lands face down in the grass. *Now's when someone tells me this is all a joke, and everyone laughs at my expense.*

Melanie glances at me and grins.

I pick up my cell and stare at it for a moment before putting the phone to my ear again. "Mum, are you orchestrating this?"

"No, love, but your father is. When Ethan approached him regarding finances for a surrogacy, he decided a baby might well be the perfect stimulus for your maternal instincts."

"Mrs. Fairbairn would never—" *You wouldn't suggest Melanie as a nanny unless her mother had already approved of such an arrangement.* My stomach muscles tighten, and the air grows thick around me while I wait for my mother to speak.

"Laura and I have already chatted. If Melanie agrees to act as surrogate, Randolph will draw up a contract, and your father will oversee the finances."

I stare at Melanie and shake my head. *We're doomed. Both of us.*

"Sweetheart?" Mum's voice becomes tender again. "If you don't wish to do this..."

"No, Mum. You know I want children." *And everyone else expects this of me.*

Melanie

The M-Path train sways, a gentle back and forth motion a mother might use to soothe her baby. Kinda makes me wanna barf.

Dani's been fidgeting for days—her thumbs never leave her phone. I sidle up beside her and block the screen with my hand. "What's going on?"

"Hmm? Oh. Ethan wants to have children right away."

"Does he know you can't have kids?"

"Yes. I talked to him after we started dating."

"So what's the big deal? Adopt."

We roll to a stop at the Santa Clara station. I take Dani's hand and head for the exit. Ten minutes later, we arrive at the clinic.

Dr. Pierson has her own office, but we find the door locked, so we go to the waiting area and sign in. A few minutes later, a nurse shows us to an exam room and hands Dani a gown.

"Guess you know what to do with that," I say.

Dani hops up on the table, glances at the business end, and shuts her eyes. Muscles grow tense.

Well, yeah. I don't like stirrups much, either.

I climb up beside her and put an arm around her shoulder. "It's only Dr. Pierson. She's not gonna march in here with a bunch of stupid med students."

She glances at me and nods, but doesn't relax.

Dr. Pierson does bring a nurse with her.

I hop down off the table, but Dani grabs my arm, shakes her head, and makes puppy eyes at me. No way am I gonna watch, so I lean my back against the table and hold her hand.

Dr. Pierson beams at me like I'm her granddaughter or something before facing Dani. "Ordinarily, we don't allow anyone other than staff present while we examine a patient. Melanie's free to wait in my office if she likes."

"She'll be with me for all of my exams. I get really nervous about anyone poking around down there. I think you know why."

Static hangs in the air between Dr. Pierson and Dani for a moment before the doctor nods acceptance.

What was that all about?

The girl yanks on my hand till I turn around. Pleading eyes skewer me before she slides her heels into the stirrups and scoots her tush toward the doctor.

Yeah, knees up, legs apart—every girl knows that drill.

Dr. Pierson holds up one of those stupid duckbill things my gynecologist is so fond of poking where no man has ever gone before. A tiny one, though. "I'm going to start with a pediatric speculum," she says. Let me know if you experience any discomfort."

Dani remains quiet the entire time, only nodding or shaking her head at the doctor's questions. All the while she's crushing my hand with hers.

"All finished." Dr. Pierson snaps off her gloves and drops them into the medical waste. "Get dressed and come to my office. We'll talk there."

While Dani slips on her clothes, I stare out the window at the cars below. How will the girl make it through surgery if a routine pelvic is such an ordeal?

We stroll back down the hallway to Dr. Pierson's office. Books, knitting, kids' toys, plants—the doctor made a den out of the place. I plop down into an overstuffed leather armchair. Tension melts out of me. I grin when I spy a tray with three bottles of water and a bowl of chocolates and nuts.

Dr. Pierson closes the folder on her desk and leans back. "Danièle, I spoke with Dr. Nguyen about your surgeries. He's old school regarding intersex, but he does excellent work."

The girl's face pales, like maybe she's heard of the guy. So I reach over and put my hand on hers.

The doctor pauses for a moment, flipping though some papers on her desk. "Vaginal development in PAIS varies. Many patients can gain adequate depth using a set of dilators. In your case, however, I believe surgery is appropriate."

Muscles in Dani's face relax a little, like maybe she's accepted her fate. "All right."

Dr. Pierson glances at me before continuing. "There are a number of different techniques used to create or lengthen a vaginal canal. Dr. Nguyen prefers the Davydov procedure—a laparoscopic transposition of the peritoneal colpopoiesis." She grins. "Would you like that in English?"

"Well, yeah," I say.

Dr. Pierson looks at me in surprise.

I'm here too, you know.

The doctor opens a drawer, pulls out what looks like some huge needle with a knob on one end, and turns to Dani again. "This is a laparoscope. Dr. Nguyen—or one of his associates—will insert several of these into your abdomen through small incisions. Laparoscopic surgery is safe and minimally invasive."

After replacing the gizmo, she opens a bottle of water. "The peritoneal membrane lines the abdominal cavity. Colpopoiesis is a fancy word for making a vagina. Dr. Nguyen will deepen your vaginal canal and use part of your peritoneum to line it. There's a short video of the procedure online I'd like you to watch. All right?"

Dani's eyes are about glazed by now, but she nods.

Dr. Pierson slides her chair back and stands. "We'll get together again at the house next week to talk about the rest of your surgeries. You're welcome to stay here at the clinic and watch the video. Any questions?"

She's already given us way more information than I wanted. Is she trying to scare the crap out of Dani so she'll cancel her surgery?

Well, yeah, I sure hope so. Sex doesn't have to be vaginal inter-course, you know.

I grab the crazy girl's hand and head for the door.

Danièle

On the train back, I gaze out the window and struggle to work up the courage to ask Melanie to carry Ethan's baby. In the reflection, emerald eyes study me. A smirk creeps across Melanie's lips. She leans against me and grabs my hand. "Okay. Out with it."

While Mrs. Fairbairn underwent chemotherapy, Melanie stayed with us. Through the emotional turmoil of those months our hearts intertwined. She understands me better than anyone. Perhaps she still cares enough to agree. "Will you be a surrogate mother for me and Ethan? You know I can't have a baby on my own."

After a moment, pain overwhelms the surprise in her eyes. The barest hiss of a whisper reaches my ears. "I can't."

The train slows to a stop. Melanie pushes away and runs for the door as though the car is aflame.

I struggle through the crowd and rush to catch up. "Melanie, wait!" Tires screech as I bound down the stairs. *Melanie! Oh, please, God, no!*

Outside the station, people crowd the sidewalk. Cars honk. Waves of heat rise from the asphalt. Choppy breaths bring me not nearly enough oxygen. Muscles tremble from the adrenaline.

Melanie sits on the far side of the road, hands to her head. I stumble across the street and collapse on the grass next to her. "Are you all right?"

She gazes past me at the cars stopped on Ponce. "Yeah, well, they all missed. Does it matter?" Mournful eyes pierce my heart. "Look. I'm screwed up. Okay?"

Words refuse to organize into anything meaningful, so I put an arm around her shoulder and pull her close. What can I offer that might help her beyond my friendship? And a lame Cockney accent. "It's the world what's bloomin' mental, luv. Not you."

Well, at least that coaxed a smile out of you.

Happiness fades from her eyes, though. "Dad's gone. Mom's gonna live with my sister. Me pregnant's the last thing she'd want."

"Wouldn't you rather stay with my parents than attend preparatory school?"

"Well, yeah."

"If I get your mother's blessing, will you consider surrogacy?"

She stares at me until suspicion replaces the pain. "Is this a set-up?"

I've broken promises, but never lied to her. "According to Mum, the decision's yours."

"For real?" Her warm smile burns away the morning's dark clouds.

CHAPTER 5

Melanie

Imagination swirls around me and weaves the air into wild impossibilities—me at prep school, dressed in a cute white blouse and plaid skirt, books held against my chest—another me, the mother of a beautiful little girl, with Dani beside me.

Sweet. "I get to choose?" I'm not talking to Dani, but the girl plays bobble-head anyhow.

A curious glow warms me as I examine my two pathways, like a beautiful package nestles in my lap, all wrapped in shiny paper and lace ribbons. An embossed card says the present's from Miss Danièle Aileana Welles. One choice or the other, one peek into the box means leaving this stupid place forever.

I click open my locket. The old Dani reminds me of the promise we made. Always and forever. We belong to each other, even if the old Dani has faded into the mists of time. I hold the new Dani's hand while we walk back home.

The girl would probably write down positives and negatives for all the options and give each one a value. She always makes plans and orders the world around her.

Me? I found out when my mother got cancer that I have no say in what happens. I begged God to make her better, but for a long time, she kept getting worse.

Dad said God does things for our good, but not always to our liking. Well, Dad's gone now, and either path I take leads me away from Mom as well.

Some important choices you only get to make one time, and they're done. I want to hold mine in my arms a while before sending the decision on its way. Am I gonna agree to be a mother? Well, yeah. I gave Dani my word when we were little. She broke her promise. I'll keep mine. But not before I make the girl pay.

Five days—one for each year she was away—that seems reasonable. Dani doesn't mention surrogacy again, but she gets all sad-faced, especially after the daily call from her boyfriend. I almost cave early out of sympathy.

* * * *

The next Tuesday, Mom's all chipper. She gabs the entire way through supper, and after we clear the dishes, she sets a homemade devil's food cake on the table. "This is a thank-you for all the hard work you two did around here."

We never keep sweets in the house. Ever. Dessert goes straight from my mouth to my hips. I was skinny before the pill became part of my life.

A wicked grin splits my face. Surrogacy might mean I could eat chocolate again. I cut myself a healthy slice. "Mom, is it okay if I have Dani's baby?"

The girl drops her fork, cake and all. It rattles around on the floor. *Sweet.*

Mom's eyes do a slow-motion nova, but she smiles, wicked-like. "Why of course, honey. Are you two getting married soon?"

Whoa! You know that's not what I meant. "No, Mom. She asked me to be a surrogate mother for her and Ethan."

"You'd stay with her parents?"

"Yeah. Maybe they'd help me get my GED."

Mom walks around the table, wipes some chocolate off my face, and hugs me. "You don't need my permission, honey, but I'm glad you asked. What you're doing takes compassion. I'm proud of you."

"Thanks, Mom."

"Be sure to tell Dr. Pierson you're taking oral contraceptives." She pulls us into a group hug. "I am so happy for both of you."

Dani's phone chirps. Another text. She excuses herself and steps outside.

My mother and I clear away the dessert dishes. *No way Dad would have agreed to my getting pregnant. You neither when he was alive. What happened?* "Mom, why are you okay with this?"

She hugs me again, tighter than usual. "Would you marry Tommy someday if he asked?"

Nerd, thrasher, at times a jerk—he's been my only real friend since high school. "Yeah, I guess." *If I had to.*

"You're not sure? Have you slept with him?"

He's not my boyfriend. "Mom. No. He's—never mind." The problem isn't with him, anyhow. My heart never got over the last one.

Relief calms my mother's eyes. In spite of what Mom says, she never much liked Tommy. "Is there someone else?"

"No." I bite my lip and turn my face away, hoping she's forgotten the boy who loved me so long ago.

My mother's tenderness pries open my heart. "Was there ever?"

You know there was. My cheeks grow hot. He promised me his heart. "He's gone, Mom."

"There's always hope. Perhaps one day he'll return. What if you could have *his* baby?"

Tears blur the corners of my vision. "Mom. Just don't. Okay?"

She pulls me close and holds my head against her breast. "It's all right to dream, honey."

Danièle

Melanie and I stay up past three in the morning. We chat like schoolgirls at a pajama party, and sleep past both breakfast and mid-morning tea.

Melanie shakes me awake in a panic. We dress, grab a quick snack, and rush out the door.

On the way to our appointment, I call Mum and leave a short voice-mail. Ethan will let me know when to call. No sense in texting him yet.

My heart continues to bounce from bliss to wondering about my sanity, and back again. What would the psychologists think of such emotional turmoil?

Dr. Pierson greets us and waves us toward the dining room. "Why don't you both sit on one side of the table? I need to draw some illustrations."

She sits across from us and opens a medical encyclopedia. "Androgen Insensitivity Syndrome varies in severity, depending on which genetic mutation's involved. The Quigley Scale provides doctors with a means of grading the effect of AIS on genital shape." She turns the book around and points at a chart. "Typical male is grade one—female grade six."

Melanie flashes me a look of total boredom, no doubt meant to urge me to leave my bits as they are.

Dr. Pierson writes on her notepad. "Clitoral Recession—for genitals toward the feminine end of the scale, the clitoris can be tucked further back into the body."

Melanie frowns at me. Her whole face broadcasts her opposition to my having any surgery at all. Beneath the table I grab her hand and squeeze.

The doctor points at the chart again. "The procedure reduces the visual prominence of the organ without removing any tissue. Nerve damage is still possible, and sometimes erections become painful. You're on the masculine end of grade four—your labia are mostly fused. Although your phallus is shaped like a clitoris, I'm certain it's too large to recess."

She begins to draw again. "Dr. Nguyen will remove the erectile tissue from the shaft and reduce the size of the head. The remaining tissue will then be relocated closer to your pubic bone. You may experience a significant loss of sensitivity."

Melanie squeezes my hand. Hard. Sympathy and pain flow from her eyes. She might object to my having surgery, but her support will carry me through.

I put on my most reassuring smile. "I'll be all right." *As long as I don't think about the surgery too much.*

The doctor gets up and brings us all drinks and snacks. After a few minutes, she leans back in her chair. "There's one additional procedure I'd recommend. With intra-abdominal testes, gonadal cancer's difficult to detect. An orchiopexy is a procedure for moving a testis down the inguinal canal and fixing it in the scrotum—or in your case, the groin area or labia. Testes are easier to monitor there."

Panic sweeps away my composure. They might be the same gonads wherever they live, but having them in my abdomen makes them easier to think of as ovaries. What would Ethan say about my having testes between my legs?

The doctor gathers up her drawings. "Any questions?"

I nod, but wait for my heart to slow enough to let me think again. "Yes. Melanie's agreed to act as a surrogate for Ethan and me. We'd like you to handle the IVF."

Dr. Pierson's good mood fades. "I'd love to, Danièle, but August's my last month at the clinic. I'm retiring."

"Once Melanie's pregnant, wouldn't an obstetrician be sufficient?"

Surprise and confusion widen her eyes for a few seconds before her face hardens. "How soon did you intend to start?"

Tension bubbles up out of my gut. Talk of moving my gonads left my mind unprepared for debate. "Right away?"

The doctor lets out a groan of disappointment and closes her eyes for a moment. "Having a child is a serious commitment. Have you all thought this through?"

Any arguments I might have made slip away. The path I tread has been dictated by psychologists and doctors who abhor sexual ambiguity, parents determined to see me happy, and my own desire for some semblance of a normal life. Surrogacy or adoption—marriage and motherhood is my *condicio sine qua non*—proof that I'm normal rather than some monster. Yet part of me still doubts.

Melanie's eyes plead for me not to abandon her. I squeeze her hand tight and nod my encouragement.

Disappointment clouds her face, but she hesitates only a moment. "We've wanted to do this forever, doc. I was five the first time I promised Dani I'd have her babies."

Anger simmers in Dr. Pierson's eyes. She fixes her doubts on me again. "And I suppose the only thing you ever wanted was to have children." Regret flashes across her face, but she says nothing more.

Are you happy as a girl? Want to play with trucks instead of dolls? Do you want to be a mommy or a daddy? Doctors grilled me about my gender a thousand times. Well, they can all buzz off. "I wouldn't need you if I were female. I'd be home, planning my wedding."

All the frustrations of an intersex childhood boil up out of my gut. "If I were male, Melanie and I would get married. If we had reproductive issues, we'd come to you expecting help, not questions about our determination to have a child."

I stand and lean toward Dr. Pierson, hands clamped on the edge of the table. My arms tremble as I fight to suppress my anger. "I'm well satisfied with my body and my gender, doctor, but since I'm intersex, and no one but Melanie's capable of accepting that, I'm here for surgery to make the rest of the bleeding world happy with what's between my legs. If you don't think that demonstrates my commitment to becoming a mother, then nothing will."

Melanie grins at my language, stands, and offers me a high five. We're halfway to the front door before Dr. Pierson speaks again. "Next week we'll make final arrangements for your procedures."

Might as well seal my doom. I pause in the doorway. "No. Not without the surrogacy." I pull the door closed after me and stumble toward the street.

What have I done? My parents' biggest fear becomes mine—I'll always be alone.

Melanie grabs my arm and pulls me to a stop. "Guess that didn't go so well, huh?"

"I'm sorry." My foolishness has destroyed her hopes as well as my own.

"For what? Standing up for yourself?"

"For caring more about my pride than my marriage. Or you. Or the baby."

"Yeah, well, that part definitely sucks." Melanie slides her arms around my waist. Mischief sparkles in her eyes. "So we'd get hitched if you were a guy?"

Another bit of foolishness, that. "Your mother asked if I'd rather be the donor myself. Of course I would. To father your child, or be pregnant with Ethan's—is it so bad to dream of what might have been had I been born entirely male or female?"

Those tender emerald eyes swear that she would have loved me too.

I press my lips against hers—a light caress for what might have been. My pulse throbs in my temple. If I were male, we'd spend our lives together.

Melanie Rose turns her crimson face away. "So, what are we gonna do now?"

You sense it, don't you? I've always loved you, but never felt quite like this before. My shoulders twitch up. "I have no idea." In a moment of anger, I've destroyed my one chance at happiness.

CHAPTER 6

Melanie

Dani remains quiet the entire way back across campus. The dark clouds overhead make more noise than she does. I don't feel much like talking either, but I'm used to having a life that sucks. Part of me never believed the pregnancy thing would happen anyhow.

But we still have most of the afternoon free. "Tommy's off today. Wanna learn to ride?"

The girl stares at me like I'm talking Swahili.

"His motorcycle. Buy him some gas, and he'll be happy to teach you."

Eagerness blossoms on Dani's face. "Sure."

Tommy agrees to meet us at the house. We're almost there when Dani's phone rings. She pulls it out and frowns at the screen. "Dr. Pierson. I should apologize to her."

I grab her cell and brush the call into voice-mail. "Later. Okay?"

As soon as we get home, I dig out my father's old racing leathers. They may not fit Dani very well, but they'll keep her from losing too much skin if she takes a spill. She wrinkles her nose at the stiff leather, but tries on the jacket anyhow.

Dani fills a small cooler with bottled water, fruit juice, and ice. I find some peanuts and apples and shove them into my tote.

A vehicle pulls up outside while I'm searching the coat closet for my hat. I go to the door to greet Tommy, but find my mother there instead. She gives me a quick hug. "How'd your appointment go?"

"Not so good. When we mentioned surrogacy, Dr. Pierson got all snotty, and Dani told her off."

Mom rolls her eyes, but amusement curls her lips. "You didn't?"

Dani lowers her head in shame. "I need to call her and apologize."

My mother approaches the girl and runs her fingertips down the sleeve of Dad's jacket. She glances over her shoulder at me. "Your father's leathers. You're taking her riding?"

"Yeah. Tommy said he'd teach her."

Warm contentment flows from my mother's face. "You two be careful."

A horn sounds. I rush outside, set the cooler and my tote in the back of Tommy's pickup, and run back inside the house again to grab my helmet.

Dani eases into the cab after me, pulls the door closed, and paws around on the seat for the belt. When she looks up again, her violet eyes burn with excitement. Almost like old times.

Welcome back, Dani.

Danièle

We drive west until suburbs give way to fields divided by canals and fences. Out past Krome Avenue before turning off on a desolate side road. Beyond a steel gate, gravel trails off through palms and pines. A quarter mile further on, our path ends at the edge of an open pasture.

I step out of the cab into the blazing sun and grab a bottle of water from our cooler. Wearing a helmet and a leather jacket will keep the sun's rays off my skin, but sweat already trickles down the middle of my back. Is learning to ride really worth heat stroke?

After Tommy unloads the motorbike, he waves me over. "You ready?"

The breeze raises dust—a fine grit that clings to me. I take another long drink and glance at the sky. *Maybe if I leave the jacket unzipped...* I ease my leg over the already-too-hot leather seat.

Tommy places my left hand on the grip. "Clutch. Everything starts here." My right hand he moves to the other handle. "Throttle." He gestures toward the clearing. "I want you to drive around the edge of this here field. Real slow. Keep your feet spread apart. Give it a little gas. Let the clutch out. Back off on the throttle. Clutch in and coast to a stop. Got that?"

"Yes, sir."

He spits a wad of something vile on the ground. "None of that 'sir' crap. You hear?"

"All right."

"Pull in the clutch."

When I comply, he starts the engine and steps on the left foot pedal. "That there's the gear shift. Leave it be for now. The right pedal's the rear brakes. Don't press it unless the clutch is in. Always the clutch first."

I kill the engine the first time. Tommy presses my fingers over the lever and starts the bike again. "Anything goes wrong—the clutch. Always the clutch."

Halfway around the field, the motorbike bucks and coughs until I squeeze with my left hand and coast to a stop. In the distance, Tommy yells, "You got it. Just relax."

A drop of sweat burns my eye. Sun glints off the gas tank. My heart pounds as though I'm risking my life.

I can do this. The tension melts away and I ride back around to the starting point.

Tommy sits on the motorbike behind me and places his left hand over mine again. "Clutch first. Always." With his right, he moves my fingertips over the lever. "Front brakes." He taps my right foot with his. "Rear brakes." He repeats it all again, in sequence.

He squeezes my left hand for an instant. "Clutch first. Always." Tommy pushes my left foot off the rest. "Gear shift pattern's one down, five up. If you keep kicking down until it won't go no more, you're in first." He sticks the toe of his boot under the lever and nudges it up. "Tap it up into neutral. Got that?"

He presses my left hand again, and I ease off the clutch. "I think so."

Tommy slides off the motorbike and waves me forward. "Once around the field. Shift between first and second. Both brakes."

Off to the side, Melanie bounces up and down. I smile at her, then drive off, only to stop on the other side of the field.

How does anyone control both throttle and brakes with their hand this way? After a bit of experimentation, I wrap my thumb and index finger around the throttle and pull the brake with my other three fingers.

Melanie brings me a bottle of water when I stop near the truck again. I set the helmet on the gas tank in front of me and take a long drink. "Thanks."

"You're doing a bunch better than I did first time out."

Melanie's grin reminds me of Mum after I gave my first piano recital—so proud of her daughter. What would she think of me now? "Riding feels...like being home."

Tommy glances at his watch. "Take her around again. See if you can get to third gear. Watch out for them stumps down yonder."

I reach fourth gear on a straight trail across the far side of the field. I don't scream, but my face freezes in a wild grin. Back near the truck again, I slide to a stop in front of Melanie and just let my face glow.

We stop at a gas station on the way back, to top off the transfer tank in the back of Tommy's pickup. I hand him my debit card, happy to finance the afternoon's joy.

Melanie grins as though I've won a first-place trophy for cafe racing. She tugs at one of the zippers on her father's jacket. "You're a natural, you know."

Behind her, Tommy leans forward, starts the engine, and nods in agreement. "Better'n most girls, anyways. You should buy one of them new Honda CB500 bikes."

"Thanks for teaching me." In his own way, Tommy's been an effective instructor.

The breeze shifts direction. Raindrops pelt the windscreen. For a while the air cools, and the sun hides behind grey clouds. I take a deep breath of the tropical fragrances and smile sweet contentment.

Tommy says he has an important errand, so he drops us off in front of the Fairbairn home, tips his hat, and screeches on down the road. With Melanie's helmet in one hand, I follow her inside.

Moments later, I stand in front of the bathroom mirror and survey the damage. Small bruises dot the insides of my knees and ankles, where they bumped against the motorbike's frame. A larger bruise along my thigh came from grazing a stump. No need to mention that to anyone.

A single hour on a motorbike, and weird muscles in my hands and legs cramp. Even some in my shoulders.

A layer of fine dust clings to me. Grime streaks my chin. Dirt crusts near my hairline and around my nostrils. An uninvited snicker bursts from my gut. Not the most feminine I've ever looked. Mum would not approve. Young ladies simply do not wrestle with pigs—or ride motorbikes.

After a quick shower, I wipe Melanie's jacket clean and hand it back to her. "Thanks. Freedom was grand while it lasted."

"We can go again whenever you'd like."

"I'm sorry, but tomorrow I apologize to Dr. Pierson. Perhaps she'll change her mind about the surrogacy once I've recovered from—"

The phone rings—what else? I collapse on the bed, grab my cell, and thumb connect. "Are you there?"

"Hi, Danièle. Dr. Pierson. Do you have a moment?"

"Yes, ma'am."

"I'd like to speak with you. In person. Are you free this after-noon?"

"Yes. Should I come to your house?"

"Please. Alone, if you don't mind."

"I'll leave right away."

Melanie looks up from pulling on her jeans. "Where're you goin'?"

"Dr. Pierson's."

"I'll tag along." She grabs a T-shirt from her dresser and slips it over her head.

"She wants me to come alone."

"Well, yeah. The bad guys always say that."

For a moment, I think she's serious. "Look, if I'm not back in two hours, send in the cavalry."

"Deal."

Melancholy, uncertainty, and hope follow me to the doctor's house. Has she changed her mind about surrogacy?

Dr. Pierson answers the door right away. "Thank you for com-ing."

The smell of tea caresses my nose as I enter the house. I slide into one of the doctor's high-back chairs and force myself to relax.

She disappears into the kitchen and returns with a tray. "I believe Darjeeling's your favorite?"

"Yes, ma'am. Thank you." *How did you know?*

Iced tea—a sip proves it Southern hospitality sweet.

The doctor's eyes grow serious. "The most important thing a physician can do for any patient is help them make informed and rational decisions regarding treatment. I've failed you and would like to ask your forgiveness."

"I don't understand."

"Rather than inform you of your surrogacy options, I dismissed your request out of hand. I'm sorry."

"Does that mean you'll help us?"

"Once you understand your choices, I'll leave the final decision to you."

"Thank you. Please accept my apology for being rude."

"All right." Dr. Pierson swirls the tea in her glass and takes a long drink. "Knowing what to share with a patient—and when—can be difficult. I detest keeping secrets, and—well—now that you're old enough, I want to point out something from your Virginia medical records."

What are you talking about?

"The histology report on your gonadal biopsies—back when they thought you might have cancer—indicated the presence of spermatogonia. Sperm precursors. We should be able to harvest some from your testes and use them to fertilize Melanie's eggs."

For several heartbeats my mind refuses to process anything at all. *Sperm? Me?*

Testes in a woman—that's the nature of intersex—a mixture of the sexes.

If I were male, Melanie and I would get married.

Why didn't I know this five years ago? Would it have made any difference? I still wouldn't have given up my breasts.

I'm surprised they didn't remove my testes when they found out.

"I wouldn't make a very masculine man."

Dr. Pierson fills my glass again. "I'm not suggesting you try. You assured me that you're content with your body and your gender. I see no reason to change either."

Melanie can have my baby. My baby.

"But me father a child? That's asking a bit much of Ethan."

"Perhaps. Will you try to keep this a secret from him, then?"

Ethan already understands I'm intersex. At least in his head. If I hide my fertility from him, and he finds out—what then? Relationships can't be based on lies.

"No." My fiancé has a right to know.

"If he's upset with your fertility, will you give up your testes to marry him?"

"No. I don't think so." Losing them would mean taking estrogen or testosterone for the rest of my life. Too many women with my condition have osteoporosis, weight gain, depression, or other issues after castration. He'll understand.

"And the clitoral reduction?"

My little post he'd see every day. "For now, let's plan on that. Can I let you know for certain sometime before surgery?"

"Yes. The day you sign your releases. The more time you take to consider your options, the better."

Dr. Pierson reaches into her desk drawer and retrieves a pamphlet. "The ethics of assisted reproduction are complex. And contested. This brochure summarizes some of the more popular arguments."

"Thanks. I'll go over this with Melanie." I slip the paper into my purse.

"Some clinics will do selective reduction of fetuses after implantation. We don't."

"That's fine." I pull Randy's card from my wallet and hand it to Dr. Pierson. "My uncle's an attorney. Would you call him with any requirements you have for the surrogacy? And tell him what we should do to protect Melanie?"

"Certainly. Will you be the sperm donor?"

To have a child of my own—something I've longed for most of my life—how can I throw that away? Ethan accepts my being intersex—that I have XY chromosomes, and testes in my abdomen rather than ovaries and uterus. Ethan might even accept that I'm fertile as a male. In theory. But like my clitoris, my child would be a daily reminder of how different I am. Caution reasserts control. "No. Assume Ethan will be the father." No sense in shoving it in his face.

"Once you've both signed the contract, have Melanie call for an appointment. I'll see you next week."

As I walk back across campus, my mind fails to make sense of my life. In the past month, I've returned from a year of college in England, accepted a marriage proposal, and arranged the surgery I always dreaded. Now the idea of Melanie having my baby spreads like wildflowers across a meadow in the spring.

Intersex didn't make my need to bear children any less urgent than any other woman's. Heedless of my infertility, I dreamed of being pregnant with Ethan's baby. Years ago, my imagination carried me off to another world, where I was Melanie's husband. Closer now, but still a hopeless fantasy.

I find Melanie waiting for me on the front step of her house. "Well?"

"She's agreed to help us."

Melanie lets out a screech and flings her arms around my neck. Mischief shines from her eyes. "How soon do we—you know—to get me pregnant?"

Rational thought flees, like I'm a schoolboy asking a pretty girl for a date. My cheeks burst into flames. *Brilliant. Just brilliant.* More than anything, my heart wants to ask her to have my baby. Not Ethan's. Mine. Right now. Here on the doorstep. No other girl has ever done that to me.

Mischief remains, but wonder and tenderness widen Melanie's eyes.

I close mine for a deep breath and gather the scattered bits of my reason. "My uncle has to draw up a contract for us. Then you can make an appointment to start IVF."

She smiles at my discomfort. "I imagine sometimes that things were different. That's okay, isn't it?"

"We can't live in dreams." I ease away from her and retreat into the house. *How am I going to hold my sanity together long enough to marry Ethan?*

CHAPTER 7

Melanie

A series of chirps drags me out of a pleasant dream. I fumble through the stuff on my shelf for my phone.

<< Tommy—u up? repeated a dozen times.

I am now. I thumb my response and toss the phone back on the shelf. What does he want at four-thirty in the morning?

The phone chirps again.

<< Tommy—at the door.

A quick peek through the blinds tells me nothing. I jerk on a robe and meander out into the kitchen to put on coffee. Way too early.

A soft knock brings me back from sleep. Tommy's face smiles at me through the sidelight window. I yank the door open. "What's up?"

His eyes track the coffee aroma to its source. I wave him inside and pour him a cup. Cream. No sugar. He gulps down the hot brew. "Thanks. Boss wants me to haul some junk to Orlando. Can I leave the bike here and pick it up tomorrow?"

"Yeah. Sure."

He empties his cup and strides out the door. After he unloads the motorcycle, he walks back into the house and hands me the keys. "Just don't leave the tank empty. Okay?"

"Yeah. Sweet." I pull the door closed, pour myself a cup, and plop down into a chair to contemplate life.

Around seven, Dani yawns her way into the kitchen. "You're up early," she says.

I dangle the keys in front of the girl's face. "Tommy left his motorcycle here for the day. You wanna go riding?"

The struggle on her face almost brings me to laughter.

A proper young lady doesn't ride a motorbike. Yeah, right. Enough of the old Dani—the human one—survives to win that battle.

She fidgets through breakfast, impatient to be out, and puts up with wearing my dad's leathers again.

When she's ready, I show her how to start the bike. "This is the gas cutoff. Fork lock. Ignition. Kill switch." I roll the motorcycle out to the street. "Stay on Baracoa, okay? That stop sign's Alhambra Circle. The next one's San Amaro Drive. It's busy, so turn around before you get there. Come back here and start over again. Okay?"

"All right." Dani glows, like I'm her mom and just gave her permission to ride her bicycle down the street.

"And chill, okay? Getting killed on a stupid motorcycle wouldn't be very ladylike."

She nods, turns her pretty little head both ways, and tears off down the street. I snag a lawn chair from the back yard, shake the dirt and spiders and stuff off, and set it up under the tree closest to the road. No way am I gonna let her ride without somebody watching.

An hour later, the engine sputters and goes quiet somewhere down near San Amaro. *Out of gas? Yeah. Guess so.* Tommy wouldn't have checked the tank before loaning out his bike. I jog down the street and meet Dani heading back. "Loan me the helmet, and I'll go fill the tank."

I straddle the seat, switch to reserve, and start the bike again. "Should be back in fifteen minutes." Tommy always goes to the same station. He never has any issues with water or dirt in the gasoline there. No way am I gonna risk making the boy mad just to save a few pennies. How much does two and a half gallons cost anyhow?

Puffy white clouds drift across the blue sky, like a lazy flock of sheep. The forecast calls for more of the same all day, with a quick shower here and there. Nice beach day for two fair-skinned girls. Anyhow, I'm not gonna camp out in a stupid lawn chair all day while she rides the motorcycle back and forth.

When I coast up the driveway, Dani opens the front door and waits for me to park the bike. "What's the plan?" she says.

"You got a swimsuit?"

She cranes her neck, like the answer's written across the sky or something. "Yes. And sunscreen."

"Great. Suit up. We'll grab lunch somewhere and head to the beach. Okay?"

"Sure."

Two towels, extra sunscreen, bottled water—I stick that and Dani's handbag into my backpack and hand the bundle to Dani.

Our first pass around the block is to see what kind of passenger the girl makes and find out how Tommy's motorcycle handles the extra weight. Dunno what I expected, but his bike's pretty lame. We aren't gonna be drag racing anybody. Dani, however, musta been born on a motorcycle—her balance is perfect.

We stop at a little seafood joint along the way—the only place I know that serves conch fritters. Our helmets draw a few odd looks, but the fried shrimp and other stuff taste yummy.

On the way out of the restaurant, Dani gives me puppy eyes. Let me drive, they plead.

"On the way back, okay? Let's see what traffic's like."

Even without a passenger, taking a dirt bike on South Dixie Highway would be nuts. No way we're going to Miami Beach or Crandon Park. Matheson Hammock, then.

We spend the next half hour exploring the two lane drives leading south and east toward the park. Shade trees stand guard over most of the neighborhood streets. Outstretched limbs join above the pavement.

I park the bike, and we find a spot on the white sandy beach surrounding the atoll pool. There, I strip off my T-shirt and jeans and slather another coat of sunscreen across my freckled skin. "You gonna go swimming?"

"Wading." She gathers her hair up under the old floppy hat I loaned her.

"If you meet a crocodile, don't harass him. They're protected."

She grins like she thinks I'm kidding. "I'll keep that in mind."

The girl sports a two-piece navy blue swimsuit—a cute halter top with a miniskirt bottom. Even with her hair all tucked up under her hat, her demeanor suggests a model waiting for her photographer to arrive. Dani's boyish figure has given way to feminine curves. Why does that bother me? Isn't that supposed to happen to girls—even some intersex ones?

Well, yeah. Her body converts a little of her testosterone to estrogen. And the girl's got plenty of testosterone.

I roll over and let my back absorb some rays. Warm grows too hot fast. I get up and shield my eyes. Not a cloud in the blue sky. Beads of sweat leave tiny salt trails across my skin.

When Dani returns, I wade out into the cool water. Bright reflections off the surface whisper their warning—a reminder of how little exposure will burn me. I wander back to shore and don my T-shirt and jeans again. Enough sun for one day.

"Are we leaving?" Dani brightens at the prospect. Her face expresses no regret as she dresses and packs away our towels. She grins when she hands me the backpack.

Yeah. Your turn. "Mind if we drive past the Biltmore Hotel?"

"Not at all. Why?"

"Mom and I always dreamed of staying there. I don't think we ever will now."

Out of the park, we turn north on Old Cutler Road. Heavy traffic, no passing—not the greatest place for small motorcycles. I signal Dani to take the first left. Hammock Lakes Drive cuts through to Southwest 52nd Avenue. Much safer—the few impatient drivers we encounter zip right on by us.

After a few miles, we turn left on South Alhambra Circle. The speed limit drops to twenty-five, but it isn't like we're in any hurry. A lazy drive takes us to Ponce De Leon Boulevard. I wave as we zip past Dr. Pierson's house on our way up Granada. By that time, Dani has demonstrated her ability to handle traffic. The girl drives better than I do.

The tower on the Biltmore rises in the distance as we turn on Anastasia Avenue. I motion for Dani to turn on Columbus Boulevard and park on the grass beside the street.

The girl pulls off her helmet and sets it on the tank in front of her. "Shall we take a tour?"

"No." I slide off the bike and stroll closer to Anastasia. "What a wondrous sight. A palace hidden away in Coral Gables."

"Why not go inside?"

"Not all covered in sand and sweat."

"We can come back."

"Maybe someday." I force my gaze away and leave the dream behind. Time to go home.

We head back down Granada. Traffic picks up as we approach the light at Blue Road.

A few blocks further on, the presence of danger sends a cold tremor down my sweating back. I twist my neck around like an owl searching for prey. Nothing at all behind us. Trees line both sides of the street. No threat anywhere. Except the car approaching on Granada. Half a block away. Yeah. Gotcha, Miami-Dade. I peek around Dani to check her speed.

Oblivious to the cop, Dani rolls the stop sign. Doesn't everybody? The cruiser passes through the intersection before flashing his blue lights.

My arms spasm and I scream at Dani, "Park!" The police might leave us alone if they think we're students.

As soon as the motorcycle stops, I slide off the back, put down the kickstand, and pull Dani from the bike. The girl yanks off her helmet. "What are you—"

"Cops!" I hang my helmet on one of the rearview mirrors and climb on the motorcycle again.

The officer pulls up close to us and gets out. "License and registration, please."

I step between Dani and the woman to hand her my license and a copy of Tommy's registration. "Here you go, ma'am."

Confusion flashes across the officer's brown eyes, but she takes my papers. Then the woman gestures at Dani and waits while the girl scrounges through her handbag.

"This is all I have," she says, and hands the officer a US passport.

"No license?"

"No, ma'am. Not yet."

The officer grunts exasperation and aims a finger at me. "In the passenger side." Her eyes track me as I walk around the vehicle and open the door. She speaks with Dani for a few minutes and hands the girl something before joining me in the car. "Do you know how many kids your age I've scraped off the pavement?"

"No, ma'am."

"You understand what you did wrong?"

"I rolled a stop sign."

She taps her dash-cam. "Your friend was operating a motor vehicle without a license."

Outside, beyond the officer, Dani stands beside Tommy's motorcycle. Hollow eyes stare back at me. My hand creeps up to the locket at my throat. I've gotten the girl in trouble again. "Are you gonna bust her?"

"She could face six months in jail and a $500 fine. Take her home and see she doesn't drive again."

"We can leave now?"

"Don't ever try to deceive a police officer. You hear me, young lady?"

"Yes, ma'am."

"You're free to go."

CHAPTER 8

Danièle

I'm dead. Mum's bound to find out. I set Melanie's helmet on her dresser and lie on the bed. My phone rings even as I hook it to the charger.

Randy? How'd you find out so soon? I thumb the accept button.

"Hi, Uncle Randolph."

"You at Melanie's place?"

"Yes."

"I'll be there in five minutes with your surrogacy agreement."

"Do you—" No point in finishing my question—he's already gone.

In a panic, I throw off my T-shirt and jeans, and grab a dress from the closet. My hair will have to do—no time to brush it out if I want to apply makeup. Seconds before I finish dressing, Randy's black BMW pulls into the driveway, and he steps out of the car.

I thump on the bathroom door. "My uncle's here. He's got our contract."

"Woot! I'll be right out."

Randy sits at the kitchen table and drums his fingers until Melanie finishes dressing. As soon as she settles into the chair across from me, he faces her. "I represent Danièle in this matter. You should have your family's attorney review the document before you sign anything."

She nods, but her eyes say it'll never happen.

My uncle pulls a manila folder from his briefcase and lays it open on the table. "I've drawn up a Preplanned Adoption Agreement for you and Melanie."

"Not Ethan?"

"No. If the engagement fails to result in a marriage, he has no rights under this contract." Randy plans for any eventuality, but at times he borders on paranoid.

My uncle sets a copy of the document in front of each of us. "Keep in mind that Virginia won't recognize a surrogacy contract between two single women."

"But Ethan and I will be married before the child's born."

My uncle's eyes brook no disagreement. "I practice law here in Miami. You and Melanie will return to Florida a month before her due date and we'll see this properly finished."

Melanie glances at me and shrugs.

I nod acquiescence. "Yes, sir."

He points to the first paragraph. "Florida law requires the adoption be reviewed and approved by the court. We'll take care of that when you get back."

"State law dictates that the mother be allowed to rescind the agreement any time prior to forty-eight hours after the birth of the child. Melanie, when you sign be sure to initial next to each of these next paragraphs."

Melanie retrieves a pen from her tote and signs her MRF on the paper.

Randy eyes her as though she's an unruly child. "If Danièle terminates the agreement early, the baby becomes your responsibility."

Melanie shoots me a look of confidence and trust. "She won't, but my sister would be happy to have another kid."

My uncle stares at her a moment before continuing. "The trust will pay all reasonable medical and living expenses. Danièle agrees to take custody of the child regardless of any disability."

He pulls another sheaf of papers from his briefcase. "Dr. Pierson requires that each person involved in the surrogacy provide her with access to their medical records and complete a lifestyle questionnaire. Here are your copies. I'll overnight Ethan's. Dr. Pierson will contact him regarding his sperm donation."

"There are a few more details you can read later. They're mostly included to meet the requirements of the law. Any questions?"

Melanie shakes her head. I doubt she understands all the legal jargon. I certainly don't. But I trust Randy, and Melanie trusts me.

Might as well take my lumps now. I pull the citation from my purse and slide it across the table. "A rather polite Miami-Dade police officer gave me this."

After a casual scan, he passes the form back to me. "I thought we agreed the motorbike off limits."

"A friend of Melanie's taught me to ride his."

"Were you involved in an accident? Speeding? What?"

"No. We rolled a stop sign."

"We?" My uncle blinks—an indication of dismay for his poker face. "Please tell me you weren't carrying a passenger."

"Melanie and I spent the afternoon at Matheson Hammock Park. I drove us from there up to the Biltmore. The officer stopped us just north of the University of Miami."

"All right. As soon as you return to Virginia, sign up for a state-sanctioned rider training program. Call me when you have your motorcycle license."

"Will I need to appear in court down here?"

"No. I'll represent you." He slides his chair back and stands. "Anything else?"

"No, sir."

"Then I'll leave you two to discuss the agreement."

I follow my uncle to his car and hug him goodbye. His BMW vanishes into the distant haze of evening while I stand on the front lawn and collect my thoughts.

Melanie pops out of the door and runs to me. "There's a notary on Ponce. Let's go sign this thing now."

"You sure? The contract's a complex document. You should have your attorney look at it."

"Nah. I trust you, and I want your baby."

From my earliest years, Mum and Daddy and Dr. Pierson explained my medical condition—sometimes overwhelming my young mind.

I'm a girl with XY chromosomes, and testes in my abdomen. My vaginal canal's too short and my clitoris too big, but I'm still female. Even with sperm, right?

"Are you okay?"

"Fine. Let's do this."

Signing proves surprisingly straightforward—show our IDs, sign our names, and wait for the notary to sign and stamp the documents.

By the time we're through, Melanie's bouncing up and down.

Me? I pace the front yard until I've worked up the courage to call my fiancé.

"Ethan?"

"Hey, what a pleasant surprise. Everything all right?"

"Yes. Brilliant. They're sending you some forms to complete for the surrogacy, and Dr. Pierson will let you know how to donate sperm."

"Outstanding. Wish I was there to celebrate with you."

"I do miss you so. I'm sorry I can't have your babies myself."

A moment passes in deadly silence. "Not your fault, babe."

"I know. But still."

"It doesn't matter. I love you the way you are. Okay, babe? No more of this, now."

"All right. I love you, too." I drop my phone into my bag, step inside, and close the door against approaching night.

Melanie runs to hug me. I pull her head against my shoulder and press my face into her curls. "You're the best friend a girl ever had. What would I do without you?"

Melanie

The entire week flashes by, disturbed only by lingering doubts about Ethan. What do I know about the boy? Dani wouldn't marry a creep, would she?

This is for you, girl. Not your beau. Not anybody else. Okay, except me, so maybe my life won't suck anymore.

A nurse comes in and draws blood. Another goes over all the stupid paperwork I did in the waiting room. She repeats half of the same questions the psychologist just asked. No wonder Dani gets all nervous around these people.

After my pelvic, I hop off the table and start getting dressed. No sweat, huh?

The nurse practitioner waves her hands. "You still have your ultrasound." She leads me down the hallway to another room—another examining table. I lie down and force myself to relax.

Ten minutes later, the technician arrives. "If you'll put your feet into the stirrups and slide toward me, we'll get started."

My heart thumps in my throat, but I do as she asks.

The lady tears open a small packet. Tommy showed me one like it the last time he tried to talk me into having sex with him. She unrolls the condom onto a long rod and squirts clear jelly along the side.

Whoa! That's what you mean by transvaginal ultrasound? My free hand clutches the side of the table. Muscles in my legs and back tense.

The procedure doesn't hurt, but it never ends. Like some Chinese water torture, the discomfort wraps around my head and squeezes till the tears flow.

The ultrasound technician hands me a clean towel. "Once you're dressed, open the door, and I'll take you to see to a nurse about your injections."

Yeah. Shots. Wonderful. I hop down off the examining table and wipe away the remaining goo from between my legs. I take my time getting dressed again.

Dani and a nurse are waiting in a room down the hallway. After giving me an injection pen and a college-level course on sticking myself with the thing, the nurse sends Dani and me to Dr. Pierson's office.

The doctor does her grandmother impression again—all smiles and soft words. "Congratulations, young ladies. The ultrasound found nothing remarkable."

"I'm fine? So, what's the next step?"

"If all goes well, we'll retrieve your eggs on the day of Danièle's surgeries. By then we should have prepared the donor sperm for IVF. Five days after we fertilize the eggs, we'll implant an embryo into your womb."

Dani places a hand on mine. I grin back at her.

Yeah, girl. I keep my promises.

CHAPTER 9

Danièle

Each day Melanie's cheerfulness brightens, even as I grow more apprehensive about my surgery. Nine shots, four ultrasounds, and four blood draws—nothing dampens her mood. She bounces up and down, eager to be on her way, while I dawdle with makeup and hair.

We sign in at the waiting area a few minutes early, but like every other doctor's office on the planet, appointments run late. Eventually, the nurse comes for Melanie, for her final transvaginal ultrasound.

I pick up the fashion magazine she was studying. All I've seen Melanie wear are blue jeans, T-shirts, and a few old blouses. None of her clothes will meet my mother's standards. Will Melanie be insulted when Mum insists on a new wardrobe?

A few minutes later, the receptionist asks me to see Dr. Pierson in her office. When I arrive, the doctor opens a folder and pushes several sheets of paper across her desk. "These are releases for your procedures on Monday."

I skim the medical and legal jargon on the forms. Would even Randy understand the implications? He'd remind me that a contract is an agreement to not trust someone. In that case, why would I sign anything I don't understand? But I do and pass the forms back across the desk.

All but one. I hold in my hands the death warrant for my clitoris —the focal point of the medical establishment's obsession with intersex. Do I give in to a lifetime of pressure to conform?

I like my body the way it is. Ethan insists he'll accept me. Who else has any say in the matter? "I've decided against the clitoral surgery." Tearing the release into two strips brings a smile to my face.

Dr. Pierson retrieves some additional papers from the folder, but sets them on the desk in front of her. "Your uncle provided me with a copy of the Preplanned Adoption Agreement. I assume you understand and agree to its provisions. Do I need to explain any-thing?"

"No. I'm satisfied with the terms." Not that I understand them.

The doctor rises from her seat and closes the door. "I first met your mother—and Melanie's—when they were in grade school and I was a resident at Childrens Hospital. I consider them both good friends."

Weariness shadows her features as she resumes her seat. "Laura insists this surrogacy will be good for her daughter. I still have serious reservations."

"Melanie will have permanent visitation rights."

"Yes, but that may mean she never lets go of the child."

Why should she have to? "I'll speak with her about it, but no promises."

Dr. Pierson's gentle frown emphasizes her concern. "All right."

After a moment, she leafs through the papers on her desk. "How long have you known Ethan?"

"About a year."

"Has he been taking steroids?"

"I don't think so. Why?"

"There are no viable sperm in his semen, and nothing in his medical history to indicate why."

My heart breaks for Ethan. How many times have I heard of someone melting down after they discover they're intersex? Ethan's not, of course; I'm certain of that. But even temporary infertility hits people hard. "I need to call him."

Dr. Pierson nods, so I step into the hallway and pull out my cell. I bring up my fiancé's number, but hesitate before connecting. *This isn't something you tell a person over the phone.*

A joyful eagerness flows from Ethan's voice whenever he speaks of us having children. His children. *Will he accept a baby that's not his?* I drop my phone into my purse and wander down the hallway to the waiting area.

Melanie sits in a chair, studying the same magazine as before. When she looks up, her eyes meet mine. A tender smile follows.

Canceling the surrogacy would crush her. *I'd rather lose Ethan than hurt you again.* I turn around and walk back toward Dr. Pierson's office.

Ethan insists that my intersex doesn't matter to him. He might well accept my fathering a child. Especially if Melanie's already pregnant.

Yet something desperate whispers a warning—a woman fathering a child—the very idea goes against nature.

Why haven't I the same right to parenthood as anyone else? Simply because my body doesn't fit our culture's binary idea of sex? My desire for a child—a child with Melanie—swells, pushing away any lingering uncertainty. The risk no longer matters.

Ethan will have to know.

Heart pounding, I make my way back to Dr. Pierson's office and take my seat again. "Let's proceed with the surrogacy using my—my gonadal biopsies." So much for the proper young lady bit. "I'd like to wait for the appropriate time to tell Ethan and Melanie—not that I'm sure when that will be."

Fear and the hint of remorse drift through my conscience. *How will I ever tell them?*

"Very well. I'm obligated to notify Ethan of his azoospermia, but the contract makes paternity entirely your decision. I would remind you that AIS is X-linked recessive."

Yes. If we have a female child, she'll get my affected X chromosome, making her a carrier for PAIS. "We'll love our baby regardless. What's next?"

"Surgery on Monday as planned. We'll take biopsies and see what we find."

Someone knocks on the door. Melanie pokes her head into the office. "The nurse said to come here." She takes her usual seat.

Dr. Pierson brings up a series of ultrasound images on her monitor. When she turns our way again, a grandmother's kindness shines from her face. "Everything looks fine. Drop by tomorrow evening for your trigger shot."

With a squeal, Melanie jumps up out of her chair.

Yes. Worth every last penny.

Finished for the day, Melanie and I burst outside. Melanie grabs my hand and rushes toward the station. A moment after we board the train, an afternoon shower breaks over us.

Melanie grins at me as though rain brings true happiness. "We should celebrate."

"What do you have in mind?"

"I haven't been to Dadeland in forever."

"Let's go, then." *Perhaps I can talk you into some new clothes.*

"Now?"

"Yes."

Bright sunshine and puddles greet us outside the Dadeland North Metrorail Station. We stroll hand-in-hand down the path, across the street, and under the covered walkways to the mall.

I slow as we approach the entrance. Sweet memories of childhood bring a glow to my face.

How many times did Mum bring me here when I was a little girl? I was so certain then of who I was.

Melanie drags me straight to the food court. As usual, we talked most of the night and missed breakfast. I gorge on a burger, onion rings, and a chocolate shake. Most unladylike.

Melanie sucks the grease from her fingertips. "You up for a movie?"

"Sure. Can we find you a purse before we go?"

Melanie's eyes flick to her tote and back to me. "Oh. Yeah. Guess I should buy one, huh?"

"Won't hurt to look." Unless I intervene, what Mum will see when Melanie arrives is a wild-haired waif. That impression might discolor their relationship for months.

Melanie rifles through fifty purses before settling on an inexpensive faux leather bag. Adequate, but not fashionable.

I take a deep breath and blow it out through my lips. "Mind if we check another shop before you purchase one?"

Back in the waiting area, Melanie ran her fingertips over the photo of a shoulder bag in a fashion magazine ad. The store lies near the end of the mall.

I grab Melanie's hand and lead her to the entrance. She stops there and shakes her head. "I can't afford anything in this place."

Mum and Daddy ignore prices on any item less expensive than an automobile. I was taught to weigh the value of my time against whatever I might save by an extended search. "Trust me?"

"Well, yeah." She nods, but her eyes hold doubt.

I find the purse from the ad—an embroidered forest green suede with oversized buckles and a wide leather strap. Mongolian lamb trim adds a warm and feminine touch. Mum would approve.

Melanie waves her hands and backs away. "No way. You know what that thing costs?"

"I missed five years of Christmas gifts and birthdays presents. Let me do this."

Emerald eyes search my face, hesitant to believe.

"At least consider it. Please?"

Her tender eyes search mine before she agrees.

I stand behind Melanie as she adjusts the strap. In the mirror, wonder spreads across her face. I wrap my arms around her waist and grin at her reflection. "Worth every last penny to see you smile."

When she turns around, my hand strays to the locket at her throat. I brush a fingertip across the silver heart. "I wish I'd kept—I'm sorry."

Tears break free and run down Melanie's cheeks. She slinks her arms around my waist and kisses me. On the lips. After a long embrace, she releases her grip and stumbles backwards, eyes wide. "Whoa. Sorry. I didn't mean to, you know. I'm not into girls."

My arms tremble in protest at the loss of her body against mine. Disappointment struggles to displace an unexpected joy. "I'm glad you like the purse."

With a shaking hand, I give my debit card to the cashier.

On the way out, I talk Melanie into a new dress as well.

Melanie

Monday morning arrives way too early. I slap my stupid alarm clock and pull away from Dani. She moaned on and off all night, like some little kid who lost her mommy. For a moment, I consider letting her sleep through her appointment.

What kind of friend lets somebody cut off body parts?

Me, I guess.

I shake the girl awake, point her toward the bathroom, and remind her not to eat or drink anything.

My hand goes to the locket Dani gave me so long ago. Does Ethan appreciate what all his fiancée is doing for him?

After I get dressed, I check on the girl, only to find her staring at her reflection in the bathroom mirror. She mumbles something about the circus. The nurse gave her meds to take the night before surgery. She said the pill would calm her nerves. *Well, yeah. Guess so.*

I grab her bathrobe and help her get dressed. "You don't have to do this, you know."

"No freaks." She stumbles into the bedroom, picks up her hand-bag, and dumps its contents on the floor. "No boy with breasts. No girl with a big clitoris and a little vagina."

From the pile she hands me an envelope. "Tell my parents I love them." She shakes her finger under my nose. "No freaks."

The envelope contains a medical power of attorney and a note. *In case something goes wrong with my surgery.*

I stuff the papers into my bag and kneel to gather everything else into Dani's purse.

Mom parks the car and walks with us to the front entrance of the clinic. "You sure you don't want me to stay with you? I can take off work, you know."

"Thanks. No. We'll be okay." Dani's hand is crushing mine. I kiss my mother goodbye.

Disappointment flashes in her eyes. As she turns to go, I grab her elbow. "No. Wait. I want you beside me when I wake up."

Her face brightens, and she hugs me. "Sure."

The nurse checks me and Dani in, hands us gowns, and leads us to a patient room. I check my wristband again—Melanie Rose Fairbairn. *Good. I don't need them removing any of my body parts. A few eggs maybe, but that's all.*

Still in her robe, Dani plops down on one of the beds. She lies there and plays with her wristband. A glance at my watch tells me the doctor will arrive any moment, so I hand her one of the gowns. "You can still back out."

Dani gazes up at me, eyes hollow. "Please stop. I need your help to get through this."

Shake her, slap her, scream—would anything work? I clench my teeth and turn my head away. "Time to put on your gown then, *Miss Danièle.*"

The girl stands and hugs me. "Thanks for being here." As she strips down to nothing, her motions slow, like some wind-up toy running out of energy. A tear runs down one cheek.

Naked, she looks like a marble statue of some Nordic princess. Well, except between her legs rests her little post—that thing so offensive to the world—shaped like a clitoris, but more than an inch long.

You're gorgeous. Why do you wanna screw up your body with surgery? I bite my lip to keep from swearing at her, and help her put on the hospital gown.

Dani flinches when somebody taps on the door post. A nurse walks in. "Miss Welles, if you'll lie down, I'll put in your IV line."

A tremor runs through her, but Dani lies on the bed and stretches out her arm. I perch beside the girl and grab her other hand. Slow-motion terror flows out of her eyes. Neither of us blink till the nurse finishes.

A couple of minutes later, Dr. Pierson arrives. "Any questions or concerns before we get started?"

Yeah! Who says a clit can only be so big? I know better than yelling at her, though. For once, a doctor's only doing what the patient wants. And screaming at the girl seems pointless.

"Let's get this over with," Dani says. A weak smile passes across her face.

"Very well." Dr. Pierson perches on a chair beside the girl. "Before they perform the orchiopexies, they'll shave your pubic area.

I've asked them to put you under anesthesia first, but I didn't want you to be surprised when you regain consciousness. All right?"

Dani nods at the doctor. I dig out the girl's legal paper. "If any-thing isn't right in surgery, I want to know." *Though I'll probably be in unconscious.*

Her eyes flick to mine. "Of course."

When they're ready, the nurse rolls Dani's gurney out the door.

What is wrong with you, girl? I slump on the remaining bed, roll over, and cry out my stress. *Why should I care? It's your body—your life to wreck.*

One hand wanders down to my abdomen. Two weeks of shots have left my ovaries sore and my abdomen bruised. And yet—and yet my emotions have quieted from daily explosions to a steady burn.

Somebody knocks on the door frame—the nurse with the cart again. I lie back down on the bed. They're grabbing a few eggs. That's all. I'll still have time to change my mind about the preg-nancy, won't I?

Dr. Pierson said we might get as many as six embryos. She can freeze the extras, but I don't wanna leave any of my babies to die in storage. And I'll never have the money to rescue them. *What am I gonna do?*

Chapter 10

Danièle

Well, I appear to have survived. The haze clears enough for me to recognize Mrs. Fairbairn.

"How are you?" She brushes the hair from my eyes.

Nothing hurts. Yet. "All right. How's Melanie?"

"Fine. She's resting. Sharon—Dr. Pierson says the egg retrieval went well. Oh, and Ethan called to see how you were."

Mrs. Fairbairn speaks in quiet tones with someone else in the room. A truck rumbles by outside. Footsteps pass in the hallway.

Sensations awaken as the shadows of anesthesia fade. Incisions whisper pain along both sides of my groin. Pressure swells my lower abdomen. Soft throbs of discomfort press against my tailbone, a relentless distraction from the dark sea of nausea between my legs.

I arch my back and find temporary relief on my side.

"Should I call a nurse?" Mrs. Fairbairn leans close. The empathy on her face reminds me of Melanie.

"No." I ease onto my back again, this time with both hands under my hips. *Perhaps if I hold my breath.* I raise my knees and spread my legs. That proves a little better. My back arches again. A snicker twitches through the pain in my gut. *Oh, yes. Now here's a dignified position.*

Dr. Pierson strides into the room. "How's my favorite patient?"

"A mite bit uncomfortable."

"Normally I'd recommend sitting up. Perhaps standing would be better."

Less weight on my rear—an excellent idea, that. I roll on my side and stick both legs over the edge of the bed. Dr. Pierson and Mrs. Fairbairn help me pivot upright. My feet hitting the floor jars a dull pain through my gut. I stand on tiptoes for a moment before easing down, like someone entering a hot bath. "Standing's a definite improvement."

Dr. Pierson nods. "I suspected it might be. Are you up for a walk?"

"I think so." I shuffle across the room and down the hallway with Mrs. Fairbairn holding my arm. The tightness in my gut eases somewhat. Muscles relax. The pain mellows to a steady discomfort, as though I bruised my tailbone.

Melanie ambles toward us in blue jeans and a T-shirt, but stops an arm's length away. Her cheerfulness fades as she studies my face. "I'm sorry."

Perhaps she fears hurting me. I grab her hand and pull her close. "Why? The egg retrieval succeeded."

Tears gather in the corners of her eyes. "Yeah. That part went okay. I meant your other stuff."

Mrs. Fairbairn sends a kind smile my way. "I'll leave you two alone."

Tears trickle down Melanie's face. Every drop rends my heart into smaller bits. I pull her into a tight embrace, in spite of my abdominal pain. "Please don't cry."

Agony dims the life of her emerald eyes. "A true friend would never have let you cut off body parts. No matter what."

I burrow into her cinnamon tresses and press my lips against her ear. "Want to know a secret? I changed my mind. I still have all my bits."

She pushes away. Flames burst from her eyes. "And you didn't tell me? I was worried to death about you!" Her fist lashes out against my shoulder.

The muscles in my abdomen contract. Pain ripples upward from my tailbone. Not that she hit me hard, but some muscle flinched at the unexpected assault. Hands on my knees, I wait for the echoes to die out. Time to lie down again.

Melanie lets out a soft wail. "I'm so sorry. I didn't mean to hurt you. Let me help you back to your room. You okay?"

I kiss her on the cheek and trudge on down the hallway.

Dr. Pierson greets me at the door, thanks Melanie, and helps me lie down again. "Walk as much as you like, but please ask someone to help you in and out of bed."

She tugs the privacy curtain closed and sits in a chair next to me. "All of your procedures went well. Dr. Nguyen performed your orchiopexies, labial surgery, and the Davydov vaginal repair."

Her eyes scan my face a moment before she continues. "We found intratubular neoplasia in your biopsies, so Dr. Nguyen removed your right testis to preclude gonadal cancer. The good news is that gave us a much larger tissue sample. We harvested sufficient gametes to perform intra-cytoplasmic sperm injection on all of the ova we retrieved."

My sperm and Melanie's eggs. *I'm a father. And still a girl. Always will be.*

Won't I?

She pats me on the arm, once again the gentle grandmother. "Rest. You should be ready to go home in the morning. Do you want anything for the pain?"

"Yes."

"All right. I'll have a nurse bring you something."

"Thanks." After a short talk with Mum, and a text message to Ethan, I curl up on my side and abandon myself to dreams of my new family.

Melanie

Saturday morning I wake before the alarm. Embryo transfer—five days since they took my eggs. Dr. Pierson gave me a bottle of progesterone capsules and some long-winded explanation as to why I had to take them. All I know is they make me sleep straight through the night. Every time. I breathe deep of the cool air and stretch my arms. *Life is good.*

After two restless days, Dani went back to the clinic to have her stupid packing removed. The surgeon apparently stuffed her vagina full of gauze or something. She said taking it all out hurt worse than the surgery. She's napped like a cat in the sunshine ever since. I can almost hear the girl purr.

My hand creeps up to the locket at my throat. *Today I give away my virginity.* I click open the silver heart and brush a fingertip across the photo inside. *I keep my promises, Dani.*

I slip on my robe and pad into the kitchen to set the table for breakfast. Mom joins me a few minutes later. "So. The big day. Are you excited?"

"Yeah." My eyes wander across the kitchen toward my bedroom. "Ethan's not a jerk or anything, is he?"

My mother pulls me into a hug. "Don't worry about him at all, honey. Keela assures me that Ethan's a wonderful person."

Yeah, but how well does she know the boy?

Dani wanders into the kitchen. She stretches her arms above her head and yawns. We grin at each other. No way my best friend would ever marry a loser.

Mom drives us to the clinic. She says she wants to be present when her daughter gets pregnant. She doesn't work most Saturdays anyhow, so it's not like she has to take the time off.

The nurse who leads us to Dr. Pierson's office hands me a pill and a bottle of water. "The medication's to help your muscles relax. You'll need your bladder full during the procedure, so drink as much of the water as you can and wait until afterward to void."

Muscle relaxer and a full bladder? *Not good.* I collapse into my usual chair. *Glad I didn't drink anything at breakfast.*

Dani's phone chirps. She glances at the display and walks out into the hallway.

Yeah. Probably another message from Ethan.

Mom studies my face, the way she always does when she's gonna start some conversation she thinks I might not be mature enough to handle. After a glance at the empty doorway, she puts her hand on mine. "Keela asked if you'd stay on as your child's nanny—at least until Danièle finishes college. You do want to, don't you?"

"Dr. Pierson's psychologist says a clean break is better. I need to accept that the baby will belong to Ethan and Dani."

"Honey, separation anxiety and depression come from giving up your child. Danièle won't make you leave. Wouldn't you rather stay?"

"Well, yeah." Any excuse to keep my baby. And be near Dani.

"Would you leave once Danièle graduates?"

Lose my toddler and my best friend both? "Not if I don't have to."

"You'd spend the rest of your life with her, then?"

Outside, an early morning shower struggles in vain to over-power bright sunshine. I'd have to leave Dani and my child behind if I married. "Yeah. Guess so." *Does it matter? I'll probably never meet the right guy, anyhow. Not working as a nanny.*

"Would you stay if Ethan left?"

"Well, yeah." *Leave Dani to be a single mom with my kid? Ain't gonna happen.*

Something troubles my mother's eyes as they wander from my face down to—down to my locket.

Yeah, Mom, I'm gonna spend the rest of my life with Dani. But just because I'm having a baby for her doesn't mean I wanna sleep with the girl. "I love her, Mom, but not that way—she's not a boy."

"She's not a girl either, honey."

"Mom, please don't—" The sound of footsteps cuts off my thought.

Dr. Pierson walks in, deep in quiet conversation with Dani. The doctor motions for the girl to be seated. "In a moment, we'll select an embryo for transfer. We harvested fifteen eggs. Four embryos survived. I recommend we use one and cryopreserve the remain-der." She glances at Dani and at my mother, but her eyes rest on me. "Two would increase the chance of success by perhaps five percent, but multiple pregnancies are riskier for the mother."

Twins are good. Well, better than going through another stupid IVF cycle. "What happens if I don't get pregnant?"

"We'll transfer the others."

No way am I gonna screw up the surrogacy. "Can we do them all?"

Dr. Pierson's gentleness returns. "Not today. But you're healthy enough to risk twins. Shall we select two?"

"Well, yeah."

Dani nods. Mom only grins.

The doctor switches on a wall monitor, picks up the phone, and dials. "We're ready. Two blastocysts for Fairbairn and Welles."

On the monitor, some geek in a white lab coat walks up to the camera and holds up a glass tray. Mom and Dani are talking, so I get up to take a better look. A label on top reads *Fairbairn Ova, Welles Orch R.* Dr. Pierson glances at the monitor and nods. "That's the one."

The guy sets the tray under some microscope gizmo. A moment later, the video switches to a closeup of four round cell blobs.

Dr. Pierson gives me another of her grandmother smiles. "Which one would you like?"

My heart stutters. I grab the locket at my throat and gape at Mom. Her eyes send only love. *I get to choose my baby?* My gaze drifts back to the screen. *I want them all.*

Four little round blobs—almost faces to my imagination. How's a mom supposed to choose among her kids?

"This one." I press my finger against the screen over the smallest one. A bit out of round. Different from the rest. Will she even survive if I don't pick her?

Dr. Pierson speaks into the phone, and a thin glass tube sucks up my little girl. The doctor waves Dani toward the screen. "Your turn."

The girl studies the remaining three blobs for some time before indicating one.

After the technician finishes, Dr. Pierson switches off the monitor and turns to me. "If you're ready, we'll do the transfer."

Up to now, pregnancy's been a dream. My gaze shifts back to Mom. Her face shines with tenderness. Will Dani and I spend our lives together? Leaving our children behind would kill me. *Someday I'm gonna regret this. But at least I'll be happy till then.*

Dr. Pierson leads us to an ultrasound room—the same one we used for the mock transfer. Everybody waits outside while I change into my hospital gown.

After I open the door, I get all comfortable on the table, and put my feet into the stirrups. Dr. Pierson drapes a cloth over my knees. A moment later, the ultrasound technician arrives. She greases up a probe and slides it over my abdomen till she has the image she wants.

Dr. Pierson nods. "I'm going to insert the catheter. Let me know if you experience any discomfort."

Dani squeezes my hand and grins encouragement. On the practice run, I was all tense, my muscles tight. This time my whole body relaxes.

The technician points at the screen. "Through the cervix."

A small bright spot moves across the display and stops. "At the MIP point."

"Release." The spot flashes and begins to move back the way it came.

That's it? The catheter tickles on its way out.

Ever so gently—the ultrasound lady wipes a soft cloth across my belly.

A moment later, Dr. Pierson stands beside me. "Rest for about fifteen minutes before you get dressed. Then I'll see you in my office."

Dani and I grin like idiots while my mother smiles at us. *Yeah, Mom. We're happy.*

Danièle

Nap, eat, walk, sleep—with my short cycles, the days blur. When I'm awake, all Melanie and I talk about is whether or not she's pregnant. Uncertainty's the worst part.

Flowers and chocolates arrive. From Ethan. For me a get well card. For Melanie a thank you and a dozen roses.

Mrs. Fairbairn suggests I lie on my side with a pillow between my knees. That works well for a few hours, but then I move back to the living room. With the cushions arranged just so, the plush sofa affords the most comfortable place to recline. Even with Melanie's sleeping body draped across mine.

After the embryo transfers, Dr. Pierson prescribed three days of what she termed couch rest—no exertion, no stress, and no motor-bikes.

Melanie spends most of her day either worried crazy or asleep.

Blood tests confirm the pregnancy, but Dr. Pierson wants to verify normal development with an ultrasound. Just before she retires.

So we wait.

Melanie's ginger hair whispers of raspberries and cinnamon. I brush a wayward strand away from my nose. Years ago, while her mother lay in a hospital bed, recovering from breast cancer surgery, Melanie made my shoulder her pillow. I'm happy to oblige—now as before.

Sometime later—hours, months, years—Mrs. Fairbairn walks over to the sofa and sits on the floor next to us. She holds the back of her fingers against Melanie's forehead for a moment before whispering, "Your appointment's in an hour."

Has it already been a month? I have no idea the day. "Ultrasound?"

"Yes." The compassion in her eyes proves her a mother. She brushes the hair away from her daughter's face. "Time to get up, honey."

Melanie groans and stretches her arms. Tired eyes sweep my face and leave behind a smile. She pushes herself upright and yawns.

Concern overshadows the tenderness in Mrs. Fairbairn's eyes. "I noticed a maxi pad in the bathroom trash. Are you bleeding?"

"Huh? No." After a bit, realization sweeps the confusion from Melanie's eyes. She fixes her gaze on me.

Heat flares on my cheeks. "That was mine. I've had a bit of pink mucous. Dr. Pierson said to expect some drainage."

Melanie snorts and gives me a quick hug. "Leaking from your vagina—welcome to The Girls' Club. Are you dilating?"

"Yes. That and using the estrogen cream." The doctor assured me dilation was only necessary until things healed and I was sexually active. So I've been faithful.

If wearing a sanitary napkin, oozing a pink discharge, and having things poked into my vagina are true signs of womanhood, perhaps I've made a mistake. How well would I react to menstruation? Certainly men experience fewer such indignities. I lever myself up off the sofa and make my way to the bathroom. Perhaps a hot shower will wash away my new-found sense of vulnerability.

We arrive in the waiting area twenty minutes late. A nurse rushes me to an examining room and takes Melanie elsewhere. I sit on the table for a moment before changing into the hospital gown. A great weariness settles over me.

A nurse accompanies Dr. Nguyen. She stands guard while I lie down and assume the position. He grabs a speculum from the counter. "Have you been dilating?"

"Yes, sir." *Where's Dr. Pierson? And Melanie?*

"Any discharge?"

"A little bit of pink. Less now than at first."

He grunts, nods, and slides the duck-billed instrument into place.

Pain arches my back up off the table. I clench my teeth and hold my breath until he finishes the exam. He drops the speculum into the sink and removes his gloves. "You're healing fine. Your gynecologist can handle your care in the future."

After they leave, I stare out the window and try not to succumb to depression. When my phone chirps, I hop down off the examining table and grab my cell from my purse.

<< *Melanie—baby ok*

I'm going to be a mother.

Only one. I scramble to get dressed and rush down the hallway to find and comfort the mother of my child.

Chapter 11

Melanie

While Dani's outside jogging, I start sorting through Mom's stuff. Papers she might need for filing her taxes. Old photos. A recent portrait of Dad. Lots of pictures of people I don't know.

One drawer has every last Christmas or birthday card Beatrice or Dad or me ever gave her. Even my stupid old crayon drawings.

"Oh, wow, Mom." *Either you're a true pack rat or you really love me. Maybe both.*

I make up an *open me first* box for her with some of the nicest photos. I even find an old one of me and Dani pretending to be bride and groom.

Tucked away in the bottom of one drawer is a velvet case. Hidden, lost, or forgotten. When I unsnap the cover, I discover it holds an ivory-framed picture.

Mom—in her late teens, early twenties—with some boy groping her. Well, that's what it looks like at first. His hand is farther north than I ever let Tommy's go.

All my love—Ronnie is scrawled across the bottom. Weirder still —the dude looks kinda like a guy version of Dani. Only taller and heavier.

A vehicle pulls into our driveway, so I set the case aside and walk to the door. Tommy waves at me from his pickup. We haven't talked since—when did Dani and I go riding with him? More than a month ago. *Is he my friend or not? Well...kinda...sometimes...when he isn't being too possessive.* But with Dani around, I never spend any time with the boy.

"Get out here," he shouts, and waves an arm at me. He sounds pissed.

"I'm coming." My flip flops aren't by the door, so I step outside barefoot.

He waves one hand toward the real-estate sign. "Were you gonna tell me about this? Huh?"

Sold! "I didn't know. They musta got a contract today or something."

"Come on, Melanie. I seen your danged sign when we packed up all them motorcycle parts. You coulda told me about it then. You movin' or what?"

"Sorry. Yeah. Virginia."

He thumps the steering wheel with his fist. Hard. His dark eyes shine with moisture. I've never seen him so upset before. "Don't go. Please? I'll let you stay with me."

I'll bet you would. "I can't, Tommy."

"You won't."

"Yeah, whatever." An almost careless shrug twitches my shoulders. "I'm having a baby for Dani and her fiancé."

He steps out of the truck and slams the door. "Pregnant? Without even talkin' to me?"

"Don't you yell at me! It was none of your freaking business."

Tommy steps close, his whole face twisted with pain and anger.

"You gonna hit me? Huh?"

His jaw clenches, but the rage does a slow fade. We stare at each other as his sadness grows. "Well, I guess it never will be then, neither." Tommy gets back into his truck and screeches on down the road.

"Goodbye, Tommy." *Guess that didn't go so well, huh?*

Sold. A renegade tear escapes. The drop runs down my face, drips off my chin, and loses itself in the grass. *Here's one for lost love? Yeah. Guess so.*

Nausea pummels me then. I dash back inside and lean over the kitchen sink till the spasms run their course, then rinse my sorrow down the drain.

Danièle

Six weeks after surgery, my health returns to normal. Almost. I dare not ride a motorbike yet, or sit on anything too firm. Tailbone pain whispers to me after a busy day. I still require a pillow between my knees to sleep, but at least I no longer need pain medication or sleeping pills or maxi pads.

The home buyers offer to purchase most of the furnishings. Melanie and I take Mr. Fairbairn's clothes—and some of hers—to the local Salvation Army. What remains are a few precious memories—photos, scrapbooks, trophies, and family treasures, such as the flow blue china I bubble wrapped earlier.

I tape the last box of dishes closed and push it into the corner with the others. A half dozen shipping cartons are all that remain of a once-vibrant household.

You're too quiet. "Maybe they're wrong," I say.

Melanie's cheerfulness evaporated when her first post-implantation ultrasound revealed only one heartbeat. She glances up from scrubbing the refrigerator. "Yeah. Maybe. Your dad has a jet?"

If I push her, she'll withdraw even further. "The trust owns the airplane. He leases a portion of the flight time for personal use." After I told my mother that Mrs. Fairbairn intended to sell everything, including her car, Mum offered to drop her old friend off in Atlanta. When I asked, my mother also agreed to an overnight hotel stay before leaving Miami.

Melanie closes the refrigerator door and glances at her watch. "I'm done. You wanna shower first?"

"Why don't you? I'd like to jog a bit."

We spent most of the day cleaning and packing boxes. Dust and grime cover my arms. No doubt I've smeared dirt on my face. In a few hours, my parents will arrive. Perhaps Randy as well. I have one last opportunity to run in the Florida sunshine.

Outside, a breath of cool air sweeps my face, even as hot sunshine dances across my skin. On the other side of the street, rain nourishes flowering trees. I stretch my arms above my head and yawn. What a marvelous place.

I sprint a block toward the university, but the jarring proves too much, so I slow to a brisk walk. Six weeks without running has stolen my breath away. How long will it take to get back into shape? Has losing a testis and gaining vaginal depth altered something fundamental? The psychologists always associated physical strength with masculinity.

A mile from home, I sprint back toward the house until my lungs burn. I stand then, hands on my knees, and pant until the darkness clears.

Well, what's done is done. I shake my head and continue walk-ing.

In my peripheral vision, a white van paces me. *Cooper?* I walk around to the driver's side. "What're you doing here?"

"I could ask you the same thing." The always-serious security officer cracks a smile. "You should be more careful."

I take in my surroundings then. Situational awareness, my father calls it.

Alone. On a quiet side street. A block from the relative safety of the Fairbairn home. No ID. Not even my cell phone on me. *Would anyone notice if someone dragged me into a van and sped away? Probably not.* I walk on a bit faster. No. Daddy would not approve.

Cooper backs into the Fairbairns' driveway and gets out.

I give him a quick hug. "This is a welcome surprise. Are you on vacation, or does my uncle suspect a terrorist attack?"

One eyebrow twitches up Cooper's forehead. I've been teasing him since the day he started working for the company. His eyes per-form a quick scan of the neighborhood, as though he thinks my comment serious. "I'm in town for recurrent training and a bit of R and R." He nods toward the house. "You have some packages for Atlanta?"

He insists on loading the boxes himself. After I carry out two of the smaller ones, he stops and frowns at me until I go back inside and wait. Not that I blame him. Daddy would be cross if Cooper let me hurt myself.

Cooper's the sort of man whose raw virility reminds me how little effect male hormones have on my body. I wonder what the honorably-discharged officer thinks of spending his days acting as chauffeur and bodyguard to a rich girl who ignores his security protocols.

With the last two cartons under one arm, Cooper stops in the doorway, "Anything else needs to go?"

I get up and hug him again. "No. See you tonight?"

"I'm your wheels." He nods and pulls the door shut.

Melanie strolls into the kitchen, wearing only a bra and panties. In one hand she holds the new top I gave her. "Was that Ethan? What a hunk!"

The door swings open again, and Cooper pokes his head into the room. "Don't forget to lock up."

Melanie's blouse falls to the floor. Freckles die in a panic of roses blooming across her cheeks. One hand goes to her mouth as an embarrassed squeal bursts from her lips.

The door snaps shut.

Melanie throws me a deadly warning—if I laugh, she'll kill me.

I bite my lip to keep from smiling, turn my back to her, and lock the door. When I look again, she's gone.

You two would make a brilliant couple.

Melanie

Back in my room, I finish dressing in front of the mirror. Like I actually care about my looks for a change. Dani gave me a nice silk blouse and a black skirt—not even my Sunday best is good enough for meeting her mother.

Should I care?

Well, yeah. Guess so. Dani always dresses nice. And wears makeup. I'll miss my blue jeans, but in a couple of weeks, they won't fit anyhow.

In the mirror, Dani's face peeks over my shoulder. "I'm sorry. That was Cooper—Clarence Cooper. He's a driver, bodyguard, and whatever else the company requires. Uncle Randolph hired him right out of the Marine Corps." A mischievous grin overtakes the girl's face. "He's single."

What would happen if I married somebody who worked for the Welles? Would the girl let me be nanny if I had kids of my own? "He's cute."

"So are you. Let's do your makeup."

I follow her into the kitchen and perch on one of the breakfast bar stools.

Dani brushes my cheeks, touches up my eyes, and applies a burnt orange to my lips. No layers of foundation or anything. Not like they do in the online videos. A touch of mascara, but no eyeliner or shadow either. *Good. I'm not sure I like makeup in the first place.*

"Let me know what you think." Dani puts everything back into her case and clicks the lid shut.

I stroll into the bathroom and flick on the light switch. Air rushes into my lungs—a silent gasp. *So this is what it's like to be pretty.* Doubt almost drives tears from my eyes. Too many good things are happening. I turn away from the mirror and flee to my bedroom.

Dani's makeup, Dani's clothes, Dani's baby—what happens when she doesn't need me around anymore?

The girl pokes her head into my bedroom. "Our ride's here."

Footsteps cross the kitchen—my mother by the sound of them. "Ready to go, honey?"

"Yeah, Mom." I grab my suitcase and jacket, but stop in the doorway and gaze back at the lonely remains of my old life. Bed, dresser, nightstand, curtains—my father's death erased all the pleas-ant memories of childhood and left the room barren. Even my old teddy bear succumbed to melancholy. Hollow eyes beg me not to leave him behind.

The Cooper guy waits in the kitchen. By the door. Guarding the place. When I drag my suitcase into the room, he hoists the thing like it weighs nothing at all, and steps outside.

A minute later, my mother strolls into the kitchen. "You have everything?"

"Yeah." *Nothing's left for me here, Mom.*

Desolation overtakes the living room and seeps into the kitchen. I flee outside. My gaze wanders in the dusk—from the house to the BMW and back again—but I keep them far from the black emptiness of my old memories.

Cooper holds the door for me long after Dani has already slipped into the back seat. A precious memory of Dad beckons to me then—a bright image of our final motorcycle ride before he deployed. Too late, I reach a hand toward the fading image. *I'll never see you again.*

The BMW pulls out of the driveway, and I lose sight of the house as we turn north on Alhambra Circle. In the dark silence my vision blurs.

CHAPTER 12

Danièle

The Biltmore Hotel stands less than three miles from the Fairbairn home. Melanie's eyes glow with the wonder such a place generates in those not yet jaded by their wealth or computer-generated special effects. Mrs. Fairbairn takes her daughter's hand and strolls into the lobby.

My vision climbs the marble columns up to a sapphire-inlaid ceiling. I bump into Melanie, stop, and gape at my surroundings. We've been transported to a Mediterranean palace.

Cooper never gets distracted by the beauty around him, at least not while at work. He escorts Melanie and me up to our room. We drop off our luggage and join my parents in their suite.

Melanie's mother breaks into a sunny grin. "Hello, Keela."

"Laura!" Mum rushes to embrace Mrs. Fairbairn.

Melanie's eyes burn with impatience, but she fidgets in silence while our mothers chat.

Don't make her wait long, Mum. She's not your daughter.

A minute passes. After five, Mum gazes in our direction, flashes her blue eyes, and nods my cue.

"You remember Mrs. Fairbairn's daughter, Melanie."

"Why of course. What a lovely young woman you've become."

Melanie looks as refined as any of my preparatory school class-mates. "Thank you, Mrs. Welles," she says.

Mum gives Melanie a cordial smile. Melanie's left a satisfactory first impression.

My mother fixes her searching gaze on me next. I refuse to echo the doubt she transmits.

A knock at the door provides a welcome interruption. "Room service."

Cooper signals us to leave. Mum rolls impatient eyes, but takes Mrs. Fairbairn's hand and walks down the hallway.

I nudge Melanie toward the second bedroom. "Let's go wash up." No need to explain my father's security rules.

In the bathroom, she eyes me in the mirror. "Are you in the witness protection program or something?"

"Is it that obvious?"

"Well, yeah. Everybody around you is paranoid."

"My father and Uncle Randolph worked for British Military Intelligence during the Troubles in Northern Ireland."

"But you were born in Virginia."

"My parents came back to the States just after the ceasefire in 1994. Mum was already six months pregnant."

"And people are still out to get your family?"

Are they? "I have no idea. No one ever talks about specific threats."

"But you have a bodyguard."

"Cooper? He does a lot more than security."

A few minutes later, my father strolls into the room. "Would you two young ladies do me the honor of joining us for dinner?" He snaps a wink at me. "I believe the coast is clear now."

We follow him to the dining area. When he pulls a chair away from the table, I slip a hand behind Melanie's back and encourage her forward. Part of being a lady is being treated like one by gentlemen. Manners and bodyguards—an odd mix, that.

A servant lifts the cover from our appetizer and passes the dish around. Tiny fish, dusted and deep fried—I've only had whitebait on one previous occasion. Key Lime tartare proves an exquisite dipping sauce for them.

A hand squeezes mine under the table—Melanie sniffs at a fish covered in sauce and pops it into her mouth. Seconds later, a smile overpowers her skepticism.

The servant removes the covers from the side dishes—roasted asparagus and mashed potatoes—and starts them around the table. When he lifts the dome lid from a large serving tray, my saliva runs. He slices the pastry, exposing rare beef tenderloin, pâté, mushroom duxelles, and prosciutto. Mum talked the chef into Beef Wellington. *Brilliant.*

Mum and Daddy remain oddly quiet through the main course, even after most everyone has finished. As soon as Melanie sets her fork down, my father slides his chair back. "If you two young ladies are interested, Cooper has offered to give you a tour of the hotel."

In other words, the parents want to chat without the children present. I ease my chair back and stand. "Save us some dessert."

Melanie pats her mouth with her napkin and rises from her seat. "Can we see where Al Capone stayed?"

Cooper offers a polite but firm head shake. "Sorry, but the Everglades Suite is occupied."

Melanie waves it away with a yawn. "I should get to bed early, anyhow."

Concern furrows Mum's brow. "I'd forgotten you were pregnant, sweetheart. Perhaps in the morning, then." She uncovers the dessert tray and fills a dinner plate with truffles. "Take these with you."

Melanie gawks at the sweets. "Chocolate."

Mum picks up another from the tray, sniffs at it like one might a fine wine, and relishes a small bite. "Yes. Dark chocolate, not overly sweet, and made with clotted cream—all good for your pregnancy."

Cooper escorts us—and our plate of truffles—down the hallway to our room. "Please let me know if you need anything." He shoots a glance at Melanie and waits in the doorway.

Yes, I understand the drill. Don't leave the room on my own. Don't answer the door. My father sets the rules, and I have no doubt of his love for me. Cooper acts as his right hand at times to ensure my safety.

"Thank you. We're in for the night." I push the door closed and slide the bolt into place.

Melanie saunters out of the bathroom, already in her nightgown. After she hangs her dress in the closet, she finishes unpacking.

I give her a quick hug. "You were marvelous. I most appreciated you reminding Mum that you're pregnant." I open my luggage and set out the clothes I'll need for the morning.

Melanie's emerald eyes grow wide. Without makeup, her grin and freckled cheeks lend her face a child-like innocence. "I feel like some poor orphan girl sent to stay with rich relatives." She waltzes over to the desk and snatches a truffle. "If this is a dream, don't wake me till the chocolate's all gone."

After Melanie finishes off her third truffle, she pulls back the covers on her bed. She sits on the mattress, leans into a mountain of pillows, and hugs the duvet to her chest. The cheerfulness she expressed all evening melts away. "Is Mom dying? That's the only reason I can figure for her sending me away."

I pull off my heels and sit on the edge of her bed. "She wants you to get an education. The money you would have spent on a preparatory school can go toward college now."

"Yeah. Maybe." Not a whisper of belief inhabits her eyes as they sink. Her lower lip quivers.

"I'm sorry, love. I hope she's all right." I pull her head against my shoulder. *What will I do if your mum really does die?* Melanie's soft whimpers become diaphragm spasms, but after a few minutes, her irregular breathing slows. Tremors fade. Muscles relax.

A crick in my back forces me to shift position. With Melanie asleep, I slip away from her and change into pajamas. The mother of my child sleeps on, both arms wrapped around a pillow. An occasional muffled cry breaches her lips—as in a dream.

What have I gotten you into? I pull the duvet up to her shoulders, kiss her on the forehead, and retreat to my own bed again. There I burrow into the covers and fade into dreams.

Melanie

The last few minutes of sleep are always the best, and with the bed caressing me, I have no desire to be up and about. Voices whisper somewhere in the room, but only for a moment. I snuggle further into my pillows, stretch out my arms, and embrace the covers.

Sometime later, fingers brush my cheek. My eyes open to Dani's bright smile. "Breakfast is served, Miss Fairbairn." She holds out a white chenille robe, almost as comfy looking as my pillow.

A stretch, a yawn, and I push myself upright. So much beauty and elegance fills the room. I commit it all to memory. Something to treasure later. After a wistful glance at my pillows, I stretch again, stand, and let Dani help me with my robe.

Breakfast turns out to be poached salmon, scrambled eggs, roasted tomatoes, and biscuits that Dani calls scones. "Wait until you taste Jake's," she says. "They're brilliant."

My nose wrinkles at the capers spread over my salmon. I pick them off and take a bite of the fish. *Yummy? Well, yeah, but who eats this kinda stuff for breakfast?* I eye one of the smaller roasted tomatoes before picking up a scone and holding it up to my nose. *Oh, yeah.* Cinnamon and sugar.

Salmon, eggs, scones, orange juice—I'd stuff my face, but nausea forces me to stop. I haven't puked in nearly a week, and that's fine with me. I shove my plate away and gaze at the bed again.

Dani grabs my sleeve. "We're late already. Get dressed, and I'll fix your makeup."

Chiffon and lace, soft and feminine—I slip the new dress over my head and pull the belt tight. *So this is your world, huh? Am I gonna live the rest of my life in a skirt and lipstick? Guess that goes with fancy hotels and corporate jets. What about blue jeans and motorcycles?*

The girl makes my face all pretty again. I brush out my hair and clip it back on both sides. One last gawk at the stranger in the mirror, and I follow Dani out the door. *Yeah. Sweet. But don't think I'm gonna waste my entire life bein' Miss Prissy.*

Danièle

Cooper leads us through the lobby and stands guard while a valet brings the car. For a moment, I suspect he's going to search the BMW for explosives, but then he opens the door and motions me inside. Melanie climbs into the rear seat after me, and we drive off.

Emerald eyes study me from across the car. Embers of doubt flicker there. I slide over to her and snake an arm around her shoulder. "If you'd rather not stay with my parents..."

With one hand she straightens her flouncy skirt. "Your folks are okay. I'm just not sure I wanna spend the rest of my life in a dress."

I brush her ginger curls back behind one ear, press my face close, and whisper, "Neither am I, but Mum would hand me over to a shrink if she found out."

Melanie bites her lip until the muffled snickering fades. "No. They got to you somehow. Even on a motorcycle, you're all elegance. You sweat French perfume."

Have I changed so much in five years? I was a tomboy, more the mischief-maker than ever Melanie was. With psychologists ahead and surgeons behind, I fled to the only available refuge. Under Mum's wing I took on manners and grace as protective coloration against the predators. "I suppose you're right."

Melanie closes her eyes, leans her head against my shoulder, and remains silent for the rest of the drive down to Kendall-Tamiami Airport.

My parents and Mrs. Fairbairn have already boarded by the time we arrive. Cooper sees to our bags before shepherding us through security and out to the plane.

As soon as we settle into our seats, one of the crew shuts the cabin door, and the aircraft taxis out to the runway. Melanie presses hard against me and rests her chin on my shoulder. "Is there a barf bag?"

Perfect. "As soon as we take off, I'll find you something. Can you hold out that long?"

"Yeah."

Ten minutes later, the tower clears us for departure. Another twenty pass before we level off. By then Melanie's breathing has slowed. "You all right?"

She mumbles something and snuggles closer, so I put an arm around her and dream of what could have been.

Before too long, the turbine whine sings of our descent into DeKalb-Peachtree Airport north of Atlanta. We touch down with a soft chirp of tires on concrete and taxi to one of the general aviation support hangars.

Humid air and bright sunshine flood the cabin when one of the crew opens the door. Cooper ducks outside first—no doubt to rid the area of threats. Daddy offers a hand to Mum then, and they deplane.

Mrs. Fairbairn pauses in the doorway. Her eyes scan Melanie and me, as though she's committing the scene to memory. A wisp of concern disturbs her perfect contentment. Her chest rises and falls in a deep breath, and she steps outside.

Not long afterward, the pilots finish their checklist and step out of the cockpit.

They can't leave with us here. I brush a fingertip down Melanie's brow to the tip of her nose. "Wake up, sleepyhead." *Time to wish your mother farewell.*

Chapter 13

Melanie

Oh, man. I hate flying. My stomach grumbles discontent. One last glance over my shoulder, and I'm out of the cabin and down the steps to solid ground.

Learjet—gotta admit the coolness factor there. Nice comfy seats. Lots of legroom. Way bigger than a car. *So why should I feel trapped inside the stupid thing?*

Dani bumps into me when I stop. "You all right?"

"Yeah." I bend over, put my hands on my knees, and wait to see whether or not I puke. A trickle of sweat runs down my forehead. No air conditioning outside, but the open space soothes my nerves. Nausea gives way to hunger.

By the time I straighten up again, I have an audience. My mother speaks first. "You okay, honey?"

"Yeah, Mom. I'm over it now." *Soon as I eat, I'll probably barf.*

I follow Mr. and Mrs. Welles past where Cooper is standing and into the hangar. A side door leads to a lounge area and—

"Hey!" I run to hug my sister Beatrice and her two boys.

She flashes me a teasing grin. "So you got yourself knocked up, huh?"

"Yeah. You jealous?"

"Absolutely. Dani's baby?"

"Yeah. Didn't I always say I'd have one for her?"

Mom cuts in and hugs my sister. "How's Fred?"

"Fine. Overworked and loving it."

Dani eases up beside me, so I nudge her toward Beatrice. "You remember Dani?"

My sister doesn't quite gape at the girl. "Yes. Of course." The two stare at each other for a moment before hugging. Over Dani's shoulder, Beatrice gives me one of her stupid grins, like I've announced my engagement or something.

I'm having the girl's baby, not sleeping with her. I stick out my tongue.

After the hug fest, Mom and Mrs. Welles wander off to the corner and chat. I play with the boys till Dani brings us chocolate donuts. Not just the icing kind either, but all the way through. Truly yummy. I eat two—real careful like—in front of the bathroom mirror. Not a crumb gets on my dress.

"I am so happy for you." My sister stands behind, watching me in the mirror.

I wipe a bit of icing from my lips. "Is Mom okay?"

She spins me around and hugs me again. "She sold the house for you, sis. To pay for school. You're welcome to come stay with us. You know you are, but getting your GED would be harder with the boys around. Especially with you pregnant."

"Yeah. Guess you're right."

"Let's plan on Christmas, then. All right?"

"Yeah. Okay."

Dani peeks into the restroom. "We're getting ready to leave."

I rush out the door to find Mom. Words fail me, so I hug her again. She pulls an envelope out of her handbag and gives it to me. "This is your nest egg, honey. I always wanted you to go to college, but it's all right to have your own dreams. Call me once in a while. All right?"

I hug her again and drip my sadness down her back. "I love you, Mom."

"I love you too, honey." She brushes a tear from my cheek and kisses my forehead. "Better run along."

Dani holds the door for me as I rush to catch up. Cooper follows us out to the jet, but waits at the top of the stairs. I flop down on the seat I shared with Dani on the last flight.

No way to see my mother out the window. *We shoulda talked more, Mom.*

I scoot over to make room for Dani, and buckle in.

As soon as Cooper takes his seat, one of the crew closes the cabin door. In a few minutes, we're flying over North Georgia on our way to Virginia. I close my eyes to the world, snuggle against Dani, and try to sleep.

We land in Richmond around four and taxi to a stop in front of a humongous metal building. A few minutes later, one of the crew opens the aircraft door, so I grab my handbag and rush outside.

Dani follows me down the steps. She grabs my hand, and we head for a set of glass doors. "The company flies out of this airport. This is one of their buildings. The passenger lounge is through here."

She leads me down a short hallway and stands in front of another set of glass doors. After a moment, something clicks, and they swing open.

A guy with curly white hair greets Dani with a hug. "Welcome home, Miss Danièle."

"Thank you, Jake. This is Melanie Fairbairn. She'll be staying with us."

"Welcome to Richmond, young lady."

Gentle kindness permeates the old man's face and voice—like Grandpa Fairbairn.

I miss you, Gramps. Without thinking, I give Jake a quick hug.

Dani leads me to the restroom. She attacks her face like she's a contestant for Miss America. I find a place to get sick. Nausea was kind enough to wait till we landed, but my stomach demands payment with interest as soon as I open the stall door.

"You all right?"

"Dandy." *Don't worry, Miss Danièle. I won't get any on this pretty dress.* After I wash lunch off my face, I let the girl repair my makeup. "Is there a vending machine around this place?"

"Come and see." The girl's eyes burst with mischief. She grabs my hand and drags me down the hallway. The aroma of something sweet and freshly baked sends my empty stomach into conniptions. Dani pauses with a hand on the doorknob. "Jake's are truly brilliant."

"At the airport?" Beyond the door lies a kitchen. Scones swarm over a cooling rack on the counter—every one of them glazed on top.

Jake glances up from his work. "Why Miss Melanie, would you care for a scone and some milk?"

"Oh, yeah." *Like I'd refuse?* Steamed milk and orange-cranberry scone—my stomach promises me no trouble at all so long as I eat something this good. *Does a proper young lady lick her fingertips and scarf every last crumb? Well, yeah. This one does.*

Cooper pokes his head into the room as I finish. "We're ready to leave."

Jake shoos us with both hands. "You go ahead. I'll be along in a moment."

Dani and I follow Cooper out the front door. Five people—six if Jake's coming—and we're taking a motor home? No. Cooper and Mr. Welles climb into a stretch Cadillac Escalade. That leaves four of us.

Not sure what I expected, but the interior resembles a tiny apartment, with a breakfast bar on one side and living room on the other. I nestle into one end of an overstuffed leather couch and crash. After a word with her mother, Dani joins me.

Jake disappears up front. A moment later, the engine rumbles to life, and we pull out on the highway. Weird not being able to see outside, but not as bad as the airplane.

The gentle diesel drone and slow rocking of the bus fade till it's like we're sitting in some upscale hotel room on a lazy Saturday afternoon.

I walk up front and collapse into the seat across from Jake. The old man gives me a sympathetic nod. "If you're tired, missy, there's a bedroom at the rear. I'm sure Momma Bear won't mind y'all sleeping in her bed."

I flash the old man a grin. "Thanks."

"We'll be home in about two hours."

Back in the living room area, Mrs. Welles is lecturing Dani about something.

I wait till she acknowledges me. "Jake said I could use the bedroom?"

"Why of course, sweetheart. Make yourself at home."

Sure enough—past the lounge and a bathroom, behind a door, I find a double bed. Dark, quiet, comfy. Why not? Two hours is time enough to dream of the boy who promised me his heart.

Danièle

Mum slips the cozy off her teapot and pours herself a cup. "Darjeeling, love?"

"Yes. Please." I add milk and a dash of raw sugar to mine, then help myself to a scone before resuming my seat.

My mother settles into the recliner across from me. "I'd like a word with you while your guest is sleeping."

"Certainly." I shut off my phone and lay it aside. Email will have to wait.

"Miss Fairbairn's rather more attractive than I recall. Will she stay on as your child's nanny?"

"I hope so. I'd like to finish college."

"Then you must prepare now for her continued presence."

"How so?"

"Your fiancé's a man, sweetheart, and Miss Fairbairn's pregnant with his child."

"I intend to be very active as mother."

"And as Mrs. Davis, no doubt. All well and good. But you must also satisfy Miss Fairbairn's emotional needs or your husband may."

"We're best friends, Mum. She knows she can come to me with her concerns."

"Perhaps. But will she if you spend insufficient time with her?"

"No." She'll withdraw rather than bother me.

"Are you set on finishing college?"

"Our wedding's the first week of March. The baby's due later that month. Finals are in May. Ethan graduates in June. This spring will be hectic, but I've got the summer to devote to being a mother before starting my senior year."

"You have six months remaining with Miss Fairbairn before your nuptials. To ensure the young woman's loyalty. And your husband's fidelity."

"We're already best friends."

"She's the mother of your child."

Adrenaline sends a wave of heat up my throat before I realize she's simply trying to make a point. "Yes. I suppose so."

"You must always see her in that light if she's to remain under your roof. Meet her emotional needs as you do your husband's sexual ones." She pauses, her eyes suddenly intense. "Let me be clear—I'm not suggesting you sleep with the young woman."

Mother of my child or not, I'm daft to let her stay. She threatens not only my husband's fidelity, but mine. I've broken enough promises, though. Whatever the cost to me, I'll not deny her access to our child. "I haven't the heart to send her away, Mum."

"Then do what you must for her to protect your marriage." With that, my mother ends our little chat. She stands and walks across to the breakfast bar.

I turn on my phone again and read my email, but my mind remains on Melanie and the child she carries.

Melanie

Bright light and utter silence interrupt my sleep. I blink away tears till my eyes adjust. Dani grins at me from the bedroom doorway. "We've arrived," she says.

She leads me out of the bus and across a cement floor.

We're inside. I stop and survey my surroundings. Work benches line the back wall of the building. Sunlight filters through skylights overhead. Six garage doors all in a row. One large enough for a full-sized motor home. One bay with a hydraulic lift.

Through the open door I glimpse a drive that winds through giant trees to iron gates and a stone fence. *Where are we?* Panic bares its ugly teeth at me. Prep school after all?

Dani tugs at my arm. "Let me show you your room."

We pass a laundry, a bathroom, and several closed doors before the hallway turns a corner, and we stroll through an archway.

My heart stops for a few beats while my eyes drink in wonder. A grand ballroom stretches out before us. At the far end of the dance floor a wide stairway leads up to the second level. To my right is a line of columns, and beyond them, a dining area and kitchen. On the left is a formal entryway with massive double doors. On three sides of the two-story dance area a narrow balcony provides a walkway around the base of tall windows.

Dani grins at me and bows low. She takes my hand, lifts it above my head, and twirls me around. "Mum's well known for her charity cotillions. She'll expect you to dance with any gentleman who asks—including Cooper—and do so with both manners and grace."

She leads me around the room in a waltz before bowing again. "Are you hungry?"

"Starving."

On the breakfast bar in the kitchen we find a crock pot full of what Dani says is lamb stew. Fresh biscuits wait nearby, in a bread warmer.

The girl shows me how to use the single-serve coffee maker to make hot chocolate.

Dani loads our stuff on a tray and leads me outside to a table shaded by an umbrella. "This is Mum's garden, but I think my father spends more time here than she does."

I take a seat facing away from the house so I can study the grounds. A brick wall topped by a wrought iron fence surrounds a fairytale park. A pond—or maybe a small lake—takes up almost half of the space. To one side stands a grove of huge trees. Between the house and the water, the grass lawn gives way to boulders, decorative plants, and flowers. A flagstone path leads off around the lake and out under the largest of the trees.

"Your supper's getting cold."

"Huh? Oh. Yeah." Lamb stew isn't my favorite, but I take a spoonful. "Jake made this?"

Dani does her little bobble-head nod and keeps right on eating.

I scarf down quite a lot more of the stew before nibbling on a biscuit. Minutes later, I find myself staring at an empty bowl. *Jake's gonna make me fat.* I lean back and survey the garden once again.

Dani stands and gathers our dishes. "Finished?"

"Yeah." I gulp down the rest of my chocolate and set my cup on the tray.

Back inside, Dani rinses our bowls, puts them into a dishwasher, and loads up a plate with scones. Her pace quickens then, and she rushes me up the stairs. At the top, I spin around. My imagination fills the ballroom with men in fancy tuxedos and women in their Cinderella gowns. *Mom said it was okay to dream. What if he ever did come back?* I shut my eyes and imagine he had.

Somebody touches my cheek. My eyes snap open to discover Dani brushing a stray lock away from my face. "It's good to see you smile," she says.

Down the hallway and around the corner our journey ends. Dani leans against an old wooden door. "An English cottage once stood here. My parents loved the house so much they saved some of the architectural elements and incorporated them into the new building." For a moment, her mischievous grin reminds me of the Dani of long ago. She swings the door open and steps aside.

Oriental rugs cover much of the worn plank flooring. Rough-plastered walls rise to meet exposed beams and a vaulted ceiling. A stone fireplace and bookshelves cover the far wall. A seat in the bay window overlooks the garden. A full-sized Jenny Lind bed, an antique oak dresser, and a rocking chair complete the furnishings.

I pull open a door at the back of the room to find a modern bath. *Sweet.*

The old wooden bed squeaks when I flop down on its feather mattress. Not as plush as the Biltmore, but certainly comfy.

Dani's grin turns downright wicked. "Mum suggested one of the other guest suites. They're larger and more modern. Would you like—"

"No! This is perfect." I run across the floor and hug her.

"Well, then. I'll leave you to unpack. If you need anything, my room's around the corner."

With the door closed, my imagination blossoms—my own cottage in the woods. A place away from the rest of the world. Just me. And my baby. And *him.*

I retrieve Mom's envelope from my backpack and worry it open. A check for one hundred and twenty thousand dollars falls from my trembling hands. *It's all right to have your own dreams, honey.*

God, please let Mom be okay.

CHAPTER 14

Danièle

Flowers ambush me just inside the bedroom doorway. A bevy of balloons jostles the ceiling above my bed. Chocolates wait on the dresser, along with a kilo tin of Darjeeling and a quart of Irish cream.

The aroma of latkes and aged Asiago draw my senses across the room. A magnum of vintage French Champagne relaxes in a cool bath on my desk. Two wine glasses provide formal escorts.

Leaning against the bottle stands a card. I slide a fingernail under the flap and open the envelope. *Joy of my heart and mother of my child—I love you more than life itself.*

A scene from an old Alfred Hitchcock movie flashes through my mind. Adrenaline floods my veins, but the terror soon fades. It has to be him. "Ethan? Are you here?"

He pokes his head out of the bathroom. "Yeah, babe. Hope I didn't scare you."

I fling myself into his arms and kiss his sweet lips. When we break for air, I glance over my shoulder. The decorations speak more eloquently than my fiancé usually does. *Mum.* "This is all very lovely. Were the flowers your idea?"

"Your mother suggested them. The Champagne was mine."

So she knows you're in my bedroom. Which means she approves.

The psychologists consider vaginal intercourse the fundamental measure of a person's sexual health. Without that, one simply isn't complete. Hence the importance of surgery. Or dilation. They measure the success of their treatment, however, not in width and depth, but by my willingness to have Ethan penetrate me.

If I hesitate—if I don't jump into bed with him— Unthinkable. Such would mean utter failure. To everyone. Excepting perhaps me. And Melanie.

Mum can't hold my hand on my wedding night. But she hesitates not to push me into the deep end of the pool. *Enjoy the water, sweetheart.*

Are my psychologists in on this as well?

I capitulate, Mum. "Open the bottle, will you? I think I'd like a drink." I slip off my heels and toss them aside.

Ethan sits on my bed and pats the bedspread next to him. "Relax, babe. I won't hurt you."

"I'm not like the other women you've known."

"But you had your surgeries."

"Vaginoplasty and orchiopexies. Nothing more." *Not now. Not ever.*

"So you've got a super-sized clit. I don't care."

I've fathered a child. "My testes—"

He silences me with a fingertip. "Get it through your pretty little head, Danièle—I love you. I'll adjust to your body being different. I'm a patient man."

"Dr. Pierson said there was a problem with your—"

A firm shake of his head stops me. "I read her letter. We'll sort out the details after I see a urologist in October. What counts is Melanie's pregnant with my baby."

"Ethan—" I meet his stubborn eyes before sighing my frustration. "All right."

With a practiced hand, Ethan unfastens the top button of my blouse. Heat rises in my chest. The two of us have never ventured beyond kisses and a bit of heavy petting, but the memories of childhood games rise like sweet magnolia blossoms.

A gentle kiss. A brush of his hands down my sides.

Champagne—spiced apple and fresh-baked bread tickling my nose—a hint of nuts and yeast on my palate. I savor the delay.

Another kiss. Two more buttons. One step closer to the threshold.

I can do this.

Melanie

Puffy white clouds drag their sorry reflections across the garden pond. Once in a while, some fish gobbles a bug stupid enough to fall into the water. On an old tree trunk that stretches out from the bank, a family of painted turtles enjoys the last of the evening's rays.

From the bay window I watch the sun set. When blue sky turns red and purple, I punch in my sister's number. If my mother's sick, I don't wanna know. But I gotta find out.

Beatrice picks up. "Melanie?"

"Yeah. Mom there?"

"Sure."

A minute passes as a couple of chipmunks gather some of the fallen acorns in the fading light. My imagination keeps wandering out into the garden, expecting to see the father of my child come walking up the path. *Ethan—the dude had better be some kinda special.*

"Are you settled in?" My mother's voice sounds chipper, like maybe she's okay after all.

"Hi, Mom. Yeah, I'm unpacked. You sure about this check?"

"Would I have given you your inheritance if I didn't trust you?"

"No. Guess not."

"Well then. Ask Danièle to help you invest the money. All right?"

"Yeah. Sure. You okay, Mom?"

"I'm fine, honey." One of my sister's kids squalls in the background. "I'd better go. I promised Beatrice I'd entertain the boys."

"I love you, Mom."

I toss the phone on the bed and lean back against the window frame. *My life's here now. With Dani.* The image of us standing in front of my mother's grave sends a creepy chill down my back. *Yeah. Maybe forever. Might as well be married.*

I brush a hand across my abdomen. Not much there yet. Did I really go through IVF and get myself pregnant for the girl?

Well, yeah. I promised to have a baby when we were old enough.

Not for Dani, though. Not her.

As a kid, I wanted my own little one so bad that my best forever friend pretended to be a boy so she could be the father. When the doctors told Dani she couldn't bear children, I promised to have one.

For Daniel. His baby.

Well, it made sense at the time.

I shake my head and force my gaze back out the window. Moonlight has turned the garden into a wonderland of silver and midnight blue. A breeze sends ripples across the pond's reflected stars. Jet black trees sway to some silent beat, waving their arms above it all.

Sometime later, a fat drop of water spatters against the window and down the pane. Others join in, till a steady chorus patters syncopation on the metal roof, till my eyelids succumb to the reassuring music.

Would you stay if Ethan left?

Yeah, Mom.

Movement in the garden snags my attention. The breath catches in my throat. A wraith drifts along the path beside the lake, white hair floating in the breeze, her body wrapped in stars and silver moonlight. *That you, Dani? What're you up to?*

The ghostly vision passes under the trees and comes to rest, a pale blue glow beneath sheltering arms of black. Spellbound, I perch above the garden and wait while the moon drifts across the night sky.

The wind picks up again. Lightning flickers in the distance. The trees whisper to each other above our heads.

A curious longing tightens my throat. Is this what I want—me and Dani alone in the garden of my imagination?

Raindrops start their chorus again—a warm summer lullaby tapped out on the window and roof above. A branch scrapes the wall outside. Mist rises from the ground.

Yet the apparition moves not.

Are you nuts, girl? It's raining.

Lightning flashes a portrait of her seated form. Then darkness. Her after-image floats across my vision. The garden remains shades of midnight blue and dark grey.

After a moment of indecision, I step into the hallway and ease my bedroom door shut. In the dim light I rush to the stairs and pad in silence down to the grand ballroom.

Across the dance floor, past the support columns, beyond the kitchen, a glass wall stands between me and the outside world. Rivulets of water distort my vision of the garden. *Where was the stupid door?* In the darkness, I don't remember. So I run along the wall, one hand on the glass. On the left, the barrier ends in the quiet darkness of a hallway.

I find the garden-side entrance past the kitchen in the other direction. The security panel beside it blinks red. *Wonderful. Cooper's probably gonna shoot me when I set off the alarm.*

Eyes closed, every muscle tense, I push the door open and stumble outside into warm rain, a stiff breeze, and darkness thicker than I imagined.

"Dani!"

Moon and clouds above send their ghostly children dancing in blue and silver shadows across the garden. I draw in a deep breath of the moist air and shuffle my way closer to the water. With the stone pathway under my feet, I turn back toward the manor and scan the darkness for my bedroom window.

Yeah. This way. As long as I stay on the flagstones, things should be okay. I take a step into darkness. Then two. Ankle-deep mud greets my third and steals away my balance. I teeter over a black abyss.

In a flurry of motion, something white grabs my arm, pulls me to a stop, and holds me in its relentless grip.

When the echoes of my scream die away, Dani nudges me toward the manor. Once inside, the girl punches a code that makes the security system happy.

The wall sconces seem bright as daylight after the darkness outside. Dani stands there like a statue, dripping on the tile floor.

The redness in her eyes says she'd been crying—something I've never seen her do before. Ever. "Are you okay?"

"Brilliant. Just brilliant."

"Let's get out of here then." *Before Cooper shows up.* I tug her a step toward the ballroom, but she shakes her head and leads me down the hallway to an elevator.

When we get to my room, she pauses in the doorway. "Can I borrow a nightgown?"

Her robe is soaking wet. I get that part right away. But her room's just around the corner. She must have a dozen clean ones there.

Then I notice the blood. "Yeah. Sure."

Well, okay. It's only a few drops. Like what I used to get between my periods.

I pull out one of my old nightshirts—an oversized baseball uniform top made from a soft cotton flannel. "The stains might come out if I soak your nightgown in cold water..."

After a glance down, Dani nods. Tears fill her eyes.

I draw her into a tight hug. "What happened?"

"Ethan and I—we had sex."

You just got home. "Here?"

Her head bobs in slow motion, like one of those little dolls. "He's asleep now. In my bed. His snoring kept me awake, so I took a stroll in the garden."

"Are you in pain?"

"Does it matter? I'm a normal woman now. Maybe they'll leave me the bloody hell alone."

"Huh?"

"Vaginal intercourse—that was always their measure of success. I did it. Now screw them."

Not knowing what else to do, I help Dani take off her robe. While the girl is drying her hair, I put her soiled nightgown into cold water. I strip and throw my damp clothes into the corner, then put on my own pajamas.

Dani hugs me again. "I should go."

But she doesn't. She perches on the window ledge and peers out into the night. I settle in beside her and wait till the girl turns to look at me. Guess it's my time to be the strong one. "Dani, if I'm gonna spend the rest of my life being a nanny for you and Ethan, you need to come to me when something's wrong."

Dani lets out a soft bark of laughter. "Mum thought I might need to lend *you* emotional support." Tenderness floods her violet eyes, but she says nothing more.

The girl pauses in the doorway on her way out. Her lower lip trembles, but she doesn't speak a word. I roll my eyes and move to the far side of the bed. "Come on. You've held me often enough."

She strides across the room and crawls into bed beside me. I snake my arms around her waist and draw our bodies close. The tension begins to melt away. Hers. And mine. Finally.

Chapter 15

Danièle

The ancient grandfather clock in the den below Melanie's room chimes five. Darkness still cloaks the world outside the bedroom window. Only Jake would be up and about this early.

Cashmere soft, Melanie's hair gives off the gentle aromas of coconut oil and raspberries. I ease away from her and sit on the edge of the bed.

The mother of my child murmurs something in her sleep and reaches a hand across the sheets. After all these years, her heart still belongs to the boy I can never be.

If only it were possible, love. I lie down again—just long enough to plant a kiss on her cheek. "I have to go. Sleep well."

Back in my own room, I stuff Melanie's nightshirt into the hamper, don a fresh nightgown like the one I wore outside, and slide into bed next to Ethan.

One of the benefits of Partial Androgen Insensitivity Syndrome is my relative lack of underarm hair. Personal body odor has never been a concern. Ethan's musky scent may be normal for a man, but mixed with wilted flowers, stale Champagne, and the remnants of Asiago and latkes, it leaves me wishing for coconut and raspberries.

I roll away from him, bury my face in the bed linens, and try to sleep.

Sometime later, he slides an arm around my waist. "You awake yet, babe?"

"Yes, love." I sit up and stretch.

With an overwhelming strength that sends a shock of panic through my bones, Ethan draws me into his arms. Beard stubble scrapes across my chin. His lips close over mine, but last night's food and drink spoil his romantic overture.

He hitches a leg up and rolls us over as though he's practiced the maneuver a thousand times. One hand meanders up my thigh, taking my nightgown along with it. The other seeks out my breast.

I force my muscles to yield and open my mouth to ease my breathing. Being a woman means letting a man be the center of my life—haven't they all but chiseled that into stone? *Am I any less a woman if I never learn to enjoy this?*

A few minutes later, Ethan sits on the edge of the bed, having satisfied his urgent desire. "I better shower and get dressed. I need to get on the road as soon as we finish breakfast, and I'd like to talk to your father first."

"All right. I'll meet you downstairs, then."

I lean against the headboard, pull up my sore legs, and rest my chin on my knees. A bit of something wet runs down my leg. Several spots of pink—along with small puddles of semen—stain the sheets as well as my nightgown.

Is this the preview of married life? Shag the girl and run? With the collusion of my parents, the doctors and psychologists, by their careful manipulation, have brought me to this—a leaky repository for semen.

This is what makes me a woman in their eyes.

The problem has never been my intersex; I accepted my body a lifetime ago. They never have. Nor believed I could be happy without —without *this*.

They used the psychological equivalent of the Powell Doctrine —overwhelming force backed by widespread public support. What chance has an intersex kid against the organized might of the medical profession and the approval of society at large?

Without thinking about what I wanted, I conformed to their idea of normal.

The perfect chameleon.

"You okay, babe?" Ethan drops his towel and pulls on his boxers.

"I'll be fine. But we really should talk about the surrogacy."

"October. Don't have time right now. I want to see your father about our future."

"All right. See you later, then."

He finishes dressing, kisses me one more time, and rushes out the door.

I pull off my nightgown, yank the sheets off my bed, and pile them all next to the hamper. The pillow cases follow seconds later. Even the bedspread proves to be tainted.

Small bruises dot my arms and legs. The dull ache I had the week after surgery has returned.

Do all women feel this vulnerable? This much at the mercy of men? Is this what my doctors wanted all along? My body trembles at the thought.

My phone chimes its breakfast warning. No time remains for a leisurely bath, so I settle for a quick shower. Fresh underwear, a comfortable and bright sundress, subdued makeup, braided hair—enough to make me feel almost clean again. Almost whole.

Melanie

I figure Dani wants me to make a good first impression on Ethan, so I wear a nice dress and do my hair and makeup and all. I glide down the grand staircase like some princess, trying not to make any noise.

Mrs. Welles glances up from whatever she's doing and nods a good morning. Mr. Welles stands as I approach the dining area and gestures toward the man seated beside him. "Miss Fairbairn, let me introduce you to Ethan Davis."

The guy rises and extends his hand.

Sweet. So you're the dude I'm gonna spend the rest of my life with.

He's several inches taller than Dani. And ripped. He draws my hand to his lips, kisses my knuckles, and smiles like he means it. "Good to meet you, Melanie. You're even prettier than I expected."

Yeah. Right. "Thanks."

He pulls out the chair beside him and motions for me to sit. "Jake's got breakfast ready if you're up for pecan waffles, scrambled eggs, and bacon."

"Sure. Why not?"

A true gentleman—he saunters over to the buffet line and loads a plate with goodies.

I say grace like a proper lady, then begin stuffing my face like a starving pregnant girl.

Ethan studies me over his cup of coffee. "Danièle said you're willing to stay on as nanny."

"Yeah." *I wonder if our baby will have your steel-blue eyes.*

"Excellent. That will let Danièle finish her degree."

Danièle. Yes. Miss Danièle Aileana Welles. I take another bite of waffle to hide my smirk.

"Ah. Well. Here she is." With that, he stands for Dani and kisses her like they've been apart for years.

Ah, how sweet the young lovers. Yeah. Suck her face off, why don't you?

They wander off in quiet conversation, so I finish my breakfast alone. When I set my fork down, though, Mrs. Welles strolls across the room, places a folder on the table, and perches beside me. "Your mother desires that you improve your education while under our care. To that end, I've prepared a schedule for you."

I shoulda gone to prep school.

"When Danièle is home on holidays and weekends, you'll spend your time with her. The pregnancy—your health—is your primary responsibility. Your relationship with my daughter is a close second."

Well, yeah. "Yes, ma'am."

"Three evenings a week, Cooper will instruct you in ballroom dancing. Every Friday, you and I will meet to review the books you've read—one from the list I've prepared and one of your own choosing. We shall also discuss etiquette."

That's your idea of education—books and ballet? Sweet.

She hands me a debit card with my name on it. "Randolph Welles will deposit a small sum monthly for your personal expenses. Ask Danièle if you need help balancing your account."

Mrs. Welles glances at her wrist and stands. "You have an appointment this morning with Ms. Lundsford, our hairdresser. An hour from now. One of the staff will let you know when she arrives."

But I like my hair the way it is.

"Our seamstress, Ms. Franklin, will measure you early this afternoon. Do you have any questions?"

"No, ma'am." Mornings—read. Evenings—dance. Manners. Grace. Tailored clothes. *What's gonna be left of me?*

Danièle

The lonely highway drones on toward Richmond. Melanie lies asleep, head on my lap. I brush the ginger curls away from her face. I hoped to chat on the way to school, but her eyes drooped before we crossed the river.

When we pull into the dorm parking lot, I ease from under Melanie and step out of the Escalade.

Cooper grabs my suitcase from the back of the limo. "How much do you know about your roommate?"

"Grace is Heather's younger sister. She's not a security risk."

"What about—"

"She's fine, Cooper. Trust me."

"All right." Nevertheless, he performs a quick search of my small dorm room before leaving with Melanie.

Grace arrives an hour after I finish unpacking. She stops in the open doorway, suspicion clouding her face. "You and my sister were close at prep school, but why ask to room with me?"

"She said you're a diligent student." *I promised Heather I'd look after you.*

"Did she tell you about me?"

"Does it matter?"

"Yes. And I'd appreciate an answer." Grace leans against the doorpost and crosses her arms.

I like you. "I went with your sister to visit Grayson in the hospital." *After you tried to kill yourself.*

"Oh. Yeah. I forgot you two went back that far." She tosses her backpack on the unoccupied bed and eases the door shut behind her. "I'm stealth, okay?"

"Sure. I'd prefer no one know I'm intersex."

Her stubborn frown relaxes into an uncertain smile. Then a slow nod. "Gotcha. I didn't know."

I pull out my phone and bring up Google Maps. "I'm going shopping. Want to come along?"

"Where?"

"There's a motorbike dealer on Marshall out past 195. I need a helmet."

"You ride?"

"Sort of. I got a ticket this summer for driving without a license. So I need to get one. Stat."

"Sweet. You know Brent Hamilton?"

"I don't think so. Why?"

"He's got an almost new Honda for sale. Maybe he's got an extra helmet."

"Does he live on campus?"

"Frat row. Want me to call him?"

"Sure."

Fifteen minutes later, Grace introduces me to her friend—boyfriend someday perhaps, although his eyes hold more hope for a relationship than hers do.

Brent leads us to his Shadow Spirit. *I'm in love.* When he starts the bike, the Honda purrs like distant thunder on a warm summer's night. "You interested in the motorcycle or just a helmet?"

"How much are you asking for the bike?"

"Five grand. Cash. Paid eight for it six months ago."

"If you'll take me to my bank and then the DMV, we can complete the sale today."

"Deal. You gonna ride like that?"

In a sundress? I think not. "No. Let me change first."

Melanie

I waltz on in an eternal Cinderella dream, swirling across the marble floor with Cooper. The first week at Victoria Springs, we practiced the box; the second turning. I spent most of September in the Marine's embrace, while he guided me through the moves of ballroom dancing. My body knows the steps now. And the feel of his arms around me.

I could love you, Marine. Cooper's the best dance instructor ever. Always positive. And friendly. Like a brother. Yeah, like that. Definitely not interested in me. Yeah. Marrying the guy's a hopeless dream.

Always a gentleman, Cooper holds the door to the limo while Dani and I climb aboard.

Weary, and fighting nausea, I lean against the girl in the back seat of the Escalade. "Thanks for tagging along," I say. "You didn't have to, you know."

"Even if the baby wasn't mine, I'd want to do this with you." When she puts an arm around my shoulder, I snuggle against the softness of her sweater. The girl brushes her other hand across my belly—searching for the baby, no doubt—and parks her fingers close by. The tenderness in her eyes brings my heart up into my throat.

You still dream of being the father yourself, don't you?

I imagine Dani as the gentle-hearted boy she might have been if her body knew what to do with testosterone. *Yes, I'd have married that you.* I spread my fingers over hers and smile my contentment.

Victoria Springs Medical Center—the two-story building provides what passes for medical care in the county. Cooper parks in front of the door and escorts us to Dr. Hawthorne's office.

Twelve weeks—my first trimester ultrasound—my heart stumbles in anticipation. I find a seat, but rock from hip to hip, unable to find a comfortable position.

Dani plays with her cell. She's gonna be one of the first people on the planet ever wired directly to the Internet if she gets her way. She probably won't even put down her phone on her wedding night.

The nurse calls me into the back and doesn't object when Dani tags along. I slip off my pumps and crawl up on the padded examining table. With my head propped up, I still have to crane my neck around to see the display.

Dani squeezes my hand. "Relax. I'm sure the baby's fine."

The technician walks into the room and glances from Dani to me. "Are we ready?"

When I nod, she spreads a warm towel across my lower abdomen and pushes my top up a bit further. "This is a lubricating gel."

Oh, really? Like I've never had a stupid ultrasound before?

She squeezes a blob on her wrist and slathers it around. "I'm making sure it's not too hot." Then she squirts a bunch of warm—no, make that hot—goo across the top of my all but invisible baby bump, and pushes it across my belly with the ultrasound wand.

Dani's violet eyes blossom. I twist my head around to see the screen, but the technician has already pulled the sensor away and is adjusting the machine's settings.

A smug grin has taken over Dani's face by the time I turn my head back again.

"What?"

"You'll see."

The technician rubs her wand back and forth across my belly, like she gets paid by the number of strokes. I try to watch as she points out stuff, but I get this crick in my neck and it all looks like an old black and white TV show anyhow. So I try to read the emotions from Dani's face instead.

"Can you see?" the technician asks. "She's sucking her thumb."

For a moment—just a moment—I see my baby's face on the screen. "She?"

"It's difficult to be certain at this age. But, yes, this one's probably a girl."

This one? My eyes bounce from the display to the technician to Dani's glowing face. A calm resolution shines from the girl's eyes. I grin, but she doesn't notice, her gaze still fixed on the screen.

The technician asks me to roll a little to my side before she squirts more gel across my abdomen. Nervous tension builds as I wait for what has to be coming. She rambles on about body parts being okay till I want to scream.

At last, she taps on my arm and points at a blob on the display. "He looks to be a boy."

Twins. They both made it!

She keeps right on moving her wand and taking measurements, like anything else in the universe matters.

The screen's reflection mixes with the wonder and determination in Dani's eyes. The set of her jaw says she'll do whatever it takes to protect her family—her babies.

Yeah, girl. So will I.

When the technician finishes, I wipe off the slime and straighten my clothes.

Twins. As soon as I stand up, a wave of nausea reminds me that pregnancy isn't all a party.

Dani pulls me into a tight hug—kinda like the smothering ones her father gives. "I've got a quick question for Dr. Hawthorne. I'll be right back." She disappears down the hallway, so I wander back to the waiting area and sit in the worst chair in Victoria Springs.

Dani returns before I find a comfortable position. The girl stops in front of me and takes both of my hands in hers. Mischief and joy light her face—almost like old times. "He says it's okay for you to ride a motorbike—so long as we don't get into an accident."

"You got your license?" Okay, so my voice sounds more like a squeal.

"Yes. The week we got back. And I bought a Honda Shadow Spirit—the most beautiful motorbike you've ever seen."

"And your parents are okay with this?"

"I haven't told them yet."

"Yeah. Gee. I can understand why. So when do I get my ride?"

"Come back to school with me and spend the week in the dorm."

Do I really wanna be cooped up in a small room with you and Grace? "Is there anything to do while you're in classes?"

"The campus is lovely this time of year."

And your mother won't be there. "Let's do it."

We meet Cooper in the hallway. Dani and I wait in the lobby while he gets the car. The low grey overcast of morning has turned dark. Thunder crashes in the distance. A drop splashes my cheek. The rain turns heavy by the time the limo pulls up to the entrance. Cooper shelters us with his umbrella as we rush for the Escalade. Dani and I crash in the back seat and just grin at each other like idiots the entire way home.

CHAPTER 16

Danièle

Crimson, gold, and amber leaves flutter in the cool October breeze. Melanie snuggles closer, her head pressed hard against my back. My lovely Shadow Spirit purrs as the asphalt beneath us races by.

Tree shadows and sunlight flicker past, the syncopated rhythm mesmerizing. I turn in at the dorm, find a parking spot, and kill the engine.

The afternoon has warmed somewhat, but a chill clings to my bones, one that I suspect a cup of Darjeeling won't heal.

Melanie snuggles against me as we stroll up the path toward the dorm. Her gaze at some distant wonder. "While we were riding this afternoon, I had the most incredible sense of having been here before."

I urge her to sit on a bench, where we might still capture a bit of the sun's warmth.

Tenderness spreads across Melanie's face. "After you first moved to Virginia, I dreamed of today's drive through the changing leaves. On your motorcycle. And me pregnant with your baby. I thought it all impossible then."

I'm desperate to tell her the children are mine, but cannot find the words—or perhaps the courage. So I lean close and kiss Melanie's forehead. "Whatever else happens, the children will always be ours."

"Are you really gonna let me stay forever?"

It's you I long to be with. I dare not admit my guilt aloud, but my hand caresses hers.

Melanie's eyes grow tender, her cheeks crimson.

Am I capable of blushing? I lean close again and kiss her on the lips. "Yes. Forever."

Melanie

The old highway drones on beneath us as the miles slide past. Autumn colors flash by the window. Late October paints the hardwoods in festive hues, leaving the pines a drab green under the clear blue sky.

Dani remains quiet, her body slumped against mine, head resting on my shoulder. In the cool darkness of the Escalade, heat radiates from the girl. Along with the scent of fresh-cut lilacs.

Even with a fever, you smell like flowers.

Rarely during the turmoil of my childhood did Dani ask to be held. Yet I did so whenever she got sick. I squirm around in the seat to find a more comfortable position. For her. And for me. Then slide my arm around the girl.

I wipe at the sweat on Dani's forehead. Pale violet eyes drift open and closed again as she nuzzles closer.

My hand wanders down to my abdomen. At sixteen weeks, not much shows except the weight I've gained. Something twitches under my fingers—one of the babies kicking?

When we arrive at Victoria Springs Manor, Cooper lifts Dani in his arms like some Viking warrior rescuing a fallen princess. I close the limo door and follow them down the hallway.

In her bedroom, I coax Dani awake long enough to help her into a nightgown. "You sure you don't want a doctor?"

One side of her mouth curls up. "I'm sure Mum's already spoken with Dr. Hawthorne."

"Can I get you anything?"

Perched on the edge of her bed, Dani breathes through her mouth. Tired eyes slow-blink twice. "Um. Yes. Ask Jake to bring me some tea, please—Darjeeling with honey, lemon and a spot of whiskey. She closes her eyes and slumps back against the headboard.

A fresh pot of hot water waits on the kitchen counter, along with a small decanter of amber fluid, a honey bear, and a sliced lemon.

But no Jake. I find the right canister, steep the tea for five minutes, then load the stuff on a silver tray and carry it upstairs.

Dani's eyes flutter open as I'm pouring tea, so I help her sit up and watch her while she sips the steamy liquid. She sets the cup on the nightstand without finishing more than half and lies down again. When her breathing slows, I walk downstairs to the solarium and kick back with what I hope is a good book.

An hour later, a shadow crosses my vision. Ethan perches on the edge of the chair across from me. His eyes radiate suppressed anger. "Mind if we talk?"

I place a bookmark in *Golden Boy* and set the paperback aside. "Okay."

"Outside." Without waiting for a nod, he stands and walks to the door.

Yes, officer. She fell into the pond and drowned. So sad.

Come on, Melanie. Don't be paranoid. I follow Ethan down the path into the dark shade under Dani's old walnut tree and join him on the bench.

The sun sets even as we sit. Deep red and purple drift across the garden and paint the house with shadows. Branches rustle and creak in the late October wind. Wispy clouds scoot across the darkening sky. I shiver at the chill in the Ethan's eyes.

The guy's face softens into an awkward smile, but his eyes betray a deep sadness. "Sorry," he says. "I didn't mean to be short with you. None of this is your fault."

What's wrong? "I have no idea what you're talking about."

He pulls an envelope out of his pocket and taps it against his knee. "Shortly after the clinic fertilized your eggs, I got a letter from Dr. Pierson saying I had azoospermia. Last week, my doctor confirmed that a supplement I was taking kept me from producing sperm."

"Then you're not the father?"

"No. And I really wanted to be."

"So who is?" My hand wanders down to my baby bump. The air becomes thick as molasses.

Breathe.

The dude stares past me, like he's gone mental or something. "Does it really matter? They're not mine."

Yes. It matters! My middle finger twitches, anxious to stand in front of the guy's nose. But a proper young lady doesn't flip off her best friend's fiancé. And he's not being a jerk so much as a guy who just found out the kids aren't his after all.

Ethan's attention finally returns to me. "We'll continue to provide for you and the twins. Help find them a good home." His desolate eyes wander away again. "I'll leave it to Danièle to work out the details of your severance." With that, he strides off toward the manor.

I wait for the ground to swallow me, but only silence infects the darkness. For a fleeting moment, I wish he actually had drowned me. Then I trudge back to the house.

My book lies where I left it, but I no longer care to read. Or do anything else. So I sulk in silence up the grand staircase and down the hallway to my room. Away from people. Where my dreams can die alone.

I hang up my dress with the others. Well, Dani's dress. Like most everything else I wear, the Welles paid for it. I dig around in my bottom drawer till I find the pajamas Mom gave me years ago.

Dressed in my own clothes, I crawl into bed and pull the quilt up to my chin. *Hope I get to sleep before the tears start.*

Danièle

Ethan's musky scent drags me out of fevered dreams. His hand brushes wet hair from my face. My fiancé bends down to press a tender kiss against my lips. "Sorry you're not feeling well, babe."

Pressure throbs behind my eyes. I squint at the room's brightness. "When did you arrive?"

"Here? About an hour ago. I flew in to D.C. earlier this week for some meetings. And my doctor's appointment. My return flight leaves tomorrow, but I wanted to drop by and see you before I left."

"You went to a specialist?"

"Yeah. The urologist thinks a supplement I was taking caused the problem. Apparently it was contaminated with steroids. So we'll start over—find another egg donor and surrogate after my sperm production's back up."

Start over? "All right. I don't mind having more children."

"No. Just one or two from my sperm. I explained to Melanie that we don't want hers."

I rub at the pain in my temples. "You did what?"

"No big deal. We'll give her a handsome severance package. And she can put the babies up for adoption."

"No, Ethan. They're my children. I tried to explain that. The clinic extracted sperm from my gonadal biopsies."

His face darkens with anger. Ethan drags a chair close to the bed and sits. Seconds pass as my heart murmurs discontent. "Yours," he says, finally.

"Yes." With that confession, the last of my fear departs, leaving only my throbbing headache. I no longer care to meet anyone's expectations. Not even his.

Some of the tension leaves Ethan's face before he meets my eyes again. "I love you. I can accept that you're intersex. But you and Melanie having a baby together? With me the odd one out? Sorry, but no. Just no."

I push myself upright, but the world spins me down again. "I'm keeping my children, Ethan. And Melanie will have access to them. Neither of those is negotiable."

Ethan kisses my cheek—once, twice. "You're sick, babe. Think it over when you're better."

I pull off the sapphire ring he gave me and press it into his palm. "No, Ethan. I love you dearly, but I'll never give up my children. Or their mother."

After he leaves, I stand, but only for a moment before nausea and weariness drag me back to my bed and into darkness.

Melanie

Memories of a younger Dani haunt my dreams—a fair-haired tomboy with a dusty black top hat canted off to one side, and her father's moth-eaten tuxedo jacket worn over flannel pajamas.

I arrange a lace handkerchief over my head for a veil. My mother's white pinafore stands in for a wedding gown. The scene amuses our parents—kids playing house and all—and once in a while, Dani's father acts as a pastor for our ceremony. The grownups all clap when the groom kisses her bride on the cheek.

One day, when nobody was watching, Daniel kissed me right on the mouth and slid his hands around my waist. He gave me a silver locket afterward, a promise that we'd be husband and wife someday, and not just for pretend.

They never asked why Dani was always the groom and me the bride. Daniel's being a boy was our *cross my heart and hope to die* secret. At least till Mom discovered the two of us on one of our pretend honeymoons.

Dad spanked me good for that one, and the Welles family took Daniel to some stupid intersex specialist. Talk of removing his budding breasts panicked the boy into swearing he was happy as a girl. His family moved away then and disappeared, leaving me only pleasant memories of Daniel's love and an antique locket with his picture inside.

Whispers in the night rouse me. Glad to be awake again, I push myself upright and brush a damp strand of hair away from my face. A bead of sweat rolls down my nose. Heat and the shadow of nausea remind me I'm still pregnant. But with whose baby? Not Ethan's. Even that tenuous link to Dani—an excuse to remain near her—has crumbled. She's content to be a girl now. Best for her if I'm not around, and better for me if I never see the babies, or anything else that reminds me of Daniel.

I flip on the light, get up, and go to the bathroom. On my way back to bed, I hear a soft tap on my door. I freeze and hold my breath.

"Will you forgive me?" whispers Dani's frail voice from the hallway.

"Well, yeah." *You're sick, girl. You should be in bed.* My hands clench at my sides as I struggle to keep from running to her. *I still gotta go. Me being here only brings us both pain.*

Her voice drifts in again, soft and plaintive. "Please unlock the door."

I take off my necklace and click open the antique locket. Daniel's picture grins out at me.

Time to admit he's gone.

After I kiss the boy's photo, I place his silver heart on the nightstand, turn off the light, and wait till Dani's soft footsteps drift away into the night. *Rest in peace, my love.*

I roll on my side then, and pull up my knees, but the restful sleep I yearn for escapes me. My closed eyes see only the tenderness on Daniel's face when he promised me his love forever.

Chapter 17

Melanie

Victoria Springs to the Richmond airport by car takes almost two hours. Mr. Welles woulda let me travel by helicopter, but I'm in no hurry to be anywhere except away from Dani.

I frown at Jake when he picks up my suitcase. "I think I can manage," I say.

"Miss Melanie, y'all don't want poor old Jake to get himself in trouble, now do ya?"

"No. Guess not." He's always been kind to me. I try my best to smile for him.

I found the old gentleman at the motor pool that morning. He agreed at once to give me a ride, but called Mrs. Welles in spite of my begging him not to. She asked me why I wanted to leave, but my words kept getting all jumbled up. Only tears found their way out. She hugged me and wished me well before asking Jake to see me safely on my plane.

Jake leads me to the airline counter. After he purchases my ticket, and we check my bag, he asks if I'd prefer a wheelchair.

I reply with my best icy scowl.

He grins and waves me toward security. At the last instant, I turn and hug him. "Thanks, Jake."

"You take care, Miss Melanie." He tips his hat and smiles.

When boarding starts, I cut to the front of the line—one advantage of being pregnant.

Mrs. Welles didn't want me to go, but at least she got why I had to leave. Even I could tell that from her eyes. She insisted on paying for a seat in First Class.

Somebody's nosy grandmother sits beside me the entire flight home. Chubby and short, with poofy white hair and pointy glasses. Bet she keeps a flock of plastic flamingos in her yard.

I turn my head toward the window, but she doesn't take the hint. "Are you from Atlanta, dearie?"

No need to be rude, so I shift in my seat to face her a little better. "No, ma'am. Florida."

Her eyes latch on to my baby bump. "Is your husband meeting you at the airport?"

I grimace and place my left hand against my belly to show her my ring finger. "I haven't got one."

"But you are going to marry the boy, aren't you?"

Isn't torture illegal? Who are you, anyhow? "What boy?"

"Why, the father of your child, of course."

I think about explaining the surrogacy and all, but I'm not sure she'd get it. None of her beeswax, anyhow. "I don't know who he is."

"Oh, my. You've slept with that many different men?"

"No. Only one." Except his post is small, and he hasn't got any sperm, so he can't have children. And we never really had sex—not like grownups do, anyhow.

Her look accuses me of being an idiot. "Well then, dearie, I would think he's the one."

Daniel? How I wish he'd come back to me. "Then I guess I'll have to marry him, won't I?" I fold my arms across my belly, turn away from her, and shut my eyes.

We land a few minutes ahead of schedule.

Dani left a voice-mail, but I'll only start crying if I try to explain things to her. She wouldn't like that any better than me. I compose twenty different texts, but don't send any of them. We went five years without talking before. Might as well let the emotions fade before writing.

Concourse C—Concourse B—Concourse A—the electric walkways at the Atlanta airport stretch on forever. I wander past the displays of African sculpture, plop down on the floor, and rest my head against the wall till the nausea passes.

Southerners might be known for their hospitality, but not one of the other passengers makes room for a pregnant girl trying to board the train.

Concourse T? No way. You're not allowed to throw in random letters. Baggage Claim should come next. And who checks their stuff anyhow?

Well, me. 'Cause my stupid suitcase won't fit into the overhead compartment and is too heavy for me to lift that high. So I trudge all the way to Baggage Claim, plop down on a bench, and wait for the luggage from my flight to come around on the carousel.

Beatrice and Fred live in Duluth, about an hour north of the Atlanta airport. My sister jokes that rush-hour on Friday starts Thursday night and ends Saturday morning. No way am I gonna ask her to pick me up at the airport. A MARTA train goes most of the way to their townhouse, though, so I walk to Ground Transportation and check my options before calling her.

"Hi, sis. Would you ask Mom to pick me up at the Doraville station?"

"I thought you were in Virginia. What happened?"

"They don't want the babies. Ethan claims they're not his."

"I can't believe Danièle threw you out."

A wave of heartache washes over me. "She didn't. I left on my own."

"Wow. I am so sorry. Where are you?"

"At the airport."

"All right. I'll be outside the MARTA station in an hour."

"Thanks."

The schedule says forty-one minutes to Doraville, so I walk back to the food court and buy a sandwich and a bottle of water.

On the train my thoughts wander across the past five months and find only desolation. I don't want the babies now. Whoever their father might be. My sister will love the children like they're her own.

Depression overwhelms me at the thought of being alone, though, with somebody else raising my kids. Okay, so I'll want to keep them myself the moment I see their tiny faces.

Tommy might let me stay with him. Even with the twins. I almost call, but some spark of hope remains that Dani will yet change Ethan's mind.

Not gonna happen. Besides, the guy won't want me around, so I'll never see my babies.

I pull out my cell again and stare at the screen. *Do I love Tommy? Would I marry him to keep my kids?*

No. He deserves better. And I left my broken heart on an antique wooden dresser.

The train slows to a stop. End of the line. I wrestle my suitcase onto the platform and bump it—one step at a time—down the stairs.

Outside the station, Beatrice waits in her old Honda. When I'm halfway across the parking lot, my sister hops out of the car and runs to hug me. She presses a fingertip against my baby bump. "What's it like to be pregnant?"

"Great. Now that nausea leaves me alone most of the time. It's awesome to feel the babies move inside me." I hug her again.

While Beatrice shoves my bag into the trunk, I open the back doors and hug the boys in their car seats. Little Greg squeals and kicks his legs. Joey kisses me on the cheek, like a true gentleman. Another wave of sadness hits. How will I ever give up my babies?

The fifteen mile drive takes close to an hour. "Is traffic always this bad?"

My sister rolls her eyes and thumbs the garage door remote. "Not when I'm home."

I unbuckle the little guys while Beatrice takes my suitcase into the townhouse. Joey explodes out of his seat and disappears through the door without waiting for his younger brother. I lift Greg and carry him in after he starts crying.

My sister takes the boy from me and kisses him on the fore-head. "How would you like to help Joey build a fort?"

"For real?"

"Yeah. Aunt Melanie's gonna sleep in your room tonight. Is that okay?"

"Can I be a superhero?"

"You can be anything you like."

"Sweet."

Beatrice puts him down, and he bounds off.

Fred welcomes me with a hug. "Sorry things didn't work out. You're welcome to stay with us as long as you need to."

After I unpack my things, I grab a towel from the linen closet and head for the guest bath. A torrent of steam and soap lather and water washes away the grime, but leaves me more weary than I've been in months.

Dani got their seamstress to do a maternity makeover on my favorite pair of jeans. I slip them on, along with an oversized sweatshirt, and sneak into the living room to watch the guys build their fort out of chairs, blankets, and cushions from the couch.

My sister pokes her head into the room. "Mom would like to see you."

"Okay?" *Why didn't she pick me up?*

Beatrice swallows. Her eyes flick away for an instant.

Oh, God. No! I struggle to my feet, sway, and follow her to Mom's room.

I saw that nightmare image of my mother once before. She clung to life for months while cancer and chemotherapy battled for her body. But I had Dani to comfort me then. *You're not gonna make it this time, and neither will I.*

From her bed, my mother stretches a bony hand toward me. "I'm sorry, honey. I didn't want you to see me this way."

Mom seems translucent—like some ghost who can't fully materialize. Her skin is pale, a little off color, and thin as paper. My mother's beautiful ginger hair is gone. She doesn't even have eyebrows or eyelashes. She's halfway morphed into some alien. Yet serenity hides behind the pain in her eyes.

This is why you sold the house and sent me away. Why you encouraged me to get pregnant. My legs quiver. "You're beautiful, Mom. Not even chemo can take that from you."

Darkness floods in. I sink to my knees and rest my head against her shoulder.

Breathe.

"Please don't leave me, Mom."

The terminal reality of her cancer permeates everything. My mother's weary eyes. Her rasping breath. The acrid stench of chemicals seeping from her pores. Death hovers over her, like some angel with dark wings ready to snatch her away—away from me.

"Dad can't need you as bad as I do, Mom."

"You'll have your babies, honey," she says. Her fingers press against mine, faint as the touch of a butterfly's wing. "Hold my hand against my grandchildren, will you?"

I slip my jeans down past my baby bump and press Mom's hand against my bare abdomen.

The ghost of a smile touches my mother's eyes and lips. "May the good Lord bless you all the days of your lives."

A muscle twitches. Or one of the babies moves. Does it matter? Too weak for Mom to feel. Mom's fingers press a breath harder. "The babies aren't Ethan's?"

"No."

"She really did it, then." Her hand relaxes, and her eyes close. I kiss her forehead and turn to go.

Did what?

Beatrice dims the lights. "I'm sorry. She has so little energy these days."

Nausea ambushes me outside the bedroom door. I run to the bathroom, kneel in front of the bowl, and heave till my gut cramps and my head threatens to explode.

Breathe.

Why?

A cramp twists my abdomen. I lean back against the door frame, press my eyelids closed, and will my muscles to relax.

"You okay?" Beatrice stands above me.

Another muscle twitches. I hold my breath against the pain.

Breathe.

"My stomach's kinda messed up. You got crackers or something?"

She brings me a couple of slices of toast, some graham crackers, and a glass of water.

Thirty minutes later, I push myself upright, stumble back to the boys' room, and collapse on Joey's bed. Echoes of soft muscle contractions ripple through the gloom. I bury my face in a pillow and breathe through my mouth till the spasms fade.

Chapter 18

Danièle

Despair chases me through the manor. I flee to Mum's garden—the one place no one will bother me. Not at night, anyway. The cold silence envelopes me while I wait for my eyes to adjust.

The wind picks up as I walk the stone pathway around the pond to the grove. In the west lies darkness. Far above, the first clouds of a storm front struggle against the bright glow of a full moon.

Beams of soft light dance along the garden pathways, a slow waltz of shifting grey and blue shadows. Only the great trees remain forever black, their silhouette arms swaying in time to the quiet beat of the cold wind.

On the far side of the garden, beneath the ancient walnut tree, my bench awaits. The bare branches of a weeping willow—once my childhood friend—urge me away, but I duck beneath their grasping arms and push on through dormant maiden grass to take a seat.

The moon—obscured now and then by storm-driven clouds—hangs above the garden and casts a dim reflection across the water. In the distance, Victoria Springs Manor sleeps in quiet contentment.

My heart yearns for Melanie. For her gentle touch. Her winsome smile.

The rain begins as an occasional splash in the pond and builds to a steady rustle in the treetops. The music it makes brings me a measure of peace.

Drops filter through the branches and plop on my skirt. Run down my leg. Patter against my cheek. I lean my head against the trunk and let my mind drift.

By the time I open my eyes again, the clouds have dispersed, leaving behind a sprinkling of diamonds across the heavens. God promised Abraham his descendants would outnumber the stars. Two children would have been sufficient for me, but even they have fallen from the sky.

"Danièle?" My mother's voice drifts across the darkness.

A deep sigh shudders out before I answer. "I'm out here, Mum."

When we first moved to Virginia, the limbs of the old walnut were my place of refuge from an often cruel world. Proper young ladies don't climb trees, though, so I sit on the bench below. Only my mother would think to look out here for me now.

"I'd like a word with you before you retire."

"All right, Mum. I'll join you in a moment." One more glance at the stars, and I head back to the house.

We often gather in the kitchen for snacks and informal conversation. Only silence greets me there.

More serious mother-daughter chats concerning etiquette, fashion, and romance we hold in Mum's inner sanctum—her sitting room. With patience and a pleasant smile, Mum taught Miss Danièle Aileana Welles poise and manners there. Acid bubbles in my stomach when I find it dark and lonely.

After a wistful glance at the place associated with so many fond memories, I head downstairs again.

Before I convinced Mum I wanted to be a refined young woman, we met in the den. The massive stone fireplace, the animal trophies, the antique sporting equipment—the room at one time fascinated me. Finding Mum waiting there strikes like a willow branch across my back side.

She glances up at me and looks away. "You know your condition was inherited."

"Yes, Mum." I sit in the high-back chair across from her and pull my legs up under me.

A distant pain flows from her eyes. "I had an older sister once—Veronica."

I never considered the familial aspect of my condition. Mum's an only child—or so I thought. My heart throbs in my throat as I wait for her to continue.

"The doctors performed surgery on her when she was an infant. Making her genitals more feminine was supposed to fix everything. She was never to know, and they said that if her family never doubted her gender, she wouldn't either."

Surgery, secrecy, and shame—the pillars of intersex treatment since the early 1950s—and a miserable failure. You can't hide that sort of thing from a child.

Mum's eyes bore deep into my soul. "She never quite fit in as a girl. Veronica was your age when she took her life." Something I've never seen in Mum's eyes appears then—fear.

You're terrified I'll do the same. "That's why you wouldn't let them operate on me."

"And why we never pressure you about your gender."

True—they always said the choice between blue and pink belonged to me. But their joy grew at my success as a young lady and withered the few times I mentioned being a boy. Only Melanie ever liked the idea of my being Daniel.

"Veronica fell in love toward the end—a rather scandalous affair, at least in the eyes of our parents."

"So you moved back to England."

"Yes." Mum studies my face for a moment before continuing. "You know how proud we are of you, Danièle, but if you ever decide to be our son instead of our daughter, your father and I will support you. Even now."

What if I just want to be me? "Thanks, Mum. I'm well content with my gender." I rise and kiss her on the cheek. "I'd better pack for school." *And call Melanie.*

"Don't worry about Miss Fairbairn, sweetheart. Randolph will see to her expenses until someone adopts the babies."

"They're my children, Mum, and I don't intend to abandon them. Or her." I leave before she can object and rush outside into the moonlight. To my safe haven under the ancient oak.

I hope for some word from Melanie—a text or an email. I click on her number, but my call goes directly to voice-mail.

I wait. And dial again. Until the battery fades, and I'm left alone in darkness.

Melanie

A wayward raindrop splashes against my nose. Gloomy clouds threaten more. My heart longs for the warmth of Florida sunshine. For a motorcycle ride with Dad. Or a walk on the beach with Mom. And for Daniel. Yeah. Especially for him.

He's not coming back. Not him. Not Dad. And whatever Beatrice says, Mom's dying.

The phone vibrates in my coat pocket. *Why even carry the stupid thing? If Dani calls, I'm not gonna answer. But it might be my sister.* I pull out my cell and check the number. Nope. Not her. A Virginia area code. Not Dani. Not Mrs. Welles. Cooper, maybe. Kinda miss him. But he'd only wanna talk about Dani. I shove the phone back into my pocket.

A dozen people stand in line at the coffee shop, so I plop down into a chair and wait.

One of the babies kicks. I spread my fingers over her. "I love you, even if nobody else does."

A young girl wanders over to me and presses her hand against my belly. "You have a baby in your tummy?"

"Two." I move her hand a little more to one side. "The boy's right here."

"What's his name?"

I have no idea. "Patrick." *Yeah. After Dad. And the girl after Gramms. What's Mom gonna think about that?* I shift the kid's hand to my other side. "Ellie's over here."

Some lady finally realizes her daughter's loose. "Janet! Leave the woman alone."

The kid's lips twitch. She delays a moment before speeding away.

The line fizzles out, so I buy a coffee and a hot cocoa and start back to my sister's place. To watch my mother die. Another call comes in, but I don't bother to see who it is.

Danièle

Thick darkness gives way to the dull red glow of morning as we cross I-295 coming into Richmond. Traffic is light—more so than usual. Not much longer, and we'll be at the university.

Cooper remains quiet for most of the drive, apparently unwilling to risk another argument. Just as well—my heart aches to be away from everyone—everyone but Melanie.

He pulls as close to the dorm as campus security will allow before retrieving my suitcase.

I give him a goodbye hug, then pull the keys out of my purse. "I'm sorry. What I said was out of line."

"Forget it." He nods acceptance and turns to leave.

I ease the door open, but the hinges squeal and wake my roommate. Grace sits up and rubs at her eyes. "Don't you ever sleep?"

Not lately. "It's seven. When's your first class?"

"Not until ten. How'd your weekend go?"

I lift my suitcase onto the bed and start unpacking. "Can I trust you?"

The intensity of her laugh startles me. "Of course not. But you already do."

Grace has never revealed anything I said in confidence. Her eyes proclaim the truth of that. And a touch of surprise at her own innocence.

"Melanie's gone. While I was sick in bed, Ethan sent her away. I didn't find out until it was already too late."

"Have you spoken with her?"

"She doesn't answer my calls."

"She's that pissed at you?"

"No. She retreats when she's hurt."

"I'm sorry. And Ethan sounded like such a nice guy. What happened?"

"He realized the babies aren't his."

Grace snorts. "Sorry." She holds up an index finger, hops out of bed, and punches the start button on our coffeemaker. "I can see this is gonna get complicated. Let me shower and dress before we continue. Okay?"

"Sure." I pull out my cell and check for messages before calling Melanie's number again.

No answer.

My first class isn't until mid-afternoon. Nothing to do but sit around and go crazy worrying about her.

You wouldn't abort our kids, would you? No. But you might give up on life and take them with you. A long sip of coffee calms my nerves not a bit. *I don't want to lose you.*

"So who's the father?" Grace asks.

"I am. The lab harvested spermatogonia—sperm precursors—from my gonadal biopsies."

"Sweet. Were you gonna keep that a secret?"

"The time never seemed right."

"Tell me about it. So what now?"

"I haven't a clue."

Chapter 19

Melanie

A mist settles across Steve Reynolds Boulevard. Yellow auras dance around fuzzy headlights. Nobody slows down. Not one car in the blind madness of dusk. Not in the cold rain. Not for a pregnant girl with her hands full. Not in Atlanta.

I snicker when the phone in my pocket rings. Probably Dani again.

Water pools between the sidewalk and the street. I step through the ankle-deep chill, then hurry across the road between two cars. By the time I get home, every bone in my body trembles from the cold.

Beatrice pulls the door open for me. "You're gonna lose the babies if you don't take care of yourself." Her eyes scream at me, but she speaks in a soft whisper and drapes a towel around my shoulders. Fred looks on with concern.

I set her mocha on the counter, drop my wet hoodie on the floor, and wander back to Mom's room.

The pain has fled my mother's face, leaving behind a pale contentment. And utter silence. I wrap my hands around my hot chocolate, and slump in the chair beside her.

Breathe, Mom. Please. I don't wanna be alone.

"Is that cocoa?" The faintest whisper tickles my ears. Mom turns her head and grimaces her death-smile at me.

"Yeah." I get some pillows and help her sit upright enough to take a sip. By now there's no chance of her getting burned. So I perch beside her on the bed and hold the cup to her lips.

My sister pokes her head into the room. "Melanie, she shouldn't have—never mind. You up for some soup, Mom?"

The barest nod sends Beatrice scurrying out of the room. She returns a few minutes later with a cup of thick broth, barely warm.

Mom swallows a few mouthfuls, smiles at me again, and closes her eyes.

Chills hit me then, like I'm still outside in the cold rain. Alone. "I need somebody to hold me, Mom."

My mother's eyes flutter open. Her lips tremble quiet understanding. She presses my hand once, the feather-light touch of a mother's love.

You weren't supposed to hear that.

I make my way to the bathroom, shed my clothes, and climb into the shower. After who knows how long, the hot water runs cold, so I dry off, put on my sweats, and climb into bed.

Beatrice turns on the lights before I get to sleep. "You need to eat something."

What for? But I follow her into the kitchen and warm my stomach with the stew and garlic rolls she sets in front of me. Fred and the little guys stare like I might fall over dead. I squeeze out a half-smile for them. *Maybe I won't puke tonight.*

Does it matter? Well, yeah. If I wanna keep the babies.

Danièle

Restless yearning for Melanie and our children haunts my first night back at school. The next day, concern for their welfare displaces rational thought of anything else.

Winter sun pushes through the blinds and dances across my pillow. I roll over, close my eyes, and chase in vain an elusive moment of sleep.

The aroma of fresh coffee drags me out of my stupor. Grace must have started the coffee maker on her way out the door. I pour myself a cup, pull out my phone, and stab at Randy's number.

"Yes?" His voice cracks, like he might have been awake all night.

"I need some confidential advice."

"Marry the girl."

I spray scalding-hot liquid across the floor. Most unladylike.

My uncle never jokes. Ever. I wander over to the refrigerator, temper my coffee with a spot of milk, and find a washcloth to wipe up the mess. "Somehow I don't think Mum would approve."

"You're a big girl now, Danièle."

"Actually, I was calling regarding my children and the trust." Back on the bed again, I take a pleasant sip to calm my nerves.

"Is the engagement off?"

"Let's just say I want contingency plans."

"All right. If you're not going to marry Ethan, you need to terminate the surrogacy agreement and let Melanie put the babies up for adoption."

"And if I don't?"

"Having a child while single disqualifies you from further participation in the trust. Sorry, but your great-grandfather was a stickler for such things. Once married, you and Ethan are free to adopt, but only natural offspring become heirs."

"The trust doesn't recognize surrogacy?"

"Only when the progeny's related to both husband and wife. Sorry, but the old man didn't foresee having an intersex great-grandchild."

"What if I were the biological father?"

Nothing disturbs the silence but the beating of my heart. I sip the cold remains of my coffee and wait.

"If you are—which I didn't think possible—you'd still need to be legally male when you get married. Are you prepared to do that in what little time remains?"

"No." Cutting off my breasts isn't going to win Melanie's love. Besides, how would I convince a psychologist I want to be a man when I like my body and gender the way they are? I bid my uncle goodbye and lie on the bed again.

My children's little faces on the ultrasound display, the feel my hand pressed against them—the separation from my babies gnaws at me as much as the absence of their mother.

I always considered my father a bit paranoid about family. Until my own was at risk. *College is pointless until I know Melanie's all right.*

The door swings open, and Grace walks into the room. Her brows creep up her forehead. "I thought you'd be in Georgia by now. Don't you care about your pregnant girlfriend?"

Yes. Why delay? My life's over if anything happens to her. "I'm leaving within the hour. Will you cover for me?"

"Sure. Isn't Atlanta like six hundred miles?"

"Five something. But yes. Would you tell my professors I had a family emergency?"

"You got it."

With the decision made, I pack the few things I'll need for the trip. November isn't as cold in Georgia as Virginia, but I dress extra warm. One last glance at my old life, and I walk out the door.

Melanie

My stomach grumbles, dreaming of Jake's cranberry-orange scones. And a hot chocolate. I yawn and rub at my eyes before strolling into the kitchen. No pastry, but my sister keeps fresh fruit on hand. And milk for cereal.

After my late brunch, I crash on the couch with a good book, hoping to find some of the simple contentment I lost when I left Virginia—and Dani.

Mom's off at the clinic, getting some kinda treatments. Fred and Beatrice and the little guys are on their way to Stone Mountain for a picnic. Not even half a day alone, and already darkness overwhelms my soul. *What am I gonna do?* One hand makes its way down to my babies.

I grab my phone for a distraction. Dani left text messages again. I delete them all without reading a single one. I don't need the pain. Not now. Not ever.

Somebody rings the doorbell. Probably one of the neighborhood kids. No way they need to see me in a nightgown. The phone chirps another message. I power it off. *So much for a quiet afternoon.*

The bell grows more insistent, so I meander over to the door. Through the peephole, violet eyes gleam. Violet eyes surrounded by white lashes.

Daniel? My heart forgets to keep time. Muscles refuse to do more than groan in anticipation, while my imagination has already run to him.

I ease the door open enough to peek outside. Dani never goes out without a perfect face. Ever. Yet she stands there without makeup, dressed in a fleece-lined leather jacket, jeans that look like real suede, and for-serious boots. Even if the girl was clad in motor-cycle leathers, only a moron would mistake her for a boy, though. Her curves and ballerina moves give her away. So why do I imagine Daniel behind those hungry eyes?

"Please forgive me," she says.

The babies kick at the sound of Dani's voice. *Figures.* "Why are you here?" I lean against the door frame and try without much success for my best frown. "Just go. Please."

Hopeful eyes search my heart. "I want us to be friends, Melanie."

Friends. One hand rises uncommanded to my throat, seeking a heart no longer there. I turn my head away. "I'm busy. I need to—"

The girl nudges me inside. "For Daniel. All right?"

A spike of angry pain burns through me. "No, Dani. It's not."

But her eyes know I won't turn her away. Not even with me sure I'll get hurt again.

Leaving her to close the door, I rush back to my bedroom, shed my nightgown, and rifle through the drawer for some clean clothes.

Dani shrugs off her coat and lays it on my bed. "I'm sorry. Ethan acted without my knowledge. And certainly without my consent. You'll always be the mother of my children."

You'd spend the rest of your life with Danièle?

Heat blossoms across my cheeks at the longing in Dani's eyes. Foolish of me to dream of the boy she might have been. I turn my back on her intensity and finish getting dressed.

Dani's arms creep around my waist then. I lean into the girl and welcome her embrace. No dreams—just a friend holding me while the heartbeats tick away and the pain eases.

"Is there a park around here?" she says. "I'd like to have a long chat about our future."

"Yeah. Maybe two miles. A quiet place with evergreens and a lake."

I find my dad's old racing leathers and pull on the jacket. It doesn't close over my belly any longer. My mind races back to the trip we took out River Road, to the rides Dad gave me, and to my dreams of Daniel.

Yeah, Mom. The rest of my life. If she'll let me.

Danièle

Melanie climbs on the motorbike behind me and holds tight. Healing flows from her arms to my heart. We might yet repair the damage Ethan caused.

She directs me along back roads from the apartments and malls of Duluth to the hidden countryside near Lawrenceville. In just under three miles, we pull into a secluded park adjoining some corporate building.

Canada geese forage close to shore. A few honk greetings—or perhaps warnings. As we walk a path around the lake, squirrels chatter at us and scamper away.

We huddle on a bench in the feeble warmth of November sunshine. For the moment, at least, not a ripple disturbs the reflection of pine trees, blue sky, and lazy grey clouds. I breathe deep of the crisp air and pull Melanie a bit closer. "So. About our babies..."

"I named them," she says. "Patrick and Ellie."

My eyes wander from hers toward her swollen belly. "May I?" When she nods, I slip one hand under her blouse, spread my fingers across her abdomen, and wait for one of our children to kick.

Melanie's lips twitch into a momentary frown, but wonder and a bit of fondness struggle through. Her eyelids droop then, and she leans into my shoulder. "What are we gonna do?" Contentment edges her ennui, as though the present moment is sufficient for her happiness, and darkness lies yet in the future.

"I'm not sure, love. You and the babies mean more to me than anything else, but..." *But I doubt you'd marry a woman. Even an intersex one.*

Her eyes scan my face. Once. Twice. Seeking a trace of her long lost boyfriend, no doubt.

I smile my tenderness for her. Daniel was never anything more than make-believe—a part I was happy to play for her. Like the Danièle I became for my parents. Or the proper young lady the psychologists counseled. All of these—and none—were me. "I love you and don't want to ever hurt you again." *And I desire you, mother of my children.*

"Yeah. Well. What about Ethan?" Emerald eyes radiate the pain my presence has already caused her.

Perhaps I should leave you be and let Randy find our babies a good home. My gut twists at the thought. "Our engagement's off." I seek out her hand and squeeze my affection. "Someone once told me it's okay to imagine that things were different. Now they are."

The wind picks up. Melanie trembles and ducks her head deeper into the fleece at my shoulder. "Mom says kids'll make you grow up faster than anything else."

I lean close and kiss her cheek. "We'll be okay."

A soft rain patters through the treetops. The afternoon sun retreats behind the clouds. I rise and offer her my hand. "Let's get you someplace warm. And dry."

As we enter the comfort of a local restaurant, the drizzle becomes a downpour. The hostess leads us to a booth next to a window overlooking Pleasant Hill Road. The soft beat of rain on the metal roof provides a pleasant background noise to the chatter of a dozen quiet conversations.

Now that you're a captive audience, what do I say? I love you more today than all my yesterdays. Would that I were a man; my world would be so much easier.

CHAPTER 20

Melanie

Angry black clouds hang low over Pleasant Hill Road. Cold rain pounds the window beside us. Muddy water the color of Georgia clay flows down the road and across the sidewalks.

Lightning flickers the restaurant lights. I hold my breath and count off heartbeats till thunder shakes the building.

Across from me, Dani's a study in angelic beauty. The girl would be stunning as a model, yet without makeup, her white brows and lashes lend her face an ethereal delicacy that requires no cosmetics. She brushes a stray lock away from her sleepyhead eyes and glances up at me. Pain and longing torture her face. Has she really lost Ethan?

My imagination reaches across the table to comfort her. I trace the girl's jawline with the whisper of a fingertip and remember the pretty boy who swore to be mine forever.

A wistful smile creeps across Dani's lips.

"You miss him, don't you?"

I stare out the window again to avoid the girl's eyes. Anger smolders—at her for asking, at Mom for being sick, and at my dad for getting himself killed in Afghanistan when my mother and I needed him the most.

Guilt seeps in like a deadly mist. I was away too, not even aware of my mother's cancer. Not there to support her, pray with her, or even hold her hand. Yet more than anyone else, I miss Daniel.

"Yeah," I say, to the girl who already knows my heart. My fists clench as I fight off the urge to beg her to be him again, if only for a moment. And yet, she's as much Daniel now as she ever was.

"I'm sorry I let you down," she says.

Because you wouldn't cut off your breasts? I find her violet eyes again and let her track my every thought. Even now the image of doctors mutilating Daniel makes me cringe. "I loved him the way he was."

"I was serious when I promised to marry you."

Well, yeah. Enough to trap my heart inside that stupid locket.

Time to leave. Before I start crying for a boy who's never coming home. I pull out my cell and call Beatrice. "Hey. Can I get a ride?"

"Sure. Soon as we get home. Where are you?"

"The Crab Shack."

"All right. I-285's a zoo, so we may be a couple of hours. I'll call when we get closer."

"Thanks."

As soon as I hang up, the downpour fades. Just like that.

Dani pays the tab. "Let's wait in my hotel room. All right? The Sonesta's not far."

"Yeah. Whatever."

The girl brushes most of the water from her motorcycle's seat. The mist clears as I hop on the bike behind her. Sunshine greets us as we drive out of the parking lot.

Halfway there, Dani slows, almost stops, then creeps ahead and into the right lane. I poke my head around the girl's shoulder. A muddy mess extends clear across the road. Deep, too.

Dani tenses and thrusts her feet down into the water. Her back arches, like we're gonna get hit or something. My muscles spasm in reaction, pulling me tight against her.

A wall of water sweeps across the bike as a red truck blurs past between us and the median. Halfway in our lane. The Honda wobbles sideways across the pavement and tries to go down. Time slows while Dani struggles to keep us upright.

She gets the bike straightened out again—somehow—and we drive the last half block to Crestwood Parkway. The girl pulls into the hotel, finds a parking spot, and shuts down the engine.

I jump off the bike and wave a finger in the truck's general direction. "What is wrong with you people?" Still being able to scream feels good.

Dani laughs, hugs me tight, then kisses me on the cheek. "Let's get you dried off."

Water and red mud splattered everywhere. I pull off my shoes and roll up my pant legs. We both drip our way to the elevator and up to her floor.

As soon as she has the door open, the girl strides over to a dresser and grabs a robe—a nice oriental flower print. She hands it to me and nudges me toward the bathroom. "Get cleaned up. I'll find you something to wear."

The shakes start then. Not for the cold mud and water. The truck came way too close. A little hydroplaning, and he'd have run right over the top of us. Dani, me, and the babies.

I rinse the mud out of my clothes, squeeze out the water, and hand them out to Dani.

Under a steaming fountain I lather with soap, wash my hair, and try not to think about the wreck my life has become. After a cool rinse, I dry off and comb out the snarls.

The fat girl in the mirror scowls at me. Well, I never had a perfect figure, but I've put on more than enough weight for my pregnancy. Five inches taller than me, Dani still weighs a bunch less. She's always been as willowy as an elf. I let out a hopeless sigh, wrap her robe around me, and pull the door open.

The girl looks up from whatever she's doing—probably something on the Internet. "Your sister called," she says.

I pick up my phone, flop down on the bed, and thumb Beatrice's number.

Dani perches beside me. "Please don't leave yet. We need to talk about the babies."

A spooky premonition drifts through my imagination—me in some fancy Cinderella gown, waiting for the music to start. Mom kisses my cheek and wishes me well before leaving to be with—with Dad.

The moment fades. Dani asked me something. "What did you say?"

"Please stay."

"Oh. Yeah."

When my sister answers, I explain about the wet clothes.

"Should I bring you something?"

"Nah. It can wait till morning. Dani wants to talk."

"Yeah. Definitely more fun to chat in the nude. In bed. All night."

"You're evil."

"Me? You're the one who's pregnant with the girl's baby."

"Jealous?"

"You know it. Call me when you need a ride."

"Yeah. Thanks."

A minute later, Dani strolls out of the bathroom wearing flannel pajamas. After checking her phone, she urges me to my feet. "I've got something for you. Close your eyes."

I'm not big on surprises, but I do as she asks.

A moment of quiet rustling passes before she speaks. "Imagine Daniel kept his promise."

A lost dream stirs in its grave, reviving the agony of hope's death. *Why not just poke me with a sharp knife?*

Something brushes against the side of my neck and jostles against my chest. My hand rushes to my breast. Yes. Daniel's locket —my heart—back where it belongs.

"The two of us have been married almost a year." Her whisper comes from behind now. Soft hair cascades over my shoulder. "Trust me," she says and nuzzles against my ear.

There was never any denying the boy when he wanted something. Longing for Daniel's tenderness overpowers my judgment, suppresses my reason, and releases my imagination.

A moment later, he reaches his arms around my waist and unties my robe. Daniel spreads his fingers wide across my bare belly and draws us closer. "You found out you're pregnant, and the babies are due in April," he says.

No. The absurdity of her statement snaps me back to reality. Dani was never male—or female—enough to have her own children. "Why are you doing this?"

"Melanie, I—" Tender passion consumes Dani's voice. She brushes against my ear again and whispers, "When I had my operation, the surgeon took biopsies and gave them to Dr. Pierson. She used my sperm to fertilize your eggs."

My heart beats a crazy staccato that steals my breath away. My eyes pop open, and I turn my head to gape at her. "For real?"

She grins and bobs her head. "I'm the father of your children." Then she kisses me the way Daniel always did. Something within me goes nova, igniting all my longings in one short burst of blinding starlight. *Daniel. Me. Together forever in an instant of time.*

But eternity fades—doesn't it always? I pause at last and gasp for air.

I kiss him on the lips again, worry open the top button of his pajamas, and urge the boy toward our bed. *Tonight, at least, my Daniel holds me.*

Danièle

I wake with Melanie still in my arms, her lavender-scented tresses tickling my nose. She lies facing me, one leg resting between my knees, her breasts pressed against my side. Every breath she takes —each move the babies make—echoes contentment through my senses.

How did I forget the way her nakedness against me affects my spirit? Nothing so trivial as sexual arousal compares with the overwhelming tenderness such proximity brings.

She clung to my side all night, weeping out at times her melancholy in splashes of despair that ran down my shoulder and wet the sheets. I loosened her robe and ran my hands across her back—the way I used to—to quiet her sobs.

Melanie still loves Daniel—a hopeless fantasy, that. Massive doses of testosterone might make me a bit more masculine, but at what cost? The doctors suggested mastectomies when I claimed to be a boy. Everyone thought I panicked then because I was a girl at heart. The truth is simpler—whatever my gender, I like my body the way it is.

The psychologists were eager to help me discover which sex suited me best, but their reality didn't include a boy who wanted to keep his breasts. To them, ambiguity breeds confusion. Surgery eliminates ambiguity. I soon realized it best for Melanie and me both if they all thought I wanted to be a girl.

If I believed in karma, I'd blame my situation on a promise I made—and broke—long ago. I returned my grandmother's silver locket. Nothing speaks with more eloquence than that heart—a silent reminder of Melanie's right to mine.

My fondness for her never diminished, but she—I have no doubt of it—she still loves a boy.

And yet you lie with me now. You must know I was never truly Daniel.

I brush the hair from Melanie's face, careful not to awaken her. A faint blush warms her freckles. Are all pregnant women so beautiful? Or is it only that she carries my children?

Across the room my phone chirps a message. Somewhere outside, a truck rumbles past. Melanie rolls off me, stretches, and stumbles out of bed. She rushes to the closet, stops, and glances back at me, her face red. As she turns away, the shadow of pain brushes her eyes. What I meant as a gift wounded her. Again. *I should have known better than mention Daniel. Why didn't I just explain about the babies?*

Melanie returns from the closet, wearing her maternity jeans. With all the tenderness I can muster, I say, "I'm sorry I hurt you."

Sadness edges Melanie's smile. "No, Dani. You gave me something I'll always remember—a peek at what might have been." A shadow of despair lurks behind those emerald eyes. What does she have left now but broken promises and childhood dreams?

We dress, and I drive her home in silence.

Beatrice greets us with an evil grin, "How was the honeymoon?" Fred smiles but leaves the room. Melanie turns crimson protesting our innocence.

Mrs. Fairbairn hovers at the far side of the living room, standing with the help of a walker. Cancer has ravaged her body. Her solemn face drags me back across the years to the night she caught me with her daughter. We weren't having sex, mind you, but our naked bodies lay intertwined as we slept. The guilt I didn't feel as a child overwhelms me now. "I'm sorry." *I didn't know you were on chemotherapy again. How can I ask anything of you or Melanie?*

"I'd like a word with you." She gestures toward the hallway.

Mrs. Fairbairn leads me to one of the back bedrooms and pulls the door closed a bit harder than necessary. "My daughter's rather fragile just now. She still grieves for a boy who promised her his heart." The intensity in the woman's eyes lays bare my soul. "She bears his silver locket once again. To what end?"

My own selfishness. I returned the heart so mine might one day mend. "Your daughter's my life. Were I a man, I'd ask for her hand in marriage. But I can't be Daniel for her."

"And what of the babies?"

"I will do whatever necessary to protect my children. And their mother."

A bit of amusement softens Mrs. Fairbairn's anger. Her shoulders slump as the emotion bleeds out of her features. Only a tender resignation survives.

She crosses the room then—an eternal voyage—and retrieves a manila envelope from the top drawer of an antique secretary. "When Dr. Pierson retired, she left this in my care. I was to give it to you if— well, this seems the appropriate time."

"What is it?"

"Sharon wouldn't say. Something to do with your fathering my grandchildren, I expect."

Anger surges at the thought of Dr. Pierson's betrayal of my trust. "She told you?"

"No. Not directly. I knew such was possible—at least in theory— but only guessed the truth when I deciphered what Sharon had written there."

Someone printed *12VAC5-550-450.3* in neat letters and scrawled *per legem terrae* underneath that—by the law of the land.

Legal papers? My heart pounds in anticipation.

The first sheet appears to be an extract from the Virginia Administrative Code dealing with changes in birth certificates. For hermaphrodites.

The South admits I exist? Wow. Just wow.

The second is an affidavit signed by Dr. Sharon Ann Pierson, MD.

The birth record of Danièle Aileana Welles includes an incorrect designation of sex due to congenital pseudo-hermaphroditism, which has since been clarified—Danièle is male, having fathered children via intracytoplasmic sperm injection.

Per legem terrae—would that satisfy Randy? Is this my salvation or simply one more person telling me who I should be? Why didn't Dr. Pierson give these to me earlier?

The next sheet proves to be an unsigned letter from me to the Registrar of the Commonwealth of Virginia, requesting a change in my birth certificate.

If I were male... But a physician's signature doesn't make it so. Darkness seeps into my heart as I consider what might be required to live as a man.

Can I really become Daniel?

A single paper remains—a DMV form of some sort—also signed by Dr. Pierson. I replace them all and stick the envelope into my tote.

A tremor passes through me as I face Mrs. Fairbairn. "I intend to marry your daughter. If she'll have me."

Melanie

Mom won. That much is obvious the moment she walks out of the bedroom. A glance my way promises trouble later. But my fate was sealed in that room. Prep school. Or worse. And my babies put up for adoption.

Patrick and Ellie are mine. You hear me? Nobody's gonna take them away. Nobody. I scowl at my mother till she frowns back at me.

Daniel always got real quiet when working out a difficult problem. That same opaqueness now masks Dani's features, like her mind is caught in some alternate universe.

I ignore her—and everyone else—till my patience dies. Then hand the girl her leather jacket and drag her outside. "So? Tell me what happened in there."

Dani's intensity melts into tenderness. "We're keeping the babies. You and I will raise them. Together." Fear blossoms in those violet eyes as a hesitant hand reaches for the locket at my breast. "I told your mother I want to keep the promise I made."

The babies party—they understand long before my heart does. Till death us do part, he said. A hundred times in play. My heart throbs with yearning for Daniel. For my babies to really be his. For us to marry and raise a family.

No way you fathered anybody's kids. "You're a lovely young woman, *Danièle*. Don't mess with that."

"And if I were male?"

"You're not. And I don't want you cutting off body parts."

"What if I were *legally* male?

"I'm not gonna marry a girl, Dani. Not even you."

Pain burns through her eyes, searing my heart. Her lower lip trembles. So does mine.

If you start bawling, I'm gonna have a breakdown. "Look, I'll think about it. Okay?"

"All right. I'll come back for you over Christmas."

Dani's kiss brings heat to my face and a pretty boy to my imagination. *I'm kissing a girl right here on our front porch.*

Not a girl. Daniel.

Yeah, right. I pull him as close as my pregnancy will allow. "What are we gonna do? For real, this time."

"Marry. And raise the kids ourselves." Dani grins at me again, her smile a little off-center. She starts her motorcycle, and rides off down the street.

I wait till she vanishes around the corner before letting go the tears. The bright sunshine the girl brought fades into gloom. I close my hand around a hopeless silver heart. *Better she marry Ethan. And I forget about Daniel.*

CHAPTER 21

Danièle

Red stripes painted across my bedroom wall announce the approaching dawn. I hug my pillow tight one last time, roll out of bed, and punch the start button on the coffee maker. One more final exam will mark the end of my first semester—my last, unless I give up the children or marry someone.

Long ago, I played the groom to Melanie's bride. After patiently enduring a number of our wedding ceremonies, Mum asked me if I were well and truly a boy. I pulled her close and whispered in her ear, "No, Mum. I'm only pretending. For Melanie."

With tenderness, she straightened the collar of my natty tuxedo jacket and kissed my forehead. "Well then, your *nom de guerre* should be Dànaidh Ailean Welles. After your grandfather."

Not Daniel. But perhaps enough for Melanie. A risk, certainly, and my point of no return. Once declared legally male...

Pursuant to Virginia Administrative Code 12VAC5-550-450.3, please change my—five minutes later, I print out a formal affidavit, requesting a change of given name and sex marker on my birth certificate.

After a hot shower, I dress in blue jeans and a nice top. Heavy cotton knee socks. Boots. Fleece vest. Woolen scarf. Leather jacket. Gloves. The outside thermometer says fifty-eight, but I learned early on to dress extra warm for a motorbike ride.

I drive out past the country club and Saint Catherine's to Grove Avenue to a notary. One of the employees greets me as soon as I walk in the door. "How may I help you?"

"I have an affidavit to sign."

"Certainly." She waves me toward a chair next to her desk.

I hand her my driver's license and my request to the registrar. Dark brown eyes grow large as she peruses my letter. A glance up shows disbelief, but she slides the paper back across her desk and says, "If you'll sign your full legal name, I'll notarize the document."

When she finishes, I fold the letter and seal it in the envelope I've already addressed. No looking back now. I thank her and drive to the post office.

Will Melanie accept an intersex boy with breasts? Reason long insisted such impossible. My heart—freed now from its constraints—believes.

I pull a note card from my box of stationary, and begin writing a letter to Melanie. My phone rings, though, so I set down the pen. *Ethan. Not now. Not after I've decided.*

On the third ring I press connect. "Yes?"

"I'm sorry. Will you let me apologize?"

"Go ahead." *I've certainly no time for an argument.*

"I shoulda checked with you before canceling the surrogacy."

"What do you want?"

"Your mother asked me to spend Christmas at your place. I don't want to unless you'll give me another chance."

"We'll talk." No doubt Mum trying to help me find happiness as a wife and mother.

"All right, babe. Will you do something for me? Pick out an engagement ring, and I'll buy it for you."

"I'll think about it."

"I understand. See you then."

"Goodbye." *Why did I even answer your call? Think I'm daft enough to marry you? To please everyone else rather than follow my heart?*

As soon as I disconnect, my phone chirps an email from my History professor.

<< *Foster—Excellent work, Danièle. An A+ on your term paper. You're exempt from taking the final. I'm proud to have had you as one of my students.*

No more exams. *Thank you, gracious Lord.* My head hurts too much to concentrate anyway. I review what I've written to Melanie, but crumple the note and send her a few quick text messages instead.

Cold air might clear my mind. And rings are a wonderful idea. I throw on my jacket and ride out to West Broad Street and the chain jewelry stores. Sales people lurk inside the vestibule, primed for a feeding frenzy. "May I help you, miss?" one calls as I walk past.

"I'd like to look at wedding bands. Fourteen karat. Eighteen if you sell them. Simple or with flowers."

"Oh, yes. We have the largest selection in the area." She waves me toward one side of the showroom. "White or yellow gold?"

"Yellow."

A single glance proves sufficient to reject most of her offerings. I wave off an entire tray of laser-cut rings. "Don't you have anything a bit more old fashioned? Art Noveau perhaps?"

For an hour my search bears no fruit. As I turn to go, inspiration lights the woman's face. "We have some Celtic wedding bands in the back room. If you'll wait a moment, I'll run and get them."

"All right." *Why not. I've seen everything else.*

Dragons, interlocking around the middle, and edged by two solid bands—my eyes flick from them to a similar ring with four Chladaigh designs—and another with a traditional swirl of flowering vines.

"May I see these two?" I press a fingertip to each in turn.

"Certainly."

Two hands holding a heart, surmounted by a crown—my Irish grandmother would appreciate such a traditional design. I hold the ring closer to the light. Rose gold—almost pink. I slide it on my finger. An acceptable fit. "How much is this one?"

"It's on sale this week for $1995.00."

"May I see—yes—the other?"

"I think we only have this ring in eighteen karat gold."

The swirling flowers remind me a bit of French horns. Again, the pattern wraps around the ring between two solid bands. Melanie will love it. "What's the price?"

"$2840.00."

"I'll take them both." *What will I do if she says no?*

Outside, I start my Shadow Spirit and tap the shifter into first. Melanie would probably prefer the Honda to a wedding ring. Not sure I want my wife risking her life on a motorbike. *Perhaps I shouldn't either.*

Three Chopt Road runs most of the way home, but heavy traffic and red lights keep me shifting gears. With all the loonies about, I pull into the right lane behind a police cruiser and ease off the throttle.

Some fool runs the light at North Parham Road. The officer in front of me locks up all four wheels and slides to a stop. I brake hard to keep from ramming him.

Tires screech behind, and my Honda lurches forward again. The impact wrenches both hands from the controls. My beautiful Shadow Spirit floats up off the pavement—like a heron taking flight—and I drift backwards.

My poor motorbike crumples in slow motion—caught in an unrelenting vise—until nothing remains but small parts scurrying across the pavement.

Heavy metal kisses my left thigh and side, and slips an inquisitor's steel glove under my back. Shoulders land first, and a thousand bits of glass spray across my vision. My head rocks back and meets darkness.

Melanie

I buckle Joey into his car seat and close the door. After my sister finishes with Greg, she gives me a hug. "Would you help Mom take a bath while we're out?"

"Yeah. Sure. How long will you guys be gone?"

"Two, maybe three hours."

"Okay."

Fred starts the engine. I wave at the boys as the car pulls away.

Woo hoo! Two, maybe three hours of quiet. I might even have time to phone Dani.

Mom is resting in her recliner, reading one of her old Jane Austen novels. She's put on weight since I got home, but she hasn't fully recovered from chemo yet. "Would you like me to give you a bath?" I say.

"You're an angel, honey. If you'll help me to the bathroom, I'll take a shower."

Every time Mom stands, she seems a little stronger. But she's still way too frail and thin. With one arm around her for support, I walk her down the hallway to the master bedroom. She rests on the bed while I adjust the water temperature.

Once in the shower, her face melts into pure joy. After a few minutes, she plops down into the seat, and I shampoo her fuzzy scalp. Then she cleans herself with a washrag, and I help her dry off.

My mother collapses into her recliner again and closes her eyes, but contentment has replaced some of the pain chemo left on her face. I stay by her side and hold her hand till her breathing slows and her head slumps to the side.

With Mom asleep, I clean up the bathroom, then grab my phone from the boys' room. I wander downstairs to the den, plop my fat butt on the couch, and lean back into the plush cushions. The babies bounce around for a minute before settling down to rest. I sweep a hand across my belly. Ellie kicks once. Patrick ignores me. "I sure hope you're both praying for Dani to find a way for us to keep you guys. Otherwise you'll have to stay with Joey and Greg."

That gets a kick out of my Patrick.

I squirm around till I find a sweet spot and turn on my phone. The display says I missed several calls from a Richmond number. One from Cooper. One from a Florida number I don't recognize. Tommy? Probably best not to return that one. I ignore the emails and click on a message notification.

<< *Dani—Fair mother of my bairns, I love you more than life itself.*

<< *Dani—Were I a man, nothing would keep me from you.*

<< *Dani—Yet I fear you'll not take as husband the woman who fathered your children.*

<< Dani—So for you and ours, I shall henceforth be Daniel.

For a moment, my imagination sweeps half of me off into a wild dream—Daniel and me and our little ones. The rest of me panics. I pop up off the couch and run around the room.

>> Melanie—Please don't cut off your breasts.

>> Melanie—You're a beautiful girl. Marry Ethan and be happy.

Half crazy, I collapse on the couch. *Me and the kids will be okay. But you've got to forget about us.* Heart still thundering, I get up and pace the room. *But if you marry Ethan I'll never see you again. And you'll never know our kids.*

I punch Dani's number, hold my breath, and wait for the girl to answer. The call goes straight to voice-mail. As soon as the phone beeps, I push the words out, afraid I'll run out of courage and change my mind. "Dani, I love you the way you are. Don't you dare change. We'll find some way to be together and raise our kids without any stupid surgery. I'll do whatever you want. Okay? Even marriage. Just please don't do anything stupid! I love you."

I hit disconnect. My muscles twitch so bad I dare not move. Not with my brain in knots. Not till my heart starts beating right again.

I just promised to marry the girl.

No way!

CHAPTER 22

Melanie

Days pass without any word from Dani. Texting her brings no reply. Calls go directly to the girl's voice-mail. The first day, I figure maybe she's pissed at me for—well, for whatever.

You'd tell me if you got back with Ethan. Wouldn't you?

Joey snatches a stuffed panda away from Greg and holds it just out of reach. The little guy screams like he's gonna die. I push myself up off the couch and stroll toward the kitchen. "Hey, Greg. You want a bite of my ice cream?"

He stops wailing long enough to gaze up at me. His favorite toy forgotten, he nods.

Joey rolls his eyes. "Can I have some too?"

"Are you gonna stop tormenting your brother?"

"Yeah. I promise."

I grab a cone from the freezer—one of those chocolate and peanut covered things—and peel off the wrapper. Greg tracks my every movement with his wide puppy eyes. He likes the outside best, so I let him take the first bite. Then his brother.

The doorbell rings. Greg rushes out of the room. Joey takes one last nibble from the cone and runs after him. I stick the cone back into the freezer, wash my hands, and go to see who's there.

Cooper stands on our front porch, short-sleeved in the cold wind. Muscles stretch tight around weary eyes. The guy looks like he hasn't slept in weeks.

My gut melts into nausea, but I stare at him like a total moron.

"Danièle's gone missing. I was hoping you'd know where she is."

I step out of the way and wave him in. "Not here. Last I heard from her was, um, Wednesday."

"You spoke with her?"

"No." I was never much good at lies, and Cooper probably wouldn't believe me anyhow. "She sent me some text messages after she went back to school."

"She was here?"

"Yeah. Last weekend. On her motorcycle." *Sorry, Dani. He was gonna find out anyhow.*

"No!" The ex-Marine doesn't even blink, but the tension in his voice reveals the depth of his anger. "How am I supposed to protect her if she doesn't trust me?"

"She didn't want her mom harassing her."

"I'm not a spy for her mother. She should know that."

"Yeah. Guess so."

"How long has she been riding motorcycles?"

"A friend of mine taught her to ride his dirt bike last summer. The first time she drove on the streets, a cop nailed her—said she could go to jail. Her Uncle Randolph told her to get a license as soon as she got back home. So she bought a Shadow Spirit—a V-twin 750 that looks kinda like a Sportster."

"Randolph Welles?" Cooper's muscles wind so tight I think maybe the dude's gonna explode. He whips out his cell phone, stabs at it with a finger, and stomps out the door. Even half a block away, I can hear the Marine swearing at somebody. Glad it isn't me.

Five or six minutes later, he rings the bell again. "Can we speak in private?"

"Yeah. Guess so." I lead him into my bedroom and pull the door closed.

Cooper perches on the edge of my bed. "You love her?"

"Well, yeah. As a friend anyhow."

"And more." Not a question.

"She's gonna marry Ethan, and I'm okay with that." *I gotta be.*

"Come back with me."

"I don't have any idea where she is."

Somewhere in the back of his eyes the Marine begs me to tell him Dani is here in Atlanta—just out to buy tea. He's failed somebody he dearly loves. And fears her dead. Or worse. His unshed tears flow down my cheeks and splash on the carpet. *She's gotta be okay.* "What does Mrs. Welles think?"

"The Welles are vacationing in Scotland. Somewhere without cellular service. Randolph's trying to reach them."

And Ethan? "I'll go pack, but we gotta wait till Fred and Beatrice get back. I promised to babysit so they could go out on a date."

The Marine looks like he's gonna sweat impatience, but he nods.

* * * *

Freezing rain beats syncopation against the metal roof. Sleet bounces off my window panes. A tree scrapes limbs along the wall outside. Gusts whistle through the garden. Somewhere in my sleep, my imagination hears faint cries for help. Dani's broken body lies in a pool of blood.

Somewhere. Out there. In the cold darkness.

Days pass in silence while I wait. If Dani went somewhere for surgery, she'd have let somebody know by now.

In the den below my room, the ancient grandfather clock chimes the hour. One of my babies stretches and wakes the other. My stomach growls. A bead of sweat rolls down my nose. When will I ever sleep through the night again?

In silence I pad to the elevator, ride downstairs, and find my way to the kitchen. I find two scones and a cup of milk waiting for me on the counter.

A muted thumping drifts in from the great room—something soft against one of the glass panels.

Dani? I push my snack into the microwave and stab at the minute button. *Warm milk and scones. Bless you, Jake.* No question, but the old man creates the best pastries ever. My stomach content again, I turn off the lights and head toward the elevator.

Silence grips my robe and drags me to a stop. No rain. No wind. Not even a clock ticking. Only the throbbing of my heart in time with a soft bump in the night.

Can't be the Welles—they're still somewhere in Scotland. Jake and Cooper are probably asleep. So there's only me. And whatever is making that sound.

One thing I learned from horror movies—never investigate anything strange alone. Ever. *Besides, wouldn't Cooper have searched out there?*

But it might be Dani. I run to the garden door to find only a broken branch thumping against the glass.

She's gotta be okay. But it's been a week since her last text.

Maybe this is all a nightmare. Heart thumping, I ride the elevator up and walk down the hallway to the girl's bedroom. A lamp stands on one of the tables in her sitting area, so I ease the bedroom door open, walk over to a chair, and turn on the light.

Her bed hasn't been slept in. *Well, duh.*

I yank back the covers, grab one of her pillows and hug it close. *Where are you, Dani?*

Somewhere in the distance a banshee screams—death on the prowl. The *chuff chuff chuff* of its mighty wings passes low over the manor.

A helicopter! I run back toward my room, even though it's probably only Dani's parents.

Cooper meets me at the doorway. "Pack for an overnight stay," he says. "Be in the car pool in five minutes."

Please tell me she's okay. I want to scream, but the air freezes in my lungs.

"She's alive." The pain flowing from his eyes says she might not be much longer. "Go," he says and sprints away.

I dump the contents of my tote on the floor—all the stuff I'll never use again, like Dani's medical power of attorney. I stare at the envelope like a total moron for several heartbeats before packing it away with my clothes and the other junk I *will* need.

Bag over my shoulder, I stumble down the hallway to the elevator and pound on the call button. Downstairs finally, I rush—well, as fast as a pregnant woman ever goes—toward the car pool.

Cooper grabs my hand and hauls me outside, across the blacktop to the chopper. As soon as we're buckled in, the blades spin up, and we take off.

An hour later, our ride lands in a well-lit parking lot, and we climb into the back of a limo. In the quiet darkness, Cooper closes his hand over mine. "Danièle's at Virginia Commonwealth University Hospital. They're the best in the state."

"A motorcycle wreck?"

"Yes. Traumatic brain injury. Fractured ribs."

Alive—I cling to that hope and plead with the God who took away my dad. And maybe my mom soon.

When the limo drops us off, I crane my neck to stare up at the building in front of us. Critical Care Hospital, the sign reads.

Cooper takes my bag, offers his hand, and leads me inside to the elevator. "Danièle's on the eleventh floor—in Neuroscience Intensive Care—but I'm not certain they'll let us see her until her parents arrive. And Randolph hasn't been able to contact them."

I grab my bag from him and rummage through the side pockets till I find Dani's power of attorney. "Doesn't this count for something?"

He gives the paper a quick scan and—for the first time in days—smiles.

Cooper shows the document to somebody at the nursing station. After a quiet conversation, a woman in blue scrubs leads us to a room in intensive care.

Chapter 23

Melanie

Dani lies on a bed in cold twilight, her back raised. White gauze wraps the girl's head. A little clown hat perches there, tilted at a crazy angle, with a tube running out the top. Like they drilled a hole through her skull or something. Wires run from under the bandages to a monitor.

"I've seen worse. Much worse. She'll be all right." Cooper's soft words hold no confidence.

"Yeah. Hope so."

A display to the girl's right lets out a comforting stream of clicks—one for every rise and fall of her chest—as the machine breathes for her. A smaller tube runs up her nose. Several burrow into her arms. One into her shoulder. Another couple go from under the sheets to containers hanging off the side of the bed.

Propofol 40, Fentanyl 2, Mannitol—half a dozen little pumps add some drug or whatever to her system. Bags and bottles hang above them all.

The screen on her left shows a graph of her heartbeat, and a new blood pressure every second. Who knows what all the other numbers mean? There's even some little plastic gizmo clipped to her ear.

I walk to the girl's side and squeeze her hand. *Why are they so puffy? God, please. You gotta help the girl. I'll die if I lose her.*

When I try to brush a lock of hair from her face, I discover that it ends in a melted clump.

A tremor runs up my arm. Somewhere deep inside, a door snaps shut, blocking out all my emotions. I take the girl's hand again. "Dani, it's me, Melanie. Cooper's here, too. Your mom and dad are on their way."

Nobody answers, but the clicks and beeps and flashing LEDs of the machines that care for her drone on.

I kiss her on the forehead. "You're gonna be okay."

Weird bruises discolor her eyelids near her nose, kinda like little butterfly wings. *You're gonna need more makeup to cover those.*

The quiet chatter of life-sustaining equipment whispers on in the twilight of intensive care. No day or night exists here. Only hope ticked out one heartbeat at a time. Days pass. Or only minutes. Who knows?

I jump when an alarm goes off. One of those stupid little pumps wails. In a few minutes, somebody ambles into the room, replaces the empty bag, and restores silence.

Cooper offers to get me bottled water and a candy bar, but my stomach won't suffer them now.

I stand beside Dani—holding her hand—till my legs wobble.

An hour in a hard plastic chair leaves me squirming at the pain in my butt.

A muscle in my abdomen twitches. I pace till my bladder screams, and then walk out of the room. Down the hallway, bright daylight streams through tall windows. I find a bathroom, relieve myself, wash my face, and wander back to Dani's room.

In the cool darkness of intensive care, nothing has changed. The girl's chest still rises and falls in time with a graph on the ventilator display. Her heart beats a regular rhythm—too fast—her pressure way too high.

"Miss Fairbairn?" A woman stands in the doorway, wearing a white coat over her green scrubs.

"Yeah?"

"I'm Dr. Ganesh, a neurology resident here. It would be helpful to know Miss Welles' medical history."

"She's intersex—but I'm sure you guys already got that part."

"Yes. We noticed. Androgen Insensitivity Syndrome?"

"Yeah. Partial."

"Does she still have her testes?"

"One. She got cancer in the other."

"Has she had any surgeries recently?"

"Vaginoplasty, orchio—whatever you call moving her other testis."

"Is she taking any medications?"

"No."

"Does she have any drug allergies?"

"No."

"Any other medical issues?"

"Not till now."

Her face twitches into a grimace, but she nods. "I'm sorry. She hit the back of her head. The bruising around her eyes is typical of a basal skull fracture. Her brain bounced and the contrecoup bruised her frontal lobes."

"Will she be okay?"

"Hard to say. Right now our primary concern is keeping her intracranial pressure down."

Two men in scrubs appear at the door. Dr. Ganesh whispers with them for a moment before continuing. "Miss Welles has another CT scan. If you like, I'll have someone call you when she gets back."

"Yeah. Do that."

Cooper puts an arm around my shoulders and urges me out of the room. "Let's get something to eat."

I shoot a glance over my shoulder at Dani's still form. Would they tell me if she was dying? Let me say goodbye? I rush back into her room and kiss her on the nose. "Don't you dare croak on me, girl. You hear?"

On the way out, we stop by the nursing station and leave them my cell number. One of the women hands me a plastic bag. "Her jewelry," she says.

Brand new wedding bands—too creepy. Dani might be finicky about some things, but wouldn't she let Ethan help pick them out? Or at least take him along?

She asked me to marry her. I promised I would. My heart flutters up into my throat.

Me and Daniel and our children.

The one with flowering vines and all fits perfect right where Daniel's ring would go. I stick the other on my right hand.

The girl's in a coma—maybe dying—and all you can think of is some boy?

Well, yeah. I'm messed up, okay? And I need Daniel bad right now.

* * * *

Cooper leads me down to the main floor and finds the cafeteria. He loads up on bacon and eggs and buys an extra large coffee. I get a bagel and cream cheese and a carton of milk. No caffeine for me; I'm already so wired I may never sleep again.

The reds and purples of sunset—or maybe dawn—filter through the windows. A surge of people in scrubs arrives, eats, and moves on while I stare at the crumbs on my plate.

Cooper takes away the remains of our breakfast. He returns with another cup of coffee, a packet of sugar, and one of those little stir sticks. Or maybe the thing is a straw.

Morning shines bright before my phone rings. "Yeah?"

"Miss Fairbairn? This is Dr. Ormond. Are you still at the hospital?"

"Yeah. In the cafeteria."

"If you'll wait there, I'll be down in a few minutes."

"Okay." *They never tell you bad news over the phone.*

Cooper lays a gentle hand on my arm. "What's up?"

"The doctor's on his way."

Twenty minutes later, some old guy in a white coat saunters into the cafeteria and scans the room. *Gotta be him.* I stand and wave a hand till he nods.

The doctor joins us at the table. "Good news. Danièle's internal bleeding has stopped. Her intracranial pressure's under control. She's still in critical condition, mind you, but the scans don't show any brain damage."

Cooper's muscles ripple, visibly releasing tension.

"She's gonna be okay?" I ask.

"We'll know more once she's conscious. The next step is to get Ms. Welles off the ventilator."

Dr. Ormond rides the elevator back up with us, but doesn't go to Dani's room.

Somebody removed the bandages around her head. Her clown hat—the Styrofoam cup wrapped in one of those stretch bandages—is gone. It covered the sensor they put through her skull to measure pressure in her brain. What remains now is a small bandage in the middle of an area they shaved.

The machine that watched her brainwaves is gone as well, along with all its wires.

But the breathing tube remains.

Cooper's cell is on vibrate, but we both jump when it goes off. The Marine bids me farewell with a nod and disappears into the brightness of the outside world.

The bruising around Dani's eyes has spread—a larger butterfly now, although not as dark. Her hands are no longer as puffy, so I slide the heart ring back on her finger. The other won't come off mine.

"What are you doing?"

Ethan? His words mean nothing at first, beyond the obvious. "Dani," is all my weary brain manages.

"Get out." The boy grabs my arm, wrenches it behind me, and propels me across the room.

I yelp in pain and stumble to my knees as he shoves me through the doorway. And into Cooper. The way the Marine reacts makes me wonder if he ever really liked Dani's boyfriend.

By the time I get to my feet, Cooper has Ethan's face pressed hard against the wall. Security arrives ten minutes later and escorts the dude out of the hospital. My power of attorney trumps his claim to being Dani's fiancé. Ethan says he'll tell Mr. and Mrs. Welles. Like I care.

Cooper leads me down the hallway to some vending machines and buys me a hot chocolate. Coffee in hand, he gestures toward the visitors' lounge. I sip at my cocoa. It's probably nasty, but my taste buds are offline, and the warmth feels good.

The Marine sets down his cup and studies me with brown eyes that have already seen too much pain for a lifetime. "There's a hotel fifteen minutes away. I'll arrange a room for you."

"I'm not leaving Dani."

A quiet sigh lifts Cooper's chest. His eyes wander away for a moment. "You need to get some rest. You've been up longer than forty-eight hours straight."

I swirl around the sludge in the bottom of my cup. Sleep isn't gonna happen. "What about you?"

"There's a recliner just outside Danièle's room. I'll wake you if anything happens."

"Then you sleep while I watch." *Even Marines gotta have down time.*

Chapter 24

Danièle

The memory of drowning fades, but leaves my throat raw, my lungs congested, and my heart longing for sunshine. Shadows of pain lie dormant beneath the oily surface, their opaque eyes cast heavenward, eager to rise from the mire.

My lids snap open in the gloom. I cough the brown waters from my lungs and spew them into the darkness. Too weak to rise, I roll my head to the side to clear the noisome liquid from my mouth. At last my breaths flow cool and clear.

An unknown face hovers near me, full of tender concern.

So many questions—they emerge as a rasping hoarseness that becomes a hacking cough.

"Don't try to talk. You've had a ventilator tube down your throat." The apparition coaxes something into my mouth that sucks away the mucous. After that, she wipes my chin with a soft cloth.

More of the brown slime lies puddled across my gown and bed-clothes.

I try to raise one leaden hand, but something restrains my arm.

The nurse disappears for a few minutes and returns with clean linens. She throws my soiled blanket and sheets into a hamper. Removing my gown proves more difficult. So many connections—an IV in my right arm, a second line in my left. Wires end in small pads on my chest and side. A subclavian line—like the one Mrs. Fairbairn had for her chemotherapy—enters my chest by my collar bone. Another tube comes out between my ribs on the left side. Mottled green bruises extend from my thigh up to my armpit.

A second nurse removes the padded straps from my wrists and sets them on a counter nearby. They wash me from my shoulders down to my knees, front and back, and then change the sheet under me. After the first one rolls me on my back again, she helps me don a clean gown and raises the head of the bed.

"Would you like some ice chips?"

Darjeeling with a double shot of Irish cream would be brilliant. Instead, she brings me a plastic cup, half full of crushed ice. The tiny morsels she places in my mouth prove rather pleasant, actually. My throat savors the coolness of every last one.

When I tug at my gown for a bit more modesty, a glint of metal brings my hand even closer to my face. A wedding ring? Yes, a familiar pattern—named after—after a fishing village somewhere. How does one forget being married?

Certainly not to Ethan.

Will I ever see Melanie again? I would have followed her to Atlanta, but Mum said to give her a few weeks to herself.

My distress over the loss of Melanie drove me to the refuge of the ancient walnut tree in my mother's garden. A winter storm pelted me with cold rain. And a voice called my name in the darkness.

What if she needs my help? Panic drives me to the edge. I ease one leg over the side of the mattress and try to push myself upright. Thunder shoots through my side, and I slide to the floor. The exertion leaves me panting and dizzy and in pain.

A male nurse rushes into the room. "Please don't try to get out of bed by yourself."

I have to leave. Why won't the words form?

"Relax. We let your friend know you're awake. She should be here any moment."

"Melanie." Her name comes out more static than speech.

The nurse flashes a compassionate smile, gets me centered on the bed again, and walks out the door.

12VAC5—like a bit of some encrypted message—the letters snap into place in my memory. For a certainty, they hold a secret dear to me. But what? The little concentration I muster brings nothing more.

"Dani!"

Melanie? I track her with eager eyes as she slides into the room and stops.

For the space of three heartbeats she remains there, still as a statue, and as quiet. Her lower lip trembles then, and she explodes into tears. Melanie runs to my side and throws herself into my open arms.

On her left hand she wears a wedding band. Mine. Perfect bliss overwhelms me.

Forehead, nose, lips, and neck—I kiss her with abandon. And yet with such frailty. My shaking arm drops without touching her cheek. I lie back again, soaked in warm contentment, and savor her presence. "I love you," comes out as a soft rasping.

She sits next to me on the bed, stares at me a while, then tugs on her clothes until she exposes her baby bump.

Careful of my IV, I move a trembling hand to her belly.

She places both of her hands over mine.

The baby kicks.

Melanie shifts my hand to the other side of her abdomen. Another kick. "Ellie and Patrick have both been little psychopaths with me here at the hospital so long."

Twins. A fragment of memory returns—tiny faces on an ultrasound display, and me swearing I'd never give up my children. Mine. I pull my love close again and kiss her until I haven't the strength for more. I lay my head back against the pillow, exhausted.

Emerald eyes—a bare hand-breadth away—ponder my face with tender concern. Her locket dangles close to my heart. *Yes. My promise kept.*

A man strides through the door then. Cooper. A soldier babysitting a rich girl who might be daft enough to ignore danger when it stalks her. His haggard face owns some terrible failure. Did I find trouble outside the shelter of his protection?

Do Marines cry? A tear glistens on its journey down his cheek.

My gaze drifts back to Melanie and drinks in her beauty.

One last kiss before I sleep. My hand brushes her arm, but I have not the energy to raise my head off the pillow. My eyelids settle back into the mists.

Enough that you're here with me.

CHAPTER 25

Melanie

Dani sleeps on, one hand still attached to my belly, like some little kid gripping her favorite blanket. The girl wouldn't surprise me if she started sucking her thumb. *Whatever. I don't mind playing mother for a while.*

Cooper eyes me like I have a clue to Dani's behavior.

I sniff and make like I'm gonna wipe my nose on my sleeve.

The Marine grins and pulls a handkerchief from his pocket, but he cleans my forehead and neck before wiping my nose.

Right. Like the girl would be wearing lipstick in the hospital. "Thanks."

He gives me a silent nod, leans against the wall, and closes his eyes.

Weariness creeps into my soul like a deadly fog. Sleep, it whispers. Once I succumb to its lullaby, I'll be out for a week.

Not till Dani's outta here.

Somewhere down the hallway people chatter. An alarm beeps. Footsteps soft-tap across the floor. A cabinet door closes. Something big rumbles down the hallway.

In the quiet darkness Dani's chest drifts up and down in the gentleness of sleep. An innocent smile warms her face. Even her bruises seem only shadows.

The girl's oxygen monitor hangs around ninety-eight, blood pressure ninety over sixty. Dani's heart draws a steady beat across the display. A few meds still flow into her system, but most of the tubes have been withdrawn.

I hold Dani on her side while a nurse tugs away the soiled linen and places a clean sheet under the girl. After that short interruption, hours—maybe days—pass in endless waiting.

My bleary eyes wander in the soft haze of twilight—the fathomless void of intensive care. Sleep, the darkness whispers. I sway, fighting to remain upright. Perched on the bed, I don't even have anything to lean against. I slip away from Dani and try to stand, but the world blurs, and I slide to the floor.

Cooper hoists me in his arms. Without a word, he carries me to the recliner in the visitors' hallway behind the room. "Get some sleep," he whispers.

Not gonna happen.

I close my eyes. Dreams stir in a mental haze—Daniel and me walking the beach with our children. Mom well again. Dad and me on his motorcycle. A car hitting Dani on her bike. An alien machine breathing for the girl. That last one plays in an endless loop till I climb out of the depths, struggle to my feet again, and amble back into Dani's room.

She lies on the hospital bed still, but somebody has raised her back, so she's almost sitting up. Mrs. Welles holds a cup to the girl's lips.

What happened? I've only been away a few minutes. Yet they cut her hair in a shoulder-length bob—almost a pageboy. With a bare spot on one side where the sensor was.

Dani beams her love my way. "I missed you," she mouths, her voice but a whisper.

Mrs. Welles scowls at me. Like the accident was all my fault.

Yeah, guess so. I scoot across the room and park my butt on the side of the bed opposite Dani's mother. I force a smile and nod a greeting. "I'm sorry it took you so long to get here."

Her anger flares, but fades right away. She sets down the cup, walks around the bed, and faces me. Like some Gestapo general. "Be thankful you're not Randolph Welles. My husband's rather upset with him for not contacting us sooner." She searches my eyes then—the way Dani sometimes does—lets go of her anger, and hugs me. "Thank you for watching over my daughter."

My vision blurs again. I grab the bed rail and hold tight, refusing to let my mind wander off. And. Into. Dreams.

Danièle

I wake to soft pain—as subdued as the light of intensive care. The sensation floats—mostly submerged—in a pool of numbing sedation. Tenderness ripples down my side when I move.

Melanie rests her head against my shoulder, strands of her ginger hair spreading across my chest. Both Mum and Cooper encourage her to sleep—I all but order her away—but she remains in a chair next to my bed. She no longer responds to the nurses who come and go, nor even to the few words my parents direct her way. But embers of tenderness still burn deep within her eyes.

Cooper leans against the doorpost, as relaxed as the Marine ever gets. When his gaze meets mine, I beckon him closer. "Will you help me? I'd like to sit up for a while."

He nods, but pushes the call button and asks for a nurse.

I slide my legs over the side of the bed and, with Cooper's added muscle, pull myself upright. The exertion leaves my heart thumping. I lean against his shoulder and breathe through my mouth.

Melanie sits on the bed next to me and adds her support, though she seems as knackered as me. I brush the back of a finger down her cheek. "Help me remove the EKG, will you, love?"

After a glance at Cooper, Melanie reaches through the back of my gown and begins tugging at the wires. She leans close—her face almost touching mine—as she stretches for the far-side pads.

My body aches for hers—to hold her close. I press my lips against Melanie's for a breathless moment.

Her arms tremble, and she stops, her emerald eyes searching. For Daniel, no doubt.

That's all right, love. I'll be him for you and a proper young lady for everyone else.

A nurse arrives, glances at the blank display, and transfers my saline drip to a rolling IV pole.

After they move me to a chair, an orderly brings a tray with some soup, gelatin, ice cream, and juice. I finish the tasteless bisque. The flat gelatin. Even the dairy lacks flavor. Likely an aftereffect of the anesthesia. And eating even that little leaves me exhausted.

After an orderly removes my tray, Melanie rests on the arm of my chair. I pull my wife close and kiss her with what little strength remains. Her weary eyes slow-blink, but a tired smile spreads across her face.

Sometime later, Dr. Ormond walks through the door, followed by a resident. "Miss Welles, We're moving you out of ICU today. Your parents would like me to transfer you to the Gumenick Suites. There, you'd have adjoining guest rooms for family and friends."

"Do they have real food?"

The doctor breaks into the warmest smile I've seen on him. "I believe they have a gourmet chef."

Melanie leans her head against mine. Ginger curls spill down across her pale cheeks. A single tear runs down her face and spatters on my arm.

Perhaps now you'll rest.

Melanie

Dani lies asleep on the hospital bed, free of the ventilator, IVs, tubes, and wires. Her chest rises and falls in gentle waves. Bruises give her the face of a pale racoon, but she radiates peace.

I make my way to the guest room and ease the door open. Somebody left my suitcase beside the bed. I lift it onto the dresser and click it open.

A hot shower. Clean pajamas. A good night's sleep. I'm gonna have my meltdown tonight.

A trail of dirty clothes follows me into the bathroom. I flip the water to full steam ahead and duck beneath the life-giving flood.

Shampoo lather flows down my hair and falls in clumps around my feet. I scrub my arms and legs till my skin burns bright red. With the torrent of water massaging my neck and shoulders, I close my eyes and dream of cuddling with Daniel.

After I work out all my tension, I grab a towel from the rack and press my face into its clean, cottony scent. *Now if I only had some of*

Jake's scones and a cup of steamed milk, I'd be in Heaven. I pat myself dry and wander back into the bedroom to find my comb.

Dani teeters on the edge of my bed, her hospital gown on the floor around her ankles.

I rush to the girl's side and grab her arm to keep her from falling over. "You should be in bed."

"Help me shower first." Her desolate panda eyes beg me to help.

On one side of her too-thin body, fading bruises stretch from her thigh up to her breast. Here and there, angry skin displays the recent memories of tubes and incisions.

"I'll get a nurse."

"No." Her hand tugs—light as a feather—against mine while her face pleads.

So frail—will the girl even make it to the shower?

I am so gonna regret this. I help Dani to her feet, and we shuffle toward the bathroom.

She leans against the stall while I position the shower seat under her tush. The girl slides down the wall—more like collapsing than sitting—yet still kinda graceful, considering her circumstances.

Bathing Dani takes almost as long as my shower did. I shampoo her hair and clean the rest of her with a washcloth. After a warm rinse, I turn off the water, hand the girl a towel, and help her to her feet again.

Dani leans back against the wall, slides both arms around my waist, and urges me closer. "I am so blessed to have you as my wife."

Huh? Not now. My head collapses against Dani's shoulder in utter weariness. *I got you your stupid shower. Can the brain damage please wait till morning?*

Soft breath warms my cheek. "I'm sorry I put you through this."

Such tenderness hasn't flowed from the girl's lips since—well, yeah—since Daniel gave me his locket.

She brushes a fingertip across my cheek. "When I'm better, let's find a beach somewhere. All right?"

We're not married, Dani. The accident knocked something loose. Okay? I should explain, but I don't have the courage to disappoint the love in her frail eyes. *I'm not gonna be the one who spoils your dream.*

"Okay." I kiss Daniel—a gentle brush of my lips against his—and lean my head against the boy's shoulder. Faded memories of his body against mine pull me ever closer.

Who's gonna hold me after you marry Ethan?

We make our way across the room again, one halting step at a time. Daniel collapses on the double bed. Too weary to do anything more—dazed beyond caring—I crawl in beside him and pull the covers over us.

I am so sorry, Dani. I would never have wished for this.

Danièle

In grade school, Melanie chattered on endlessly about family and motherhood. When I suggested we marry, she replied that I needed to be a boy for that. After all, it took a man and a woman to make babies.

Why not? Everyone else pretended I was a girl. Melanie didn't care that my body was intersex—my little post was sufficient proof of maleness for our childhood games.

In the guest room bed with my wife, warmth suffuses me—along with a profound sense of peace. I slide a hand down across her baby bump, in search of some trace of our children. Ironic that I succeeded at the one thing little Melanie most wanted out of her for-pretend husband. And knew I didn't have to give.

After we moved, I wandered off into a feminine puberty and the resulting struggle to show myself a proper young lady. Melanie didn't mind my getting breast development. It didn't matter that I was Danièle to everyone else either, so long as I remained Daniel for her. My family's move to Virginia crushed her heart, and my being away from her killed Daniel.

I almost succeeded as the princess in a fairytale romance, though. My Prince Charming would have been well worth the body modifications and gender bending required to make me his bride. Or so I thought.

I learned my part rather well, actually. Being Miss Danièle Aileana Welles was grand. But my true gender lies somewhere between princess and little boy. In the end, only Melanie accepts that.

I prop myself up on one elbow and tug the sheet down. My wife has never been more beautiful. I run a fingertip—light as a breath—down her forehead to the tip of her nose. Her mouth curls into a smile, and she murmurs my name.

I press my lips against hers once, but have not the energy to do more. A dull throbbing in my side has grown too difficult to ignore. A more subtle pain caresses my hip. I lay my head on the pillow again and stroke my fingers through Melanie's cinnamon curls.

A line of brightness splits the dark and widens, like some portal through space. Cooper stands in silhouette in the doorway. I pull the sheets back up far enough to hide my breasts.

He strides across the room and leans over the bed. "I promised the nurse you'd take your medications." He sets a glass of water and a little cup of pills on the nightstand.

"All right." *Do I need so many?*

"Your parents have ordered breakfast. Would you like to eat with them?"

"We're a bit indisposed at the moment."

Ever the gentleman, Cooper fetches our bathrobes and drapes them across my legs. "I'll get your ride."

While he's out, I slip from under Melanie and don my robe.

Cooper returns a moment later, helps me move to the wheel-chair, and chauffeurs me into the dining area. I stand long enough to secure one of Daddy's overwhelming bear hugs and hear him whisper his love for me. Mum holds me as well, though anger and disappointment taint her enthusiasm. "Will Miss Fairbairn be join-ing us?"

Miss? "No. Let her rest."

Cooper shuts the bedroom door. I ease down into the wheel-chair again.

My mother sits across from me. Her eyes wander between my hand and the closed door as Cooper serves me poached salmon and scrambled eggs.

Yes, Mum. Married and deliriously happy. Get used to it.

Daddy prays for our meal, but remains silent afterward, his eyes distant.

My mother searches my face again before speaking. "Sweetheart, perhaps it would be more appropriate to sleep in the hospital bed."

Rather than with my wife? "No, Mum. I'll heal faster in Melanie's arms than anywhere else. And she needs me to hold her."

Ignoring my parents' frowns, I relish my first bite of breakfast. The mental haze has cleared. My body aches from head to thigh. Proof positive I'm alive. I throw a smile at the closed bedroom door, then grin at my mother.

Mum studies me over her tea.

Tea. Darjeeling? "May I have some?"

"Certainly." She pulls the cozy from the china pot and pours me a generous cup.

Now if I only had some Irish cream.

Melanie

Voices murmur outside the bedroom door, a long but hushed argument. I roll toward Daniel, but my husband's gone. Only the memory of his body against mine remains. A plaintive sigh parts my lips. Even if life's only a fantasy now, I need the boy to hold me till we're both better.

Is it so evil to hope he never leaves me? I slide out of bed and stumble toward the bathroom. A hot shower does little to ease my yearning. For Daniel. And—to my surprise—for Dani to come back again.

For the first time since leaving Victoria Springs Manor, I put on a nice dress and do my makeup. For Dani. Memories of our stay at the Biltmore drift past like leaves on a fall day. The night she cried in the rain drips down my cheek. Visions of our motorcycle rides together leave me wanting to hold her. I stop by the bathroom again to wipe the mascara from my face. *I'd give him up forever to have you well again, Dani.*

Someone taps on my door. I pull it open to bright light and Mrs. Welles' stern face. "I'd like a word with you while the speech therapists are evaluating Danièle."

I follow her to the dining table, where a pot of tea waits. As always. I pour us both a cup before sitting. A little cream. A little sugar. Yeah, and a scone would be yummy. I ease down into a chair and straighten my skirt. *What do you want?*

Dani's mother takes the seat across from me, but sips at her tea before speaking. "How close were you to marrying Danièle before the accident?"

Does it matter? Everything's changed now. "I'm pretty sure she bought the rings for us. But I don't think we'd have gone through with actually getting hitched. I'm not really into girls."

"You promised to marry her."

Do you always spy on your daughter's voice-mails? "I panicked, okay? You know—maybe she was gonna cut off her breasts or something. I didn't want her doing that. Not for me, anyhow."

"But you welcome her descent into fantasy."

"Look. I want Dani back as much as you do." *But is it so wrong to be Daniel's wife till the girl wakes up again?*

The woman's blue eyes search me for a long time before she replies. "Dr. Ormond attributes Danièle's behavior to frontal lobe bruising—and its attendant suppression of her inhibitions."

So being married to me is what your daughter really wants. Yeah, well, so get over it.

Mrs. Welles takes a long sip of her tea. "Perhaps you should encourage her toward reality."

You mean away from loving me. "What does Dr. Ormond say? I don't wanna risk hurting Dani till she's strong enough."

The woman's eyes echo the wounds of a battle lost. "He credits your relationship with Danièle for her remarkable progress."

Then why mess with that? "Okay. So we wait till she's better then."

Blue eyes promise me trouble in the days to come.

Chapter 26

Melanie

Daniel lies nestled in my arms, peaceful as ever. The physical therapists worked his too-thin body, till his lower lip twitched in pain. But over the past two days he's gone from sitting to standing to walking short distances.

Time was pretty weird in the ICU. Even in the guest rooms, it keeps its own pace.

The second hand on the wall clock sweeps around again. *Eight twenty-five. Morning or evening?* Memory fails me.

Somewhere in the distance, chimes play an old carol. Or maybe it's another ambulance rushing somebody to the hospital.

I grab my phone, and turn it on. *Tuesday, December 25. 8:26AM Oh, wow. Christmas Morning.*

Daniel's angel face smiles at something in his dream. Violet eyes flutter open. He flexes his hand in a feather-light caress of my baby bump. Then he kisses me. *Guess I got what I wanted most, huh?*

The boy's drowsiness gives way to joy. Clouds of disappointment and pain shadow his face, though. "I was hoping I'd remember something more during the night. Tell me about our wedding."

We're not married. The words form behind my lips, but the frailty in Dani's eyes keeps me from speaking. *It's okay to imagine— to cheer you up till you're better. Isn't it?* "Guess," I say. Daniel and me—we'd have an awesome wedding.

Concentration wrinkles the boy's brow. Violet eyes scan the ceiling. He chews on his lower lip. Then a burst of illumination hits his face. He dips his head—the slightest nod. "We had the ceremony and the reception at Victoria Springs Manor. Out in the garden."

In Virginia? "Go on."

"Your dress was straight out of a winterland fairytale. Mum designed the gown herself."

A princess. I can deal with that. "Yeah. Satin and tulle and velvet —all trimmed with feathers and fur."

Excitement glows in Daniel's eyes. "You wore my grand-mother's sapphire bracelet."

"Well, yeah. Fancy earrings, too. Like I was Cinderella or some-body."

The boy nods certainty. "Yes. You're the fairest of all women, even now."

And a liar. If we keep going, you're gonna hurt more when the truth comes out. Better to fess up now. But how do I explain without hurting you? I turn my head away long enough for a tear to escape. "Our marriage is only pretend, Dani. Like when we were kids. Any-how, I'm no more a proper lady than you are a man."

Hurt and confusion torment the girl's eyes. With her warm hands against my bare back, she pulls me closer, till my baby bump presses hard against her abdomen.

The tension flows out of me. *Yes, the truth is better.* "You were hurt bad. I was afraid of losing you. And my heart longed for Daniel. I'm sorry."

"Whatever for?" She caresses the side of my belly. "I'm not entirely male. 'Tis true. But I've given you for real what I promised in pretend—a loving husband, and children."

"But we're not—"

The girl seals my lips with a fingertip. "Not one more word, love. Would I have donned a top hat for our wedding if I didn't appre-ciate your calling me Daniel?"

"Your father's old top hat? The one—the one you always wore?"

"Didn't I tell you? I took it off before the processional. Cooper held it during the ceremony."

"You don't mind?"

"No. Mum—and probably Daddy as well—will always call me Danièle. All they know is the proper young lady. You love the rest of me as well."

I'm not gonna be the one who wakes us from this dream.

* * * *

Back at Victoria Springs—finally home again—Daniel lies still most of the night after taking his meds. I find a comfortable place for my head on his shoulder, my baby bump pressed against his side. Ignoring the bright morning rays streaming through the blinds, I cuddle tighter.

Even the twins rest in quiet contentment now. The few times they kicked during the night brought a sleepyhead smile to Daniel's face. And mine.

Time for the dream to end, though. I brush my lips against his— whisper soft. *Goodbye, my love.* Surely a kiss should awaken the princess. *What's become of you, Dani?*

Nothing at all. The accident knocked loose her inhibitions— nothing more. No longer pretending to be Danièle for them or Daniel for me. Simply the intersex Dani nobody knows.

Even asleep she radiates serenity, as though the truth freed her from all earthly concerns. Yet she dreams of marriage to me—that she kept Daniel's promise. My hand reaches unbidden for the locket at my throat. No way I'll part with that yet. Or him. Not till Dani comes back.

I swing my legs over the edge of the mattress, push myself upright, and survey the room. My dress lies draped over a high-back chair, my bra on the seat, both shoes on the floor. I was too tired to do more than grab a nightgown, slip it on, and collapse into sleep.

Such a blessing to be in my own room—well, in Dani's anyhow —still a delight compared to sleeping in the bed at the hospital.

After a quick shower, I browse the girl's closet till I find one of her belted smocks. It fits as good as my maternity clothes. I grab my dress and shoes and sneak back to my own room.

Dani's supposed to spend the morning being evaluated by physical and occupational therapists—and probably psychologists, so I snatch a book from the shelf and retreat to my favorite sanctuary—a rattan love seat in the solarium. My legs up over one armrest, I lean back into a small mountain of pillows and begin reading.

Around ten, Jake drops by with a cart. "Top 'o the mornin', Miss Melanie. Care for some tea and scones? Got your favorite—cran-berry-orange."

The babies have pressed the appetite out of my stomach, so instead of large meals, I snack all day. Scarfing a couple of warm scones with clotted cream has become a daily ritual. I grin at Jake and nod my eagerness. "May I have two?"

He fills a cup with black tea, adds milk and sugar the way I like, and hands me a plate of his delightful creations. I thank him, set my tea aside to cool, and lean back to savor my first morsel of the yummy pastry.

One hand strays to my baby bump. Motherhood still feels sur-real at times, especially with Daniel—with Dani being the father. To have childhood dreams that lay dead for so long spring to life again has left me—as she might put it—gobsmacked.

One day or an entire lifetime—I'll be Daniel's wife till the princess awakens, and she remembers her love for Ethan.

I take another bite of scone and lean back so the sunshine warms my face.

"Good morning, Melanie."

My eyes snap open. Mrs. Welles sits in the wicker chair across from me. On her lap, she holds a journal or something.

"Ma'am." I nod and take a long sip of tea, hoping my nerves don't show.

"Your face was glowing just now. Did I miss some bit of good news?" Her eyes examine me, reading my emotions much the way Dani might.

Glad you're not my real mom.

I sweep one hand across my belly and let all my love for Daniel warm my face. "Oh, just daydreaming about my babies' father."

Her eyes shine with the curiosity of a bird of prey. Game on, they say. "I thought you didn't know who he was."

I straighten up and grin. "Oh, but I do now." One hand creeps up to Daniel's heart. "Turns out he's somebody I've loved my entire life."

Another bite of scone and clotted cream—I savor it while Mrs. Welles glares at me. "He gave me this locket when he promised to marry me."

Mrs. Welles moans in frustration, but anger grows on her face. "Would you hold a lovely young lady hostage to your foolish childhood dreams?"

Me? I'm the only one around this place who doesn't. "As you do Danièle? No. I love her more than that."

The woman's anger slow-fades to pity. "Sweetheart, Danièle's had a traumatic brain injury. She's no more the father of your children than you are her wife. Don't enable her delusions."

I pick up the last fragment of scone. She won't appreciate my talking with food in my mouth, but at the moment, I don't much care. "Dani told me before the accident."

"I'm sure she was only trying to comfort you."

"She would never lie to me. *Ever.*"

Clearly, the woman doesn't give a flip about my opinion. Her shoulders twitch up—a proper old lady's shrug. "Well, Melanie. Perhaps she believes it then. Her psychologist thinks her confusion springs from her desire for children and her fanciful childhood experiences with you. He says we should encourage her to embrace her gender."

Of course. Force her to be your version of normal. "Why should I believe some stupid shrink over my best friend? Go ask Dr. Pierson if you don't believe your own daughter."

"Indeed. Randolph spoke with her successor." The woman slides a folded sheet of paper out of her journal and hands it to me.

I open the heavy stationary—a letter from Randolph Welles, Esq. to Theodore Welles, PhD.

Dr. Villanova assures me that, even were it possible—which is doubtful—the clinic would never use sperm from a woman. So that much is illusory.

At this point, Danièle has limited options. If she marries a man before the children are born, she can keep the children. Otherwise,

*she must give them up for adoption or lose her share in the trust—
now valued at a little over one hundred and twenty million dollars.*

There's more. Does it matter? I fold the letter again and hand it back—as my life bleeds out on the marble tiles.

Not Dani's children? One hand flees down to my baby bump again. *Whose?*

Anyhow, if she marries me, she loses her family and her fortune. For what?

Everybody knows Prince Charming lives happily ever after with the princess. He's supposed to. What kind of fairytale ends with the heroine getting hitched to somebody's ugly step-sister?

Mrs. Welles tucks the letter back into her journal. The victory in her eyes makes me want to puke. But what follows is an earnest plea. "Melanie, the best thing for my daughter—and for you as well—is to let someone adopt the babies."

The woman pauses. Like she didn't just shred my heart. I might let Beatrice keep the kids, but they'll still be forever mine.

"What I'm asking," she says, "is that you stay in Atlanta until the children are born. Give Danièle a chance to recover without the constant distraction of childhood fantasies."

All my life, I've waited for Daniel to return, only to realize I love Dani too. Would I give up my happily ever after for the girl? Do I care for her that much? Yeah. Guess so. "You'll tell her we're not married?"

"I shall."

So that's it. The end of all my dreams.

Before placing Daniel's silver heart—and my crushed soul—into the woman's outstretched hand, I click open the locket and say goodbye.

I tug at my wedding band, but it won't budge. The emotional turmoil of the past month bursts loose somewhere deep inside. I stand, but Mrs. Welles pulls me into a hug before I can escape. She strokes my hair like I'm some upset little kid. "I'm sorry. In time you'll forget all of this."

Not gonna happen. "No. I won't. I'm carrying Dani's children. And nobody's gonna take them away from me." *I'll never see Dani again, though. Especially if she marries that creep.*

Chapter 27

Danièle

Cold soothes and calms my throbbing side. I lean back in the recliner and close my eyes. Three hours of therapy—speech, occupational, and physical—have left me exhausted and sore. Amazing what two weeks in a coma does to a body.

One of the therapists helps me move to my wheelchair and pushes me as far as one of the tables near the garden-side windows in the kitchen.

Jake brings me a fresh pot of tea there. "Would you like anything else, Miss Danièle?"

"Thank you. No. Have you seen Melanie?"

A deep sadness darkens the old man's face, but he shakes his head. "She and your mother were in the solarium an hour ago."

Outside, the uppermost tree limbs sway in the breeze. I sip at my tea and struggle to remember my life.

Ethan realized the babies weren't his and sent Melanie away. Halloween—or thereabouts. Early in December I got into a motorcycle wreck. A mournful sigh shakes me at the thought of my lovely bike ruined.

"May I?" Mum pulls out the chair across from me.

"Certainly."

As she sits, my mother lays a silver locket and chain on the table.

My heart stops beating. "What did you do to her?"

Mum reaches for my hand, but I snatch it away, unable to bear any human touch—especially hers. My mother's eyes flash with anger, but only for an instant. "Melanie loves you, sweetheart. Enough to acquiesce to the foolishness resulting from your head injury. But you're out of the hospital now."

I reach for the locket, but Mum denies me even that comfort.

A faint hope still encircles my finger. And Melanie's. "And what of the rings?"

"Ethan says he asked you to pick out one. Perhaps you wished to give him a choice."

A fragment of memory swirls—like a crimson leaf in the breeze—and falls into a pile with the rest of my mental detritus. He called and apologized. But my heart refuses to let go of Melanie. To believe our relationship a mirage. "I love her, Mum."

"Of course you do, sweetheart. But you must let her go. She has duties that call her back to Georgia."

"The children are mine."

"No, Danièle. They're not. The clinic made a mistake with the sperm." She hands me a letter from Uncle Randy to my father. "You and Ethan decided to let Miss Fairbairn put the children up for adoption. Randolph will make certain they go to a good home."

I'm sure he will. A quick scan of my uncle's letter proves nothing. Nothing. Except they'll all disown me if I follow my heart. I tear up the letter—a childish act of defiance—and drop the shreds on the table.

Unable to bear more, I wheel myself down the hallway to the elevator. Melanie steps out when the doors open. Her desolate eyes stare past me as she walks by. The doors close with her on the other side, cut off from me forever. *My life's over.*

Melanie

Azure blue reflects in the garden pond. Not a ripple disturbs the calm serenity of another January afternoon. Cooper perches on the bench in the shade of the old walnut tree. Beside him Dani's pale form—like some marble statue—slumps in her wheelchair.

I turn my face away from the girl's forlorn eyes, unable to bear her suffering.

Even my old teddy bear refuses a smile for the sunny day. Storm clouds darken her eyes, a reflection of the despair in my own soul. I grab her and hold her tight.

Mrs. Welles taps on the door frame, walks into my room, and settles on the edge of my bed. "In some ways, you're more mature than my own daughter, you know. You grieve the loss of your dreams, but you'll recover and move on with life. You place duty above desire."

Recover? Ain't gonna happen. "If you say so."

"I'm planning a soirée for Danièle's twenty-first birthday. I'm hoping that will give you and her both some closure."

"Tuxes and fancy dresses?"

"Yes. I have a vintage gown that is rather frail now, but I think you'll like it. Ms. Franklin will alter the dress for you. She's waiting downstairs."

"Now?"

"Yes, love. Now." On her way out, she pauses in the doorway. "Please. It might cheer up Danièle.

The woman has always been polite enough, but she usually assumes my obedience. That she asks surprises me. I stand and follow her.

One of those fancy dress forms wears the antique gown. I bite my lower lip hard when I see it. The pink velvet fabric has faded till it seems almost white. A fur-trimmed cape rests on lace sleeves and a bodice worked with beads. Perfect for a winter wonderland Cinderella. "You can make that thing fit me?" Almost seven months pregnant, I'm not exactly princess shaped.

"Yes. With a few alterations..."

Way cool.

Danièle

Swollen grey clouds rumble low across the afternoon sky. Winter's chill whistles through the treetops. Here and there an errant snowflake swirls to the still-warm ground. Jake rocks the wheelchair back, lifting its front wheels clear of the gaps between slate tiles. "You sure 'bout this, Miss Danièle?"

"I'll be fine, Jake. Check on me in an hour if you're that concerned. All right?"

The old gentleman stares at me in uncertainty, then dips his head and walks off toward the house. Through the dormant maiden grass, past barren shrubs, and back up the trail around the pond.

I open the thermos and sip at my tea. Well, more Irish cream than Darjeeling, actually. But hot and sweet and full of caffeine.

Shattered memories drift at the edge of my vision, taunting me. The truth lies close at hand, hidden in the shadows of recent trauma.

Melanie sits in her bedroom window, staring down at the garden. Perhaps at me. *I hope your heart doesn't ache as much as mine.*

Did I abandon my love when Ethan sent her away? I remember not. I've lost November and parts of December to the void. *We were so happy together. What have I done that you reject me now?*

Mrs. Fairbairn's stern gaze flashes by. Did I anger her as well? My heart thumps up into my throat. She's been through chemo again. *I must have gone to Atlanta.*

Another bit of memory, more felt than seen, flickers through my senses—Melanie's hot tears running down my shoulder. Her body pressed against mine. And a silver heart. *She was wearing Daniel's heart in the hospital. I must have returned the locket to her. Which means I renewed my promise.*

I slip my new phone out of my coat pocket. The old one was never recovered. And for some reason, the text message history disappeared along with my memory.

Melanie's mother won't be in my contacts, but I step through them anyway. And find a home number for Melanie, with an Atlanta area code. *I don't remember that being there.* My gut clenches in fear, but I press connect.

"Danièle?" Melanie's sister answers, sounding none too happy.

"Yes."

"What do you want?" she says, her voice colder than darkest winter.

"May I speak with your mother, please?"

Seconds pass in tense silence before she agrees.

"What can I do for you, Danièle?"

"Mrs. Fairbairn, I remember very little from the time Melanie left Victoria Springs until I woke up in a hospital bed. I was hoping you'd fill in some of the gaps."

"They say true love never forgets. Why should I help you?"

Touché. "Your daughter's my life."

"So I've heard. Yet you—or at least your family—break her heart at every turn."

The wind changes direction, announcing a winter storm. A drop splatters against my hand. More on my lap. Waves race across the pond. "I don't know what to do."

"Where's your heart, child?"

"With Melanie and our babies—whosever they are."

"Whosever? Did you lose the papers I gave you?"

"Papers?"

"The ones from Dr. Pierson. In an envelope that says 12VAC5-something on it."

Memory hits with such force that I flinch. I know where to look for an answer now. "Thank you, Mrs. Fairbairn." I slide the phone back into my pocket and begin wheeling myself toward the manor. Inside, I find my way to Jake's office.

He stands to greet me. "What do you need, Miss Danièle?"

"I'm looking for my personal effects from school."

"Your mother asked me to shelve your books in the den. And I think Miss Melanie returned your clothes to your room." He studies me for a moment, his face thoughtful. Then a bit apologetic. "I forgot about your briefcase." He rises from his desk and retrieves my portfolio from the supplies closet.

The only unusual paperwork I find in my case is a Department of Motor Vehicles Form DL 17 signed by Dr. Pierson, stating that my gender is female. Rather pointless, that.

"Miss Danièle, I've been holdin' your mail." Jake pulls a bundle of envelopes from his desk and hands them to me.

I accept that faint hope from his steady hand and thumb through the pile. Someone opened my Visa bill and marked it paid. I stick it into my pocket. Most of the rest are advertisements I drop into Jake's trash can.

One remains—Virginia Department of Health, Office of Vital Records. My hands tremble as I worry it open to find two sheets of paper. An affidavit signed by Dr. Pierson—proof the children are mine. And a birth certificate for Dànaidh Ailean Welles.

I grin at Jake's uncertain face. "You just saved my life." I make my way down the hallway to the elevator using my wheelchair, but do a happy dance as soon as the door closes. *Now to plan our future.*

Chapter 28

Melanie

Man, is he good, or what? Cooper rocks his navy blue tuxedo, like the country's honor depends on his dance moves. The guy's lead leaves no doubt where my next step should go—and yet I have to concentrate to even notice his gentle pressure against my side or my hand.

The Marine pauses between sets and offers Dani a turn. The girl paired up with her father once, earlier in the evening, but she gives Cooper a polite shake of her head and sends him back to me.

Grace and Brent drove all the way from Richmond. Dani's old roomie dances a few times with the Marine while I sway to the beat in the arms of her boyfriend. But Cooper and I are definitely the best dancers there.

Dani wears braided extensions in her hair. Tortoise shell combs hold the white-blonde tresses in an up-swept style, like some ice princess on a formal visit. Her long gown sparkles in the dim light. She's always been more into glamor than my barefoot and blue jean ways. And yet, the proper young lady's the father of my children. Whatever Mrs. Welles says, my heart—and my babies—know the truth.

Every time my gaze meets Dani's, love and true happiness flow from her eyes. And vindication. The composure of a princess has driven all uncertainty from the girl's face. Everybody else might be wearing their formal best—even Jake—but Dani owns the night. Maybe the girl remembered her love for Ethan and settled back into her role as his fiancée.

That's what we all want. Isn't it? *So why do I feel like puking?*

At ten o'clock, Grace hugs Dani and me farewell. She and Brent have classes early in the morning. Mr. and Mrs. Welles drift away shortly thereafter. Just Dani and me and Cooper remain.

The Marine pulls me closer as the music slows. My weary head falls against his shoulder. A year earlier, I would have danced till sunrise. With the twins, midnight's already well past my bedtime. "I think that was my last one."

"All right." He escorts me to an empty seat at Dani's table. "Can I get either of you ladies anything?"

Yeah. Food. "You're my hero. Tea with milk. And anything Jake made for the party that isn't sweet. My blood sugar's been high, so I gotta behave."

Dani just shakes her head and smiles at me.

As soon as Cooper leaves, the girl moves to the chair beside mine and spreads the fingers of one hand across my belly. Like she owns the place. Both of the babies kick for her. Why not? They know their father's touch.

In the dim light, the girl's violet eyes glow like moonlight. The tenderness in them probably isn't all for Ethan. Nah. Part of her is still married to me.

Hope your heart doesn't hurt as bad as mine.

Her eyes do that little scanning motion—searching for a reaction. "Why are you running from me?"

"You gonna live in a dream? Daniel was never any more real than our marriage."

"Or our wedding bands?" Her hand brushes across my belly again. The little traitors both party in response. "Tell me I'm not the father of your babies. Say you don't love me, and I'll leave you be."

"You're a beautiful young woman, Dani. Why mess with that? Marry Ethan and adopt a bunch of kids."

"That would certainly make everyone else happy. What about us?"

My date returns with tea and a plate-load of Swedish meatballs.

Dani watches with amusement as I dig into the savory morsels.

Cooper leans close and kisses me on the cheek. "Thanks for the pleasant evening. I have other duties to attend to now."

"Yeah. Thanks." I stand and give him my best hug.

After he leaves, Dani rises and holds out a hand. "May I have the last dance?"

"Yeah. Guess so." *But do you have to make this more difficult?*

The girl leads me out into the ballroom. Her feather-light touch draws me close as the music starts—another slow dance. After a few hesitant steps, she pauses. "Sorry, love. I seem to have forgotten how. Bump on the head, don't you know?"

So I lead. Well, mostly we lean against each other and sway to the beat. Like some high school kids at their first prom.

When the music stops, Dani's eyes beg me for one more, but the girl's legs wobble, so I guide her back to the table. "You should be in bed."

Dani slides into her wheelchair. Small twitches at the side of the girl's mouth give away her pain. She bends forward and pulls her skirts up off the floor and away from the wheels.

And just how are you gonna wheel yourself anywhere? "I'll push you to your room."

When she has everything arranged just so, she throws a sleepy smile over her shoulder. "Sit with me a while first."

I push her down the hallway, far from the bright lights. Beside the elevator, I lean against the wall, breathe deep, and rub the back of my hand across my forehead. *I'm losing everybody I care about.* "I'm tired, Dani. More so than I've ever been."

"I won't keep you long."

I don't have anything left to give. "All right. Someplace warm?"

"I know the perfect spot." The girl's infectious smile and enthusiasm break through my gloom. She gestures toward the end of the hallway "Beyond yonder portal."

Behind those carved wooden doors lies darkness, disturbed only by the flickering amber light of a fire. Soft waves of heat ripple through the air.

I turn on a couple of small lamps, adding a mellow background glow to the room.

Dani motions me toward an overstuffed couch in front of an enormous fireplace. River rock climbs up the wall to the ceiling. An elk's head glares down at us from above the hewn cedar mantel. The scent of pine needles and dried flowers permeates the air.

After I help her move to the couch, I pull off my high heels, lean back into the supple leather, and stretch my aching muscles in the warm glow.

The girl squirms around till her back faces me. "Unzip my dress, would you, love?"

What moron designs clothes you can't take off by yourself? I undo the little hook thing and pull her zipper down far enough for her to reach the tab.

Dani kicks off her shoes and draws her feet up under her gown. For a long while, she stares in silence at the crackling fire. When the girl turns my way again, a single tear escapes and leaves a glowing trail down her cheek. "I'll never see you again if you leave."

Please don't make this forever. I start to object, but Dani shushes me and pops up off the couch, "Give me a minute before you say another word."

In the flickering light, the girl rummages through a large trunk. When she returns, she brings an old top hat and a white handkerchief.

"We're not kids anymore, Dani."

She arranges the cloth over my head—just so—the way I always did when we were young. With the top hat at sort of an odd angle on her head, she kneels in front of me. "Marry me." The yearning in her eyes insists the girl isn't joking.

Don't you get it? None of this is real. One hand drifts up to the emptiness at my throat. We were serious about our future. Once. Long ago. A brain injury—nothing more—led us back to an impossible dream. Will broken memories forever haunt the girl? As they do me? *It's all from a blow to your head, Dani.* I want to laugh at the insanity of her proposal, weep at the damage the wreck did to her brain, but the sudden terror behind the girl's eyes clamps a hand over my mouth. *What do I say that won't hurt you more?* "Ethan adores you, Dani. Don't waste your life chasing stupid childhood fantasies."

The girl leans close and kisses me on the forehead and again, on the nose. "Our promise—our love—was real. Was it not?"

"Well, yeah." *Still is.*

Dani kisses me on the mouth. Her lips whisper memories of the boy I lost. My heart drinks it in. Me. Daniel. Together. But there's no tomorrow. 'Cause he's gone. Forever. I ease back from her embrace and shake my head. "It's over, Dani."

Somewhere behind those dreamy eyes burns the desire to use what God placed between her legs—that little bit of manhood. Daniel's shadow falls heavy across her feminine face now. And yet no surgeon's blade can divide male from female, he from she. What a cruel schizophrenia to try to force on her. She isn't two people.

Dani rises and stands with her back to the fire. "All my life, people have encouraged me to choose boy or girl. Well, I've decided." She plops down on the couch again and slides close. "I'm happy with my body and my gender as they are—princess, little boy, father of your children. Ethan will never accept that. But you already do."

"Well yeah."

"Will you, then?"

"Will I what?"

"Be me trouble an' strife. Me better 'alf, luv."

Marry you?

Ethan wouldn't accept Dani fathering children. Am I any better, dreaming of the boy? The pretend one at that?

I tug at one sleeve of Dani's gown, till it slides off her shoulder and down her arm. Daniel's breasts had already started to bud when we made our promise. Why should the blossoms bother me? Would it be such a big deal to admit I love all of her?

It still can't happen. "No way your parents will let us get married."

Those violet eyes track my every emotion. Dani grins in triumph and hops up off the couch, sending her top-hat rolling across the floor. "But you want to." She urges me to my feet and pulls me close, her whole body demanding I surrender. "Admit it."

My hand creeps down to my belly for reassurance of my sanity. *Dani's babies.* "Well, yeah. But how?"

She glances toward the door. "I have some ideas, but let's get you to bed."

Chapter 29

Dànaidh

Morning arrives too early. With my arms still around Melanie's waist, I press my face into her ginger tresses and wait for one of the babies to move.

What do my psychologists know of life? They showed me videos—they called them educational—of couples having intercourse. "Which of the two would you like to be?" they asked.

I cried and hid my eyes, not understanding the rough, almost violent passion flowing from the screen. On my pretend honeymoons with Melanie, our lovemaking was soft touches and tender kisses.

One of my children shifts position beneath my hand. Thanksgiving and contentment overwhelm me. As Ethan's wife, I would have missed this glorious experience.

I ease my arms from around Melanie, press my lips against her cheek, and slide out of bed. After a quick shower, I dress in a soft and feminine skirt suit—something appropriate for meeting with executives.

My portfolio rests on the dresser. During the few weeks I lived as Daniel, Daddy spent father-son time with me, teaching me about his business. Randy opened an online trading account using some of the money from the trust fund, and my father taught me how to buy and sell stocks.

After I returned to being Danièle, we never talked about business again. Daughters were to be protected, pampered, and trained in the art of keeping a household. Don't worry your pretty little head about that, Mum replied whenever I asked about Daddy's ventures.

Everyone forgot about my account. Except me. In my portfolio are itemized lists of stocks and bonds—the results of all I've learned about the market. When I sell the stocks, the funds will provide for my little family until I finish college. I thumb through the folders one last time before heading downstairs for breakfast.

My father spends most weekdays in his study. Business partners join him via the video-conference room. A few times a month he travels to one manufacturing plant or another. I tap on his door and poke my head in. "May I speak with you?"

Daddy looks up from writing something and gives me a tender smile. "Why of course, love." He drops his pen, stands, and waves me to a seat. "What can I do for my little girl?"

"A number of years ago, you and Uncle Randolph opened a brokerage account for me—for Daniel."

He nods, but his eyes look well beyond the room. Perhaps into the past, because he says, "My boy showed an interest in the markets. I wanted to encourage him."

Always the disconnect between Daniel and me. *I'm the same person, Daddy.* "After I—you stopped teaching me about stocks."

"Your mother thought you'd be happier studying manners, and dance, and other things a young lady should master."

Silence hangs in the air between us, a thick mass that keeps me from speaking. I tried a hundred times to tell my father who I was and always retreated in fear—that I'd hurt him, that he wouldn't understand, that he'd reject me. Or perhaps I was afraid to admit to myself that I was never entirely a boy or a girl.

Melanie understands. Melanie, the mother of my children. Melanie, my one true love. I take a deep breath and start my pitch. "Melanie and I are getting married. I'd like your blessing."

Almost apologetic, he shakes his head. "I wish the surrogacy had worked out. The best thing for everyone involved now is to find a proper home for the babies."

I close my eyes and pray that God will grant my father an understanding heart. "They're my children, Daddy. What would you do if someone you loved more than life itself was pregnant with your babies?"

Only the ticking of the wall clock disturbs the silence as Daddy's face grows somber. He married Mum over his parents' objections when she was pregnant with me.

He glances away before speaking. "I'm not blind to the happiness you two shared in the hospital. But your mother and I want you to move on with your recovery." A painful hardness spreads across his face. "You've made no progress this week. I was going to send you to a rehabilitation center in Richmond, but your mother thinks a hospital in Cambridge will be better. You'll have company there."

"Ethan."

"He's agreed to visit you daily beginning next week."

"When do I leave?"

"Tomorrow. Your flight departs an hour after Melanie's."

"But I don't love Ethan, Daddy."

"I know." He walks around the desk and pulls me into one of his giant teddy bear hugs. "Give him—and your heart—one last chance though, will you?"

No. "Let me say a proper goodbye to Melanie, then."

Daddy's gentle frown sums up his opinion of my relationship with her. "Do whatever you must. But make this the end of it."

I rush back to Melanie's room, but she's not there. Not in the quiet of the solarium. Not under the fair sky and winter sun of the garden. Not in the dark warmth of the den. Nowhere in the barren wilderness of my life.

Melanie

Packing doesn't take long. The Welles bought me a bunch of maternity clothes, but I keep only my old jeans, some tops, and a couple of dresses. I stuff them all into the fancy shoulder bag Dani bought me.

Somebody took the Cinderella dress, probably downstairs to storage. No way the thing would fit into my bag, anyhow. And I don't need fancy stuff.

With soap, hot water, and some petroleum jelly, I finally get the wedding band off my finger. I almost leave it on the dresser, but then figure I should give the ring back to Dani. I owe the girl that much.

I don't buy any of those happily-ever-after endings. Once I leave Virginia, I'll never see Dani again. Mrs. Welles will make damned sure of that. So I stand in the doorway of the little room I call my home and study every last detail.

Drops patter against the metal roof—the beginnings of one more winter storm. I walk over to the window seat and scan the barren garden. The old walnut tree waves an arm at me—a solemn goodbye. Now and forever.

No more dreams, but I'll have memories. I nod once to my old friend and walk out into the hallway. I ease the door shut and make my way to the kitchen.

They all stare, but nobody greets me. Not even Jake smiles. I get a great big bear hug from Mr. Welles, but his eyes hold some far-away sadness. Mrs. Welles says her polite goodbyes and lies about wishing I would stay.

Miss Danièle Aileana Welles is dressed to the nines for her trip to see Ethan and his mother, but her face has lost the joy we shared the other night. Her eyes say nothing at all about her promise—Daniel's old promise—to marry me. *Like that'll ever happen.*

And the Marine—wonder he doesn't break his teeth, he clenches his jaw so hard.

Are we all in some stupid soap opera or what? Glad I'm bustin' outta this place.

I follow Cooper to the Escalade, slide into the back seat, and chill while Dani hugs her parents and all. As soon as the girl slams the door, Cooper starts the car, and we drive out the fancy iron gates. Victoria Springs Manor fades into the distance. And into my past. Dead. Like everything else in my world. Never to return.

"Don't give up on your dreams. We'll be back here someday. Together." Dani's eyes urge me to trust her. To let myself get burned one last time.

"I'm all out of hope." I put my wedding band into the palm of her hand and close her fingers around the ring. "No more impossible dreams."

Dani must read the pain in my eyes, because she draws me close and pulls my head against her shoulder. "Be patient, love. A few days more."

I snuggle as close as the twins will allow. *Just hold me.*

"Can we stop at the DMV?"

I peek out of my hiding place to see Dani's hand on the inter-com button.

"What do you need?" Cooper's voice.

"I still have the dorm address on my license. And I should can-cel the motorcycle tags."

"All right."

Silence again. I burrow back into the softness of her shoulder. Time slides away till a steady thump-thump takes over from the asphalt rumble. I poke my head up again. *Yeah, the old bridge across the river.*

We stop a few minutes later, and Cooper drops us off in front of a brick building. "Don't be all day."

Department of Motor Vehicles—I follow Dani inside and mosey over to a chair. She goes straight to the nearest open position. Soon the girl has everybody who works in the place collected around her. Like she's a celebrity or something. When she points at me, they all gape like they've never seen a pregnant girl before. *Yeah. Nod. Whatever. Like I care.*

Finally, they wave her over to a camera. Somebody musta com-plained about her hat, because she pulls it off and shows them where the pressure sensor was. A small group gathers again before some big shot sends them all scurrying.

Dani waves her new license at me like she's never had one before. *About time.* "What was all the drama for?"

"I didn't want them to take a new photo until my hair grew out again."

"Yeah. Guess not."

A few minutes later, we're back on the road. Two hours, maybe three, before my flight leaves. I press my head into her shoulder again and snake a hand around her back.

Two hours, maybe three, and I'll never feel her touch again. Dani unbuttons the front of my dress and spreads warm fingers across my baby bump.

Two hours, maybe three—somebody weeps like a little kid.

The girl kisses my cheek, then my ear, and pulls me tight.

We stay in our own little time warp, oblivious to the outside world. Till the Escalade stops, and Cooper opens the door. Dani kisses me one last time, steps out of the car, and offers me a hand.

The girl acts a little strange when we check our luggage, insisting she use her phone for the boarding pass rather than the paper one Jake printed for her.

When we get to the security checkpoint, Dani gives Cooper a big hug. "Thanks. I'll accompany Melanie to her gate."

Cooper's grin reminds me of my old high school principal—or a prison guard. The Marine holds up a boarding pass. "I promised your mother I'd see you both aboard your flights."

Bitch.

Dani shoots me an exasperated glance, but gets in line.

A couple of minutes later, we find our way to B15—DL2452 to Atlanta. I plop down into a chair beside Dani. The girl belongs in bed. "You okay?"

"Yes, love. A wee bit knackered is all."

What gives your mother the right to crush our dreams?

The girl starts playing with her phone.

Our last hour together, and all you can do is look at the Internet? What is wrong with you? "What am I gonna do, Dani?"

She glances up, but keeps right on typing. "You'll be fine, love."

The money Mom gave me won't last long enough. I can't mooch off my sister for the rest of my life. And I don't wanna give up our babies.

Way too soon, the airline lady announces our departure. "Anyone needing assistance may board at this time." She looks right at me. Like I might need help or something.

First Class boards without me. It's not like anybody'll take my seat. Group Two bunches up around the entrance while Group One files down the ramp. After a while, nobody remains but me.

"Final boarding call, Gate B15, flight 2452 to Atlanta."

Oh great. Here come the tears.

I'm done. I hop up out of my seat and hoist my bag over one shoulder. *Maybe I can make it down the ramp before I have my breakdown.*

Dani grabs my arm and drags me to a stop. "Not even a kiss goodbye?"

"No." *Not after you ignored me for the past hour.*

She kisses my forehead. And my nose. Violet eyes study me, waiting for an answer.

I've never kissed a girl before, not even an intersex one.

Not fair to count Daniel, you know.

Okay, so he had buds of breasts. And a small vagina. But he had a little post between his legs. And he said he was a boy. Even if only for pretend.

He's gone, and you're here. Yeah, well, I'll show you what you'll be missing.

I slink my arms inside Dani's jacket, around her waist, and pull us closer till we breathe as one. I kiss my intersex girl—the father of my babies—like we'll never see each other again. 'Cause we won't.

Nothing else even exists.

Dani blinks first, and gasps for air.

My feelings for her bleed down my cheeks. "Come with me. Please." *Otherwise, I'm gonna die.*

"I intend to." She wipes my cheeks dry, then nudges me toward the ramp.

The airline attendant checks my boarding pass. Dani hands the lady her cell to scan.

"Danièle?" Cooper strides up to us and grabs the girl's wrist. "What are you doing?"

She never gets mad. Ever. But Dani's glare leaves ice crystals hanging in the air. "Unhand me."

"Your mother suspected you might run. If you leave, you're on your own. Entirely. Even the trust will cut you off."

Dani, are you really gonna give up everything for me? I open my mouth to protest, but somewhere deep inside enough hope survives to still my objections. *We'll be okay. Somehow.*

Dani slips her phone into the Marine's shirt pocket. Her debit and credit cards soon follow. The girl shakes free from Cooper's grip and takes my hand. "Let's go, love. We've a wedding to attend."

Chapter 30

Dànaidh

We descend through broken storm clouds into a rainy Atlanta afternoon. Droplets scurry down the window next to me while our plane taxis to the gate. Melanie snuggles against my shoulder and waits as impatient travelers jostle for their carry-on luggage and work their way down the aisle.

After the last person disappears, I follow Melanie out of the aircraft. We take the airport train from the terminal toward baggage claim. A familiar face springs from the crowd waiting outside security. Melanie shrieks and runs on ahead to greet her mother.

By the time we reach baggage claim, my hip throbs, so I collapse into a chair and wait for my luggage. Melanie sits next to me. "You okay?"

"Yes. Just worn out."

"Yeah. Me too. My legs are swollen and this weird pain runs down my leg from my butt. Mom says that's normal for a pregnant girl."

"I'd like a word with you, *princess*." Randy steps out of the crowd, his arms crossed and his face a battle of fierce emotions.

How did you get here? There wasn't near enough time.

Mrs. Fairbairn grins at me from behind him. "The girls have already won, you know."

My uncle—not quite the gentleman at the moment—scowls at her.

I retrieve an envelope from my purse and hand my uncle a copy of Dr. Pierson's affidavit. "Exhibit one, counselor." *...having fathered children...*

Melanie eyes me with angry curiosity. She never did like my keeping secrets from me. I unfold a copy of my new birth certificate and give it to Randy. "Exhibit two." *Dànaidh Ailean Welles.* "Proof the children are mine. And that I'm legally male."

My uncle spends more time than necessary inspecting the documents. Almost, he keeps emotions from his poker face. Almost. "I doubt these will sway your mother."

I slide the papers from his grasp and pass them to Melanie without breaking eye contact. "Perhaps you can persuade Mum, then. If she wishes further contact with her grandchildren or me or Melanie, she'll relent."

"Very well. Send me copies of both of those papers. As well as your marriage license when you get one. The trust will continue to cover medical and educational expenses."

"Thanks. We'd love to see you at the wedding Saturday."

"I'm in town for a conference, but I'll see what I can do." After taking a dozen steps toward the exit, he returns and hugs me. And Melanie. "Congratulations. Both of you."

Melanie turns to me after he leaves. I expect anger, but find in her eyes only tender concern. "Dani, what happens the first time you have to show ID? Huh?"

"My driver's license still says female."

"And when they find out you changed your birth certificate?"

"They already know that, love. My legal sex is male, but Dr. Pierson filled out a form that says my gender's female, so the DMV kept that on my license."

"Somebody's not right in the head."

"Lots of people have a mismatch between sex and gender."

"You don't."

"No. I suppose not. But Virginia won't put hermaphrodite on my paperwork."

Melanie eyes me like I'm crazy to even mention that.

Yes, for your sake I'm glad my license says female. But I'm not ashamed of being intersex.

Melanie

Beatrice and Fred have a feast waiting for us when we arrive—food on parade. Hors d'oeuvres and sweets overrun the kitchen countertops. I grab a sausage roll and crash on the couch in the living room. I close my eyes and relish the quiet.

"Is that any way to greet your favorite sister?" Hands on her hips, Beatrice stands in front of me, trying hard to appear upset.

I hop up off the couch long enough to hug her. "I gotta keep the little ones fed, don't I?"

Greg runs into the room, screaming, and jumps up on the couch. "Can Joey and me build a fort again?"

My sister plucks him off the couch. "Tomorrow. Okay? And no shoes on the sofa."

"Aw, Mom. Aunt Melanie's here. Me and Joey gotta sleep somewhere."

"She and Danièle are staying on the new sofa in the den. It folds out into a bed. Remember?"

"Oh, yeah. Can I have one of them little pies?"

"Yes. But only one. I don't want you ruining your supper."

Dani strolls into the room, hugs my sister, and collapses on the couch beside me. "Your mother would like a few minutes alone with us. Whenever you're ready."

"Now's fine." I struggle to my feet again and follow her into Mom's room.

Somebody painted the walls since the last time I saw the place. And banished the scent of death. Maybe even replaced the carpet.

My mother pulls the door closed. She nods at Dani, but takes my hands in hers. "You're sure you want to get married?"

The tight ginger curls covering Mom's head bring a snarky grin to my face. "Yes, ma'am."

She hesitates a moment. In surprise at my politeness, probably. "All right. Dani asked me to arrange things for you two. Pastor Hawkins has agreed to perform the ceremony at the park."

"The one with the lake? Isn't that place private?"

"The company's agreed to let us use it this Saturday. We can try to find something else if you'd rather."

"No, Mom. The park's awesome."

"Good. Shall we invite the Welles family then?" While Dani and I gawk at her, she picks up her phone and dials, then puts the call on speakerphone.

"Hello, Keela."

"Are the girls safe?"

"Yes, they made it here just fine."

"Then you'll send Danièle back home?"

"They're old enough now to make their own decisions. And what's so wrong with their dream, anyway?"

"You'd allow your daughter to marry another woman?"

"I'm stage four, Keela. I'll be gone soon. Our daughters are getting married Saturday. If you want them—or your grandchildren—in your life, you need to be here."

"Grandchildren? Yours certainly. Not mine."

"Like it or not, Danièle's their biological father. Randolph recognizes the twins as heirs. Why don't you call him?"

"I most certainly shall."

"See you at the wedding, then."

Mom sets her phone on the nightstand. "She'll come."

"What's stage four?" Fear runs down my throat and pools in my stomach.

"I'm sorry, honey, but the cancer's back."

No. The air freezes in my lungs

Breathe.

"You can do chemo again."

"It's spread too far for that." She pulls me into a gentle hug. "After your wedding, I'm moving to Saint Andrews Island to stay with an old friend."

"No, Mom. You can live with Dani and me."

"I want you and Beatrice to remember me the way I am now."

"You gotta at least let Dani and me visit when the babies are born. Or come see us."

Mom's eyes glisten with unshed tears.

The doctors don't give you that long, do they? "It's okay to dream, Mom."

After a moment, a faint hope lights her eyes. "If I'm still alive—yes, I'd like that."

"I love you." I close my eyes and bury my face in her shoulder.

Yeah, Mom. I've got Dani. But I'm sure gonna miss you.

CHAPTER 31

Melanie

A lone Canada goose leads her yearlings across the withered grass and splashes into the water. Fish play in the shallows. Maybe bluegill—Dad would know for sure. Winter sunshine spills through the pines and sparkles off the lake. I pull up my skirts and step wide of the mud. No way am I gonna let my Cinderella gown get dirty.

Mom said the dress arrived a few days ago in a package Jake sent. Maybe it reminded Mrs. Welles too much of me. Or could be the old gentleman thought I needed some cheering up. Anyhow, I'm happy to wear the dress again. Even though the thing is falling apart.

Behind me lies a crazy trail of feathers and beads and little bits of lace—the antique gown giving up everything to delight a young bride.

Mom saved the old lace handkerchief I used in our childhood ceremonies. Like she expected me to need it when I grew up. The thing has gotta look horrible sitting on top of my head, but Beatrice insists it's fine.

My sister offered me a necklace to cover the one bleak spot of my outfit, but I turned her down. Nothing can replace my missing locket.

Fred checks his watch. "Five minutes yet." Somebody has to give away the bride, you know, and my sister volunteered him. He's not my father, but the thought's still nice. The guy rented a suit that some English butler might wear. The tails hang down almost to his knees.

One of those stretch limos drives up the narrow blacktop that runs through the park. Sleek and black, with heatwaves rising from the hood even on a cool winter afternoon. I pull up my skirts again to make sure the car doesn't run over them.

The limo stops beside us, and the driver's door swings open. Out steps Cooper—all dressed up like he's the best man or some-thing. He gives me a genuine smile before opening the passenger door.

My heart pounds, trying to break out of my ribcage. The last thing I need's an argument with Mrs. Welles.

Breathe, girl. Just breathe. She can't stop you now.

Dani's mother steps out and closes the distance between us—in no particular hurry—till she stands facing me. "I had hoped better for you, child. You have a natural charm my daughter never quite mastered."

Mrs. Welles slips off her gloves, hands them to Cooper, and retrieves a fine silver chain from her pocket. "I understand now that Danièle's heart was never mine to give. I'm sorry. In that, at least, I erred." She fastens the necklace—along with Daniel's locket—right back where it belongs.

I clench my hands tighter on my dress to keep from grabbing my silver heart. I dip my head and thank her.

She chews on her lower lip for a moment. "Please come back to Victoria Springs when—when you're ready. I promised your mother I'd look after you when she's gone." The woman's eyes glisten. She turns to leave.

I gape at her back in stunned silence. Too late, I reach out a hand.

As I stare at the retreating limo, the processional begins. Irish pipes float on the breeze—a fairie melody that brings a smile to my face. Daniel and I never had proper music at our pretend weddings.

Fred holds out a white-gloved hand. In my imagination, though, my father stands beside me, dressed in motorcycle leathers and boots—his idea of formal attire. I take his hand and coax my eyes away from his face, lest the illusion fade.

Longing for my father pulses ragged through my body. *I miss you, Dad.*

Fred squeezes my hand tight and urges me forward. *Everything will be all right.*

No. Not till this pregnancy's done. Pain and numbness radiate from my butt down one leg. I pause long enough for a trembling sigh to work its way out. Then take one step. And another. I waddle down the lane.

As we round the bend a gazebo comes into sight—an open-air structure made of cedar. In front of it stands—

Daniel? No. Dani cut her hair in that ubercute pixie style she always wore when young. Her locks tumble down over her cheeks and into her eyes. Atop her head, at a wild angle, is her father's dusty old top hat. Draped over the girl's shoulders, like a cape, is the still-too-large tuxedo jacket. Black satin pants and a frilly white blouse replace her old flannel pajamas.

Sweet.

Mom and Beatrice wait on the stairs, off to one side. Grace, Dani's old college roomie, and Cooper stand on the other. In the shade behind them gather the Welles.

Dani takes off her hat and hands it to the Marine. Then she steps close, brushes a fingertip across my locket, and absolutely beams at me.

Memories sweep me back to the time Daniel first gave me his heart, swore to love me forever, and promised me his children. The sun shone bright over Miami that day.

It was you I loved all along. Small cumulus clouds skip like lambs across the Atlanta sky, chasing the cool February breeze. Pine trees wave at the passing flock. Geese honk in the distance.

Fred-as-Dad kisses me on the cheek and escorts Mom and Beatrice up the stairs to seats around the edge of the gazebo. Opposite the Welles. Cooper offers Grace his hand and leads her up to the center, where Pastor Hawkins waits.

I stand in the dread silence, Dani quiet beside me. Even the birds remain still. The throbbing of my heart pounds loud in my ears. In the cool shade, a bead of sweat rolls down my nose. Darkness clouds the edge of my vision. My body sways.

Breathe. Dani presses a tender hand against the small of my back and urges me forward. Up the stairs to embrace our dreams.

My hair floats unruly on the breeze—even with my veil. Something tugs on my skirt as I near the top—the hem snagging on one of the steps. Grace pulls it loose, leaving behind one more memory of a once magnificent gown.

Cooper, Dani, me, and Grace—we stand abreast, facing the pastor, surrounded by family. In a fairytale park under an azure sky. An impatient squirrel chatters at us to be on our way. Leaves rustle overhead.

"Dearly beloved," Pastor Hawkins begins. The man says the words I've heard a hundred times before. They echo still in my night visions. My heart knows them true.

Heat spreads across my cheeks. I grin my happiness at Mom. Even Mrs. Welles surrenders a half-hearted smile when I catch her eyes.

Dani takes my hand in hers and slides a ring on my finger. That cute one with the vines. "I, Dànaidh Ailean Welles, take you, Melanie Rose Fairbairn to be my wife. To have and to hold. From this day forward. For better, for worse. For richer, for poorer. In sickness and in health. To love and to cherish. Till death do us part."

Dani says it with such conviction—her promise kept. *Yes. Kept. My dreams abide indeed.* Grace presses a ring into my hand. The one with two hands and a heart.

Mom smiles contentment at me. *You've got Danièle now, honey.*

You can't leave yet, Mom. You gotta wait long enough to see your grandbabies.

Dad, I sure wish you could be here too.

The love in Dani's violet eyes enthralls me when my gaze turns her way again.

I always imagined you this happy married to me.

"I, Melanie..." Pastor Hawkins prompts.

The smallest cloud of doubt whispers across the calm serenity on Dani's face. Do you truly love me? her eyes ask.

Well, yeah. You know I do. I will always love you. I slip the ring on the girl's finger. "I, Melanie Rose Fairbairn, take you, Dànaidh Ailean Welles to be my—" *My intersex girl, the father of my children. By whatever name.* "—um, yeah—my husband. To have and to hold. From this day forward. For better, for worse. For richer, for poorer. In sickness and in health. To love and to cherish. Till death do us part."

Our ceremonies were always simple—the sort a child might invent. I look up at the pastor and wonder if he knows what comes next. He smiles back at me and raises a hand in blessing.

"By the power vested in me by the State of Georgia, I now pronounce you husband and wife."

We did it. My intersex girl pulls me into a tight embrace and kisses me. The way Dani always did. Time slows. My heart thumps loud in the silence. Maybe I do believe in happily ever afters.

THE END

Also from Lianne Simon

Confessions of a Teenage Hermaphrodite

From the heart of an intersex teen, one who must ultimately choose male or female—family or true love—comes the story of a deeply emotional and perilous journey home. This is a young adult novel unlike any other—an authentic portrayal of the issues faced by a child growing up with a sexually ambiguous body.

Jameson can be like other boys after minor surgery and a few years on testosterone Well, at least that's what his parents always say. But Jamie sees an elfin princess in the mirror, and male hormones would only ruin her pretty face. For him to become the man his parents expect, Jameson must leave behind the hopes and dreams of a little girl. But what is so wrong with Jamie's dreams that they can't be her life?

www.ingramcontent.com/pod-product-compliance
Lightning Source LLC
Chambersburg PA
CBHW050038180626
46810CB00002B/780